CW01085410

RIDE A COCK HORSE
TO BANBURY CROSS

by
Andrew Gorman

CON-PSY PUBLICATIONS MIDDLESEX

First Edition

© Andrew Gorman
1997

Published by

CON-PSY PUBLICATIONS

22 KINGSLEY AVENUE
SOUTHALL
MIDDLESEX UB1 2NA

ISBN 1 898680 09 4

INDEX

Nazareth House, Aberdeen, Scotland.

INTRODUCTION

Family life ended for myself, two younger brothers and three younger sisters when, we were sent to a Catholic Orphanage after our parents split up when I the eldest was six years old. Under the care of Nuns we were separated and ill treated. Under the 'brutal' regime, boys and girls were kept apart. We were separated by fear more than anything else. The treatment was brutal and sadistic and cunningly executed by Catholic Nuns.

You will be aware of the horrific hatred that exists between sections of religious groups and the destruction of human lives that such religious fanatics bring, e.g. Catholics Vs. Protestants in Ireland and elsewhere. I, my two younger brothers and three younger sisters were born of a Catholic father and a Protestant mother.

In numbers the boy intake averaged eighty. Each of us on entry were allocated different numbers that were stitched into our clothing, stamped into our boots and shoes and either etched or engraved into our minds for life. The numbers were also a substitute for our names, a number being easier to remember and often preferred. The numbers 77 and 78 were given to my brother Bill and myself, I the owner of number 78 and it is worth while remembering.

Under the 'brutal' regime, (to the Nuns it was 'The House Of God'), the numbers '1 and 2' were given new meanings .... not to be found in any dictionary. In the 'House Of God' we could not and dare not say we wanted to go for a 'wee-wee' or a 'pooh' or when we were older a 'piss' or a 'shit', no; what we had to say is we wanted to go for a number '1', when we wanted to urinate. To open our bowels we had to say we wanted to go for a number ' 2 '.

The Beano and all other comics were banned under the 'brutal' regime, all comics being tagged the 'works of the Devil'.

It wasn't all sadness !

Alive amidst the fear, the confusion, the evil and hypocrisy were laughter and joy, dares and excitement and everything that could happen under such circumstances happened.

The story continues when, at the working age of 14 years I was reunited with an alcoholic father. It was during those turbulent years that I was aware of something that was 'in' and 'around' me. In the year 1953 I joined the Royal Air Force and after six glorious years I returned to civvy life after receiving a medical discharge. Two years after my return to civvy life I married, 21 years later I, after a see-saw life was to join the 'FREE' brigade. Omitted from my story is the privacy of that marriage, only the non-prejudice talked about. And I assure you there is plenty of that.

As I became more relaxed in mind and body I began searching for

5

something, that something was with me but it took years before I truly discovered what it was. But before my mind could accept Spiritualism I had to rid myself of the hatred of the Nuns who introduced me to Hell, also I had to rid myself of Catholicism.

In my writing I tell you how I did it. I have thought deeply and pondered long over my strange and wonderful experiences I have had during my life especially as a spiritualist, experiences so strange that I readily understand the difficulty many of you readers must have in accepting what I have written. I can expect only those of you who have had similar experiences, to accept what I have written without any question or doubt.

My amazing good 'luck' and misfortunes during my adult life are, so I am told, extraordinary, I hope you will say the same when you reach the end of what I am sure is an interesting book.

For the readers who have an interest in astrology, you will find the following interesting.

Uranus was square Pluto during the 1930's.
This square is an indication of a Generation
(born during that period) who live in times of drastic upheaval.
Often their lives are disrupted and shattered by natural catastrophes.

(Taken from The Astrologers Handbook)

Self : Date of Birth ..... 8-4-1934 *
Bill : Date of Birth ..... 8-4-1935 *
Yvonne: Date of Birth 12-2-1936
Anne : Date of Birth . .... 8-4-1938 *
Tony : Date of Birth 19-3-1939
Betsy : Date of Birth 21-5-1940

Aries is my Sun Sign with Sagittarius rising. Libra holds the Mid-Haven position, with Gemini, controls my Descendant. Where was the Moon? that was moving in the benevolent Aquarius.

DAY ONE

We shared the same home, cramped we were, unhappy we were not. I didn't like leaving behind Mr and Mrs Bill and Bessy Finney or their son and daughters Bill, Doreen and baby Sheila. To me they were part of the family, kind and big hearted Mrs Finney my other mum. Mr 'pipe smoking' Finney my dad, I rarely saw my own. Bill and Doreen my brother and sister, they being a little older than I whilst Sheila was just a few months old when we were taken away from them.

Fifty years on and I still house those same feelings.

- - - - - -

From the small market town of Keith in the North of Scotland we travelled the short journey by train to the Silver City with the golden sands. Standing on the platform at Aberdeen railway station with my mother, father, brothers and sisters, with babe in arms my mum asked me for her coat. I turned around to see the train pull away from me leaving us in a cloud of smoke. I didn't like to see my mum upset, my father didn't appear to be that concerned. Within seconds of the train leaving the platform we were approached, the two Nuns were dressed slightly differently from those I left behind in Keith. Waiting for all of us outside the railway station was a large dark coloured van with dark and small windows either side. As soon as we and the two Nuns were seated the rear doors of the van were closed leaving us in a strange kind of daylight. The Nun driver then returned to her cab. Seconds after hearing the cab door close we were on our way on a ghost journey to what, for me was to be Hell on earth. Normal daylight again entered our lives on the opening of the rear van doors once we arrived at our destination.

My mind was full of inquisitive thoughts when looking up and at the large imposing building which, to me looked like a massive and solid granite built castle. My thoughts didn't change much either once inside the building where we were met by other Nuns. After a spell of talking between the Nuns and our parents we, that is Bill and I together, were separated from Yvonne, Anne, Tony and baby Betsy. And before parting from our mum she took me to one side and, knowing I wouldn't remember where she was going to live, hugging me close to her repeated several times the words, "Ride a cock horse to Banbury Cross". Immediately my mind filled with self pity and of sorrow, I couldn't find the strength to lift my head or to answer, "Oh Andrew!" my mum said, at the same time giving me another and closer hug before releasing me into the care of the Nuns.

It was with our father and in the company of the two Nuns that Bill

7

and I set off on our preview of what was to be the roof over our heads for years ahead.

We were taken along what seemed to me to be a long and narrow green coloured corridor with a door at the end of it. Arriving at that door it was then opened by one of the Nuns for us to view a vast playing yard with swings and things almost in the centre of it. Then it was inside again and the room immediately to the left of us opened, I was gazing at a long room with a highly polished ballroom like floor. To the left of me were four tall shuttered windows. Along that highly polished floor we gingerly trod then through the doorway at the other end of it which led us to a small concrete landing. We followed the leading Nun into the wash room where, down the centre ran a double row of wash basins anchored to a green coloured spotless terrazzo floor identical to that of the long corridor. The stillness in that room was eerie, I didn't feel comfortable in it, knowing nothing about the ear piercing days it held in store for me at a later date.

The room next to the wash room housed the toilets with a urinal, standing room' for about five, to the immediate left as we entered. In line with the urinal were five small cubicles where I was to do my 'number 2's.' And yet again there was that green terrazzo floor and matching walls. I was a little startled when the urinal flushed, months and years later I was to be more than a little startled when in that toilet.

We didn't climb the seven sets of terrazzo stairs that formed a spiral, leaving Bill and I in the company of one of the two Nuns, our father and the leading Nun continued their journey, after we had all viewed the hundred seater boy's dining room. On rejoining us, our father with a smile across his face, then described the large bathroom, I wasn't interested either when he told us of a lovely two bedroomed attic room used as a 'sick room' of which appeared to impress our father more than anything else. Probably having agreed there was no need to view further afield Bill and I were gently ushered back down to the playroom with the others following immediately behind.

Once in the playroom we then all made our way to the door through which we all first entered, and at which we all came to a sudden halt. After more talking between the three adults, my father turned to me taking me to one side away from hearing distance of Bill, he crouched down and facing me in the eyes said: "Andrew, look after your brothers and sisters. You are here only for a holiday until your mum and your dad can find somewhere for all of us to be together." Months later those words spoken by my father were to be used as nails in a coffin.

After the farewells our father, accompanied by the leading Nun left us, they returning along that corridor, presumably to be reunited with our

8

mother and the other Nuns. Leaving the playroom Bill and I were escorted up two flights of other terrazzo stairs, the building was full of them, to a room called the workroom, so called because clothing and bedding repairs, etc. were carried out there. It also stored several musical instruments, locked in a large white painted cupboard.

In the workroom, Bill and I were examined for lice, that took place either before or after our new style of haircut which left me feeling cold with a continuous feeling of a draught around the back of my head. Then we were taken out of the room and across a landing to and through the large dining room onto yet another landing, of course it was of terrazzo. There was a strange smell wafting down the two flights of stairs that we climbed to the bath room. Never before had I experienced the smell of industrial 'Jeyes' fluid. In the bath room that smell was more powerful and I was about to feel its burning affects, it being generously used in the bath water that Bill and I were about to be gently cased into. And never before had I been in a proper bath, consequently I was clinging with all my might to the arms of the Nun who was washing me. After that unforgettable experience I towelled then donned the new styled universally used clothing handed me by the Nun. Then, when Bill and I were dressed, we were escorted back along the route whence we came to the workroom where we had to wait some time before being introduced to the boys who were sitting at their tables in the dining room, waiting for their early evening meal. Bill was given a table place at the front of the room, I the table at the end of the room and in front of the rooms other doorway.

Although we all had food on our plates nobody was eating. It wasn't long before I found out why. Prayers had to-be said. Not having a clue as to what was being recited by the boys I just sat and waited, then got stuck into what was in front of me when the boys at my table got stuck into theirs. I had hardly swallowed my first intake when a Nun, pushing in front of her passed me then out through the doorway behind me. From the other side of the then closed door came the sound of leather on the palm of a hand, but it didn't quite sound like leather, it was something different and indeed it was.

The Nun was using a Cricket Wicket, known to all as the 'STICK'. Every time the Stick landed the boy let out either a painful sounding "Ouch," or an equally painful sounding "Ah." In fear and horror I cringed at what I was sensing and what I saw when the punished boy passed me with his hands firmly tucked under his arm pits.

After the meal I went with the others downstairs to the playroom not before more prayers were said. Naturally I was bombarded with questions from inquisitive boys of all ages during which time I was also being bumped into from all sides. Freeing me from the rough and tumble I was asked by a Nun to sit on a bench which she pointed out to me. Alone I sat while Bill was enjoying being the centre of attraction. I can' t remember what I then was thinking, probably nothing.

Out of breath and panting heavily, Bill came and sat beside me, seconds later he made an effort to tell me he had made friends with one boy and was looking forward to the following day. Shortly afterwards we were told it was time for us to go to bed even though it still was bright sunshine outside. Bill went with others around his age whilst I, with others, were held back as we were going to another dormitory a little later. Bill had four flights of stairs to climb to get to his dormitory, I had a further two flights to get to mine. Awe stricken I stood a moment and gaped at the three rows of hospital like beds either side of an aisle and again there was a highly polished wooden floor. My bed was half way up the middle row to the right of the door entrance.

After undressing and into our pyjamas we all knelt by our beds for more prayers, again I hadn't a clue what was being said, little did I know I soon was to begin learning those prayers. It was during my undressing I noticed tucked in a corner a small room with a small window, on inquiring I was to learn it was where a Nun slept.

Slipping between the white snowflake starched sheets I found little room for movement, the bedding being tightly tucked into and under the mattress. So tight was the bedding I fell asleep using what energy I had by trying to make freedom for my legs.

BLOOD SAMPLE

Drowsiness was with me on my first morning when I got out of bed and followed the example of the others, going on my knees at the side of my bed, others muttered words whilst I stared silently at the floor in front of me. It was only after the prayers ended did I hear the sobbing from boys nearest the main entrance to the dormitory. Those boys were the high risk bed wetters hence the occupation of those near door beds. It was the closest they could be to the toilet at the bottom of the flight of stairs immediately outside the dormitory.

Again I witnessed punishment handed out by Nuns, the bed wetters the victims. While I was being shown how to remove the bedding from my bed and fold the sheets and blankets in military style, the poor unfortunate bed wetters were still in their soaking wet pyjamas. Seemingly those poor unfortunates had to remain in that condition until someone could attend to them.

All having dressed, we then filed our way down the stairway to wash before going to the 'House' Chapel, after which we breakfasted. Prayers were said before and after that meal which I thoroughly enjoyed. Holy Mass and the Chapel were to be my first detest, they being in my early days, not understandable and weird. Unknown to me at that time I was to visit the place every morning for Holy Mass and every afternoon for Benediction, Saturdays excluded.

After breakfast we were allowed to play out, in the playing yard, that is all except myself, I having to be an onlooker for my own safety. This isolation during all recreation times went on for weeks until the Nun decided I should take my chances and mix in with the other boys.

After about three weeks in those strange surroundings I had my first quarrel and it was with a boy favourite of the Nuns. As with a few other boys this one thought I was being stand offish because of me not joining them for rough and tumbles. "I don't like you Gorman. I am going to spread it about you don't like going to Chapel, then let's see what happens when the Nuns find out."

It would be about the same time I witnessed my first bare listed fight. While most of the boys were out in the playing yard others were inside. On entering the playroom two boys of about ten years of age were facing each other, looking into each others eyes. I was seeing anger mixed with disgust, then two sets of bare knuckles began hitting the particles of dust that were floating in the still sunlit room. A cry of "FIGHT" is heard and soon the two bare listed fighters had an audience that soon were jumping out of the way with yells of uncertain laughter mixed with delight at what they were seeing.

It took only a few minutes before both fighters were clumsily wrestling on the floor, both struggling for dominance. From behind me came the order for the wrestling to stop. "Stop this at once. Do you hear me?". Then the racket from the onlookers died suddenly into a silence but the two continued retching on the floor. "Stop this at once," and this time with a smile on her face that brought giggles from the then silent few. Then the relief Nun beckoned two of the onlookers from the group to pull apart the two who were in some kind of wrestling hold.

I enjoyed watching my first fight and my individual antics as a wishing participant.

Holiday or not I wanted to be a family again, after all we had been in strange surroundings for over three months I had been thinking to myself for several days. And I wasn't the only one with those thoughts.

It was a chilly evening and we were all playing in the playing yard when I was approached by my brother Bill. "You liar! We are not here for a holiday! Nobody ever comes here for a holiday. We are here forever!" shouted Bill and only inches from my face. "Where are mum and dad?" Bill demanded. On not able to convince Bill he then screamed at me; "YOU liar! I hate you!" His face was void of colour from the temper he was in, he turned away only to come straight back to me. Seizing me by me clothes Bill yanked me towards him and I walked straight into an accidental knee in the stomach. Although not painful, I was in some pain as Bill continued yanking and shouting. Letting go of me, hesitating for a moment, Bill then said he wouldn't speak to me again. Then with a single hurt hating look Bill walked away from me.

All that day, all night, and all the following day, as well I was in a trance resulting in what Bill had said to me and mickey taking from a few of the boys, and remarks such as, "You sulking little baby, pull your lip in," coming from the two Irish Nuns. Then I was beginning to feel a dislike of my surroundings coupled with a dislike and distrust of the Nuns in charge. In a sense I was fearful of them. Everything about them seemed unreal, so to try to form a sort of good relationship with them a great deal of effort was required from me.

From the time of my brothers angry outburst I couldn't understand why the Nuns didn't let Bill know what our dad had said to me in their presence.

For another sample and of schoolboy behaviour I am taking you back to the day and time when my brother Bill was upset and angry. Presumably still under supervision, I was around the corner and out of sight of the Nun watching and partly taking part in a ball game played with a small ball thrown from one young boy to another. At that same time I was also interested in what other boys were doing on the steel 'rings'.

The boys playing with the ball were from time to time falling out with one and other, just typical school yard antics. "Butter fingers," shouted one of the boys to Fatty. "You haven't got butter fingers," was the reply coming from another boy as he approached Fatty. "No I haven't got butter fingers," Fatty shouted at that boy as they were almost nose to nose from each other. "Leave him alone!" It was the voice of one of the other boys shouting to the group that was surrounding Fatty. In reply it was said Fatty was one of the Nun's pets. "He is one of the Nun's pets aren't you Fatty?" said one of the boys as he poked his finger several times into the fat boys stomach. "I'm not! I'm not!" was Fattys' answer. That same boy sneered saying, "yes you are," and went on to grip Fatty by the arm. "Leave me alone or I will punch you in the face," were the words used by Fatty. "You will do what? I'll show you," the boy replied. Immediately there was a scuffle, both boys fell to the concrete; then they were joined by a couple of others. Only bare hands were used in all fights, anyone using anything else were branded cowards.

Walters always seemed to be in favour with the Nuns, nobody could understand why that was, he being popular with almost every one of us. There were about five playing on the 'rings' attempting to do what all boys attempt in their school gymnasium. A call from a Nun brought Walters over to her. During an exchange of soft voice talk about three other boys, myself included, had been standing a little apart looking on as we usually did when the Nuns spoke to Walters or any other of their pets. At the end of the conversation Walters rejoined his pals and continued playing on the 'rings '. Walters, as always, didn't mention what had been said by the Nun. Someone informed that Nun about the brawl that was going on around the corner from her. At the sound of her whistle all stopped fighting, brushed themselves down with their hands then stood looking at the Nun. She then blew her whistle three times and then brought her arm to shoulder height, straightened it out and pointed a rigid finger in the direction of the playroom.

It had taken approximately three minutes to clear the playing yard of all the boys. Some walked, some ran into the building, several wore disgruntled looks on their faces as they filed past the Nun as she stood by the entrance. Few of us appreciated being indoors, the atmosphere wasn't exciting. I was never to fully understand why everyone was punished when only a few defaulted.

About half an hour had passed after we were all on the playroom when, a Nun standing at the main doorway, blew her whistle. Two names were bellowed from the face of the Nun, bringing Fatty and the other boy involved in the brawl close to her. One of the boys was told to stand facing the corner close to that of a colourful picture of the Sacred Heart of Jesus, the other boy was then ushered into the corner at the other side of the room, the window side. Neither boy could see what was going on behind them, several times, boys most of whom were trying to make an impression on the Nuns, bumped into Fatty and his opponent. Every now and then hand balls were thrown, so were other objects such as paper balls, paper made aeroplanes and other small objects. When caught turning round to see what was going on and to try and find a culprit, the boys were quickly reminded by the Nuns they were on punishment.

On one occasion one of the Nuns on duty approached the boys, tapping the boys on the shoulder with a Cricket Wicket. A black plimsoll hit me on the side of the head as I sat alone watching what was going on around me. Laughing, a boy ran up to me, picked up the plimsoll that had fallen on the bench I was sitting on, then he ran to the opposite end of the room. Moments later I decided to go and have a word with the boy. He was going round in a circle pretending to be an aeroplane, on seeing me he ran to find his older brother avoiding pockets of boys to do so. Approaching me his older brother threw threatening words at me, promising to flatten me if I laid a finger on his brother. Having explained what had happened the older brother, after an exchange of words said, "Ach, so; we now understand each other." The younger brother said nothing, tucking his shirt into his pants he walked away to mingle with his pals.

I had been receiving my daily pre-breakfast dessert spoonful of my Radio Malt and a tea spoonful of Cod Liver Oil from about the second week of my arrival at the place. Both were denied me on a morning shortly before Christmas. The large brown jar of my Radio Malt was not in the usual place, it being on a shelf higher. When the other boys were preparing themselves to receive breakfast, I, before Adelmia began supervising the distribution of the morning meal, asked her if she would get my malt for me. She hesitated for a second then she said, "It is all gone. Go to your table."

The following morning I noticed a jar of Radio Malt on the same shelf and in the same position as that of the day before. With my feet firmly placed on the bottom shelf I just managed to ease the malt jar towards me then I brought it down to the lower shelf which was about shoulder high. Try as I did, I was unable to unscrew the jar lid, that was to be a catastrophe for me when, the thinner of the two Irish Nuns asked what I was trying to do. Then immediately from behind her loomed her mate Adelmia. It was she who whispered something into the ear of the Nun Adelmia, I then receiving a slap across the side of my head before being told to get to my table.

14

The following morning I was in the dining room before anyone, the Radio Malt was nowhere to be seen, neither was the ghastly Cod Liver Oil. I was furious and full of resentment, both malt and the oil were important and necessary food supplements for my ailing fragile body.

It was nearing Christmas within the granite walls of the building, often described by the two Irish Nuns as the 'House of God'. I was receiving undivided attention from those Nuns, they being eagerly interested, I learnt as much as possible before Christmas Day about the birth of baby Jesus. On a day shortly after the celebrated day, I alone in the playroom, looked up and around at the colourful variety of handmade paper decorations. During that time idly did my thoughts wander to my classroom in my home town of Keith. I had the urge to run away but my mind and body then seemed to be anchored to the floor beneath me. On release, thoughts crossed thoughts, for the first time in my life aversion was inside me. That hatred was like a whirlpool and I didn't feel comfortable with it. Unaware of silent footsteps behind me, I almost jumped out of my skin the second I heard the voice of a Nun. Fortunately it was the voice of the relief Nun, she being much kinder that the other two. Having listened to what I had to say the Nun then walked over to a cupboard, after unlocking and opening it the Nun the produced a jar of wrapped sweets of which she handed two of them to me, after she raised her hand to brush a quill of hair from my forehead. As in every household domestic work still has to be carried out at Christmas and so must it in institutions, where punishment didn't escape either.

That, my first Christmas in the orphanage, I saw a boy older than I on his hands and knees half way down five flights of stairs with cold water from a galvanised mop bucket and with the use of a hard hand scrubbing brush and vim, he was scrubbing the stairs. I was in the toilets having a 'No. 1' when that boy brought his bucket into the toilets to be emptied, having finished his punishment handed out by one of the Nuns. While beside me I noticed the condition of the boys fingers when he was emptying the bucket, they were white, crinkly and soggy around his finger nails, they looking as if they would fall out at any time. Smarting and also very sore the boy assured me his fingers would soon heal.

ST. PATRICKS DAY

As well as Christmas, the celebration by the Nuns of March 17th and of the days running up to it were greatly disliked by me. Sometimes I wondered if Saint Patrick's Day was more meaningful to the Irish Nuns than any other event in the Catholic calendar.

Before I continue with the story of Saint Patrick's Day, I would like to mention that a couple of days prior to my confirmation I had decided to take Saint Anthony as my confirmation name.

I wasn't in the playroom so I am assuming it was either in the choir room or in a cleared area of the dining room, where Adelmia was sitting on a bench accompanied by an unfamiliar Nun. There were about a dozen of us in line formation waiting to go forward on hearing our names being called by one of the Nuns. I was towards the end of the queue and having witnessed a happy conversation between the Nuns and the boys before me, I donned a pleasing smile when hearing my full name being called. I was feeling confident that my choice of Saint Anthony would be warmly received by both Nuns.

"Hello, are you Andrew Brookes Gorman?" the Nun sitting next to Adelmia inquired, after taking note of the name from a book on her lap. Having answered the Nun she asked me who I had chosen as my confirmation Saint. I had no sooner mentioned my choice when Adelmia with a sardonic smile on her pretentious, pious face turned her head towards her associate and said, "Put him down for Saint Patrick," the other words spoken were drowned not by tears, but from rain in my heart as I turned and slowly walked away from the Nuns.

Returning now as to why Saint Patrick's Day has unpleasant memories for me....

The central heating did keep out the howling, bitterly cold March winds but did little for the temperament of the two Irish Nuns. By this time I had learnt the names of several Catholic idolised Saints, none better than the second God of the two Nuns, Adelmia and Alemenia. The week prior to March 17th were days devoted mainly to the saint of that date, convincing me that the saint was another God in the eyes of the two Nuns. And I am of the opinion that he had some kind of mystical hold over his Irish counterparts. For those of us who were in the choir, (I was for about one year), our vocal chords were stretched to near breaking point from the number of times we had music lessons and choir practise in preparation for the Nuns big day. For those of us who were not in the choir, well most of us, our eardrums were battered by the Nuns story of their other God. The sound of a raw egg being whisked in an enamel cup wasn't exactly music to the ears of the choir boys, especially when the egg was then forced, (in a pleasant manner), to slither its way down ones throat. The reason behind this compulsory intake was because the Nuns believed it would

16

greatly assist in turning out sweet flowing, honey like voices in the Chapel on the day of the Irish idol. Well the Nuns never did get the Chapel filled with mellifluous voices, but I am sure it was the voices of heavenly angels they were hearing from above, especially when the hymn 'Hail Glorious Saint Patrick' was being echoed throughout the tiny Chapel. The patron saint of Scotland didn't receive adoration within the granite wall of the 'House of the Lord'. Something else was also guaranteed during Saint Patrick's week and that was not one of us would be mistreated by the worshippers of the Emerald Isle Saint.

Following that day I was to learn about and experience other popular days in the Catholic Calendar such as Ash Wednesday, a day on which a dark substance was placed on my forehead by a priest at the rails of the Chapel alter. Palm Sunday, when I had a flat piece of fawn coloured raffia type straw representing a cross was tied to the head metal frame of my bed. Fearing the Cricket Wicket, the symbolic item remained tied until ordered to remove it. My first Good Friday and Easter period will, with others, never be forgotten.

The servants of God are not directly responsible for my first remembered Good Friday turning out to be a Black Friday. My brother Bill approached me almost on the spot where the incident took place over his disbelief of us being in the orphanage for a holiday. Bearing a similar temper as on that occasion Bill accused me of being a liar and that I also was insane. Bill, myself and our sister Anne were all born on April 8 but in different years. This my brother couldn't understand, he preferring to believe other boys, didn't want anything more to do with me.

"And I am not supporting Hearts, from now on I am a Hibs supporter," Bill sneered at me before leaving to rejoin his pals. Greatly hurt at what I heard, I went directly to the Nun who was sitting on a bench in her usual place. She didn't take any interest in what I was saying despite my determined efforts that she would. Desperately wanting to be friends with my brother and determined not to be branded a liar, I on several occasions harassed the Nuns to have my name cleared and for them to inform Bill that we did share April 8 for our birthday. My efforts were all in vain, the two servants of God didn't want to know me either, this I didn't understand.

Foolishly I locked myself in a toilet cubicle and remained there until the Nuns and the other boys returned from Sunday morning Mass. Somehow the Nuns knew of my absence from Chapel and after a brief interrogation I received my first taste of the Cricket Wicket. Grimacing with pain I did not know where to put my hands or what to do with them, blowing at them was futile.

Within the solid granite walls the discipline was absolute and brutal in its efficiency with only one purpose ..... to produce God and Nun fearing children.

17

UNDERPANTS

Epsom Salts, diarrhoea and the shortage of paper were an awesome nightmare for the vast majority of us in our earlier months behind the solid silver granite walls of the 'House of the Lord'. Friday evenings were chosen for underpants inspection and beware those of us who were in possession of excreted underpants.

Apart from a few who were fortunate not to have bowel problems, the up to eight year olds and a small number of older boys were rounded up by the Nun on duty and made to stand in line with their underpants on display. This ordeal always brought fear, sadness and to some a little light entertainment. My earlier memories of those Friday inspections had me wondering why I wasn't one to be chosen for the ordeal and the times I felt a numbness creep into my body, it certainly was a weird experience for me. Then came the day when I was selected, it was a day or two after being refused my Radio Malt medicine.

Whether it was a coincidence or not I will never know, but it did seem rather strange that it happened when my clean pair of underpants were replaced by a not so clean pair. Of course that wasn't the first time that had happened to me but it was somewhat unusual. Now I had found myself a Friday evening victim. It was then I truly realised the torment felt by the unfortunates. You see not every boy in possession of excreted underpants were the actual culprits, like myself on that day others had their underpants cunningly swapped and that put one in a raged mood as well as an embarrassing and fearful one.

Well that first Friday evening I was standing shoulder to shoulder in a straight line with a number of other boys sharing and feeling just as they. Many of us with tears in our eyes were frantically trying to rub away the hardened excreta before the inspection began. A few of the underpants held by some of the other boys weren't too bad, probably at one time there was no paper in the toilets and they had to make do by using their fingers. I believe I witnessed a much younger boy holding his underpants for all to see and they reminded me of a sun baked 'cow plop' in a field. Naturally this exhibition brought its admirers and one by one they filtered across to have a closer look bringing a few giggles and sniggers from some of the viewers.

As always those in the line up were displaying their inside out underpants on the palm of their hands and were at about waist level, this order was carried out when the Nun on duty approached us slowly waving her Cricket Wicket. The younger boys were punished by receiving a slight tap on their covered hands, the Cricket Wicket was not so friendly with the others, they were in severe pain for a while after their ordeal. On that

18

evening I was lucky but I will never forget the frightening synthetic smile on the face of the Nun.

Of course underpants were not only swapped on Fridays. Anytime one had an accident in their underpants one would seek out an unsuspecting customer. Bedtime usually was the safest time to have a dare at swapping and this was carried out when a boy left his bed to go to the toilet, or when the victim was in bed unaware of what was going on around him.

I was about twelve years old when on a bright summers evening I was lying peacefully in my bed daydreaming, looking out of the bay window where next my bed stood, I was wishing all sorts of wishes until Adelmia called to anyone that wanted to use the toilet to do so before the night light was switched on. I was one who accepted the Nuns invitation. On my return to the dormitory the night light had already been switched on and there was that usual chilly quiet atmosphere that the occasion always seemed to bring. And when I approached my bed I was horribly faced with a pair of recently excreted underpants, whoever put them there was obviously in a hurry because he didn't do a very good job of hiding his cast offs. Pretending not to have noticed anything, I slipped into bed and apart from my heart thumping in my chest, I was motionless. I lay there thinking who on earth could do such a thing to me, after all I was experiencing a relatively quiet period of my stay. Just as most others before me in the same dilemma, I lay awake in wait for an opportunity to act. That opportunity was long in coming and I was in really good luck; the boy in the bed next to me vacated his bed for a visit to the 100. Just as others before me, I slipped out of and under my bed and crawled across and under the vacant bed, did what I had to and returned to my own bed feeling a sense of great relief.

The next morning the boy didn't show any signs out of the ordinary or at anytime during that day either, which left me baffled at what happened to the underpants, or if anything did happen. That was the way things were in that place!

It was laughter at first sight of a newish seven year old boy going to school with his obviously too large underpants showing below his short trousers. Where did he get them from we all wondered? I remember it being either the morning or afternoon of underpants inspection day because the boy was in the line up with myself and some others. No; he wasn't displaying the too large underpants, what happened was ... At a time either between breakfast and getting ready for morning session at school or on arriving back for dinner, the boy probably sensing his excreted underpants would bring him trouble, got into the workroom whilst no one was in and grabbed the first pair of underpants he could get his hands on and made a hurried effort to hide his own. I know the boy was satisfactorily questioned by one of the Nuns because in the line up he was in possession of his own underpants and what a horrible state they were in.

It wasn't that often we witnessed a nasty fight, but that can be expected when there are a number of people cooped up in the same place for several years. Animosity was live between one or two of the boys, such was the case between MacClusky and the boy Kirby who was equal in stature to his arch enemy but of darker complexion, both were about ten years of age at this time. There was an air of anger in the playroom shortly before the Friday inspection. MacClusky scowled at Kirby, hating him for seeing through him, hating him for trying to form an alliance against him and hating him for making fun at him. Kirby received a blow to his face sending him staggering back only to be pushed forward by one of the onlookers. Being hit again, this time on the nose, Kirby dropped to the floor and placed his hands on the floor to steady himself. As Kirby got to his feet he was met with a punch to the mouth by MacClusky. The punch spouted blood which mingled with the blood from Kirby's nose. MacClusky always regarded himself as a tough guy and was about to deliver another blow to Kirby's face but prevented from doing so when a senior boy spotted Alemenia enter the room. "Get out of my way," snapped the Nun at the group of boys enjoying and encouraging the fight. "In Gods Holy name, what is going on?" she asked seeing Kirby's bloody face, then several boys started shouting their version to the Nuns question. "Quiet, all of you!" snapped Alemenia ... There was instant silence. "Here comes Sister Adelmia, someone shouted. The big framed Nun stood framed in the doorway and looked sternly around. "What in the name of the Lord is going on?" she shouted when she approached Alemenia and the gathering around her. Having heard what had happened the big Nun Adelmia dispersed everyone.

The conclusion of this particular episode is that the fight took place because MacClusky and Kirby disagreed as to who was responsible for swapping someone else's underpants.

GOING HOME

It was a day well into my seventh birthday when I was told my father was arriving in the afternoon to take me home. It was a bright and sunny morning during school holidays when I was singled out from a group of us who were in the playroom excitedly talking about spending most of the day at Hazelhead. Hazelhead was a large playing field surrounded by woodlands situated somewhere in Aberdeen. To all of us and especially to me Hazelhead was an exciting place, it giving me a sense of freedom and with it the desire to be free. On a couple of occasions when I was there the older boys formed two football teams and played barefooted, except for a chosen few, who were fortunate to own football boots given to them by the school. At other times the playing area was occupied by outside youth organisations such as the Scouts and the Boys Brigade. We were forbidden to speak to anyone of them and none of us dared.

"You are going to live with your father," Adelmia said. My heart was pumping. I was scared, terribly scared. The words also left me stunned and stupefied. Then I heard the Nun say, "Don't say anything to anyone, not even your brother. We don't want to spoil his day, do we?" Looking away from the Nun I didn't answer, I couldn't answer, I just shook my head. Then I was asked to go into the washroom to wash and then make my way to the workroom where nice new clothes were waiting for me. I passed through the playroom on my way to the workroom, the others leaving behind an empty shell. I felt a little nervous as I made my way passed the rays of sunshine that beamed through the tall shuttered windows on to the highly polished wooden floor. On the large oak table was a small pile of clothing, resting on top were a pair of brown sandals. An older boy pointed to the pile and told me to undress and put on my going away clothes. I don't know how long I was waiting for a Nun to appear, when she did arrive she was holding a hair brush in her hand. Before brushing my hair my head was closely examined for nits, this time the steel comb was being gently used. Satisfied all was to her liking, the Nun asked me to make my way to the playroom. The tone of her voice filling me with nauseousness I shuddered a cold shudder bringing goosepimples to the surface of my frail body.

Arriving at the playroom I selected a bench opposite one of the tall windows. During what seemed an endless time of waiting I crossed and uncrossed my legs and arms several times, otherwise I was motionless on that wooden bench. As time passed on bringing with it an awareness of total isolation I filled with a chilling coldness. The long oblong shuttered room was filled with still air, all that was in motion was the atoms of dust that seemed to be swirling around in the warm sunrays that penetrated the tall windows. Life was slowly maturing through my body, the first signs being the hardness of the wooden bench that I was sitting on. I eased myself from the bench but other pains were taking place, they were the pains of total isolation, fear of solitude and the sharpness of fear itself. Gradually the rays of sunshine that flowed through the tall windows turned into streaks of shimmering cold steel. My heart that should have been filled with the rays of the days sunshine was housing a dark grey cloud. The vast empty room was suddenly transformed into a small, singled window prison cell that brought with it a frightened prisoner. By now my mind was operational but only for a few moments. Slowly the words "Don't tell your brother," were reincarnated in my mind. "Why," I asked myself .... "WHY?"

Thoughts began to cross thoughts sending my mind into painful cogitation throwing those thoughts into animistic confusion. The door opened and suddenly the room became a room again. A Nun was standing in the open doorway to the left of where I was sitting. Injected warmth suddenly sent the pump of my heart into operation, adrenalin gushed through me. Was it good news? Has my father come -for me? The Nun who closed in on me was a stranger to me and on closing she said, "What are you doing here all on your own?" To that I nervously answered, "I'm waiting for my father to take me home." "I have not been informed of that," she replied with a sympathetic smile on her now puzzled face."Yes," I said. "The Sister told me before the boys went to Hazelhead.Have you been sitting here all on your own all this time?" asked the Nun. Looking up and looking straight into her eyes I didn't answer verbally, I just nodded my head several times. "Well you are looking very smart and a credit to the Sister and when your father sees you he will be thinking what a good well looked after boy you are." Those were the words I believe were spoken by the Nun before she turned away and walked towards and through the doorway in which she entered. I was feeling a little better having seen and spoken to someone, but I was still terribly confused and my head was throbbing.

As the time passed the sunbeams were gradually getting shorter until they withdrew through the tall windows returning to the sky from where they came. My heart gave an excited leap when the door again opened .... a Nun entered, it was Adelmia. In a loud cynical voice she said, "Your father will not be coming for you now. Go and get changed into your old clothes, they are still in the workroom. Wait there until the others return, then join them." A wave of nausea and depression of heart made me think dark and extirpatory thoughts. The devil was surely in control of me then.

THAT DAY IS FIRMLY FIXED IN MY MEMORY AS IF IT WAS DEEPLY ENGRAVED IN A TOMBSTONE.

22

COMICS

A dickie bird twittered that there was to be a comic interrogation before we were to go out and play. Nick laughed. It was a hearty laugh. Apparently three boys of junior age were caught under a table in the dining room reading a comic, either the Dandy or the Beano. Grim faced, the three boys came out from under the table. Alemenia sternly demanded, "Who brought that 'work of the devil' into this house?" "Sister, Sister, it wasn't me," spluttered one of the boys. "Get out of this room and get downstairs to the playroom," Alemenia again demanded. With a short blast on her whistle, Alemenia brought the usual silence to the atmosphere. "All in your lines, sitting on the floor," was the order following the blast from the Nuns whistle. One of the three junior boys slowly approached the line of boys and pointed a finger in the direction of Robert. Roberts' eyes widened but he said nothing. My brother Bill laughed at the look on Roberts' face, who was gaping at him openly.

Alemenia made a grab at an arm of Robert and pulled him across the room hitting him with a Cricket Wicket. It hurt everywhere it landed. Alemenia was now gripping Robert by the neck as in a vice, and he had to force her fingers from his neck with both hands. "Oh no you don't, you little worm, oh no you don't." But he did and the Cricket Wicket came down harder on him.

"I'm going for a 'No. 2' Sister, I've got the skitters" blurted a boy as he, (right hand between his legs and firmly on his bottom), scuffled his way past Alemenia. Another boy moving hastily towards the door said, "I'm going for a 'No. 1' Sister." A "Hee - Hee" came from Nick at the sight of the two younger boys making a hurried departure through the playroom door. Alemenia glanced sharply at Nick and reminded him that it wasn't that long ago when he did the same thing. That brought a few hefty laughs from the boys in the immediate area. With a couple of quickie blasts on her whistle Alemenia had us all out in the yard, all except Robert. He attempted to sneak out by the back of Alemenia, she instinctively grabbed him as he tried to do so. "You had two comics, where is the other?" demanded Alemenia, as she made to. grab Roberts' arm. Robert tucked his chin onto his chest and firmly closed his eyes. "Do you know where that other comic is?" again Alemenia spoke using that demanding voice. Robert shook his head very slowly. The Nun grabbed Roberts' jaw and forced his head upwards and scorned, "If you don't tell me where that comic is you will be punished in the same manner as the others who have been caught with the 'work of the devil'." Robert understood what was to happen and still he didn't talk. Alemenia released her vice like grip, then produced the Cricket Wicket. Robert threw a glance at the Nun and said, "Don't start beating me Sister," his voice was low and soft, his eyes showing signs of fear. "Who did you give the comic to?" Roberts face had suddenly gone white and strained, "To ... to ... Andrew Gorman," was Roberts' reply as his appealing eyes met the piercing eyes of Alemenia.

Without delay the long swooping hand of the Nun cracked against the face of Robert, sending him crashing to the floor. Unknown to both, I observed all through a gap in the door, and as soon as Alemenia made a move towards the door I scarpered to the playing yard and made my way to and through the south set of doors. Closing the doors behind me I stood for a moment to ease and slow my heavy breathing before entering the playroom door immediately to my left. Removing the comic from my cupboard, I immediately made my way for temporary sanctuary in one of the toilet cubicles. Before entering my selected cubicle I quickly tore my comic into four squares and dropped the pieces on the floor of the cubicle next to the one where I seeked temporary sanctuary. I knew it wouldn't take Alemenia long to satisfy herself that it was a waste of time searching for me in and around the playing yard, and that the toilets would be her next port of call.

Alemenia's left hand grabbed at my shirt collar and hoisted me from the toilet seat. Shorts and underpants twisted around my ankles, the Nun hauled me out of the toilet and into the playroom. I let out an almighty yell as the servant of God brought the Cricket Wicket crashing down on my nine year old back, sending me flying on my face as soon as I entered the playroom. "Cover yourself, pull up your pants," Alemenia shouted several times as I hurriedly tried to obey her commands. Coming towards me the Nun pushed me again to the floor saying angrily, "Cover yourself you little evil good for nothing. All of you," (surely meaning my brothers and sisters), "will burn in hell for what you are." My vest and shirt did little to assist my lower garments to cover my private parts from Alemenia, and she didn't like it. As I got back onto my feet I immediately felt a dull pain across my back, exactly where the Cricket Wicket bounced off. "Ow!" I sympathetically said to myself, and thinking, "Please God, get me out of this place."

With a couple of blasts from her whistle Alemenia brought all the boys into the playroom from the yard. By the time the first of the boys arrived through the door of the playroom, I had regained my dignity. With a couple of blasts from her whistle, Alemenia brought all the boys to a stand-still. "All of you get your boots ready for inspection," she commanded. Then she brought down her Cricket Wicket onto the radiator near to where she was standing, the metallic end of the wicket bringing out a doing from the radiator at the time she bellowed, "NOW!." That command sent a shiver through my spine. Just then Alemenia stretched out her arm to grab me, I wasn't there, having moved from my original place. My relief was short lived because on seeing where I was Alemenia's arm shot out in my direction with the speed of a rattle snake,

24

that left hand was soon gripping my neck bringing me to my knees without her loosening her grip. With the Cricket Wicket in her right hand Alemenia brought it across my upper arm. Those fragile bones didn't splinter, but they sure felt as if they had.

Let me say here and now that when the Cricket Wicket was used on parts of our body other than our hands, the Nuns Alemenia and Adelmia used it with consummate skill.

The delivered blow sent me sprawling on the floor. A splinter penetrated the inside of my right thumb as my hand travelled the highly polished floor boards. "Where is that comic?" raged Alemenia. "Holy Mary Mother of God, tell me the truth," Alemenia again raged. Before the Nun could say anymore, two forks of lightening blazed the darkening sky. Roars of thunder following the lightening and immediately torrential rain followed the thunder. I wanted to be out there! I wanted to be out there! Perhaps the Nuns were afraid that their God had sent the thunder and lightening to frighten them into leaving me alone. Certainly the look of acute apprehension on the face of Alemenia when she asked me to go and join the other boys, relayed that feeling to me. Phew! .... what a relief. I scrambled to my feet and quickly obeyed the Nuns request. Another blast from a whistle and then we were told to put away our boots to play quietly.

The rain had long stopped and the skies were getting brighter when the two Nuns returned to the playroom, Adelmia holding the pieces of a comic in her hand. I at that time was watching a small circle of boys playing marbles. Pretending not to notice Adelmia coming in our direction, I slowly turned my back on the approaching Nun, only to have her scatter the marbles in all directions when she forced her way through the circle of boys to get her hands on me. "You sly little devil, you tore this comic and put it in one of the toilet cubicles hoping it wouldn't be found, didn't you, you little monster?" I lied when I said I didn't, to a very angry Nun. Crossing herself with the sign of the cross and saying, "Holy Mary, Mother of God, he is lying again." Adelmia grabbed me by the shoulder and shook me almost senseless. During that ordeal names of several Saints were used by the Nun, requesting help to know what to do with me. Saint Peter, Saint Patrick and Saint Paul were the Saints most often used by the two Nuns when in prayer. This time I wasn't brutally treated, but I did receive verbal warnings regarding my future behaviour and, "You will go to Hell when you die. Comics are the works of the devil. When you go to the Confessional you will tell Father you are a liar." Those were a few of the words spoken by the irate Nun before ordering me to return the pieces of comic to the toilets.

A five year old boy was leaving the toilets as I entered, he lifted his fingers and sniffed them.

25

THE COBBLERS

I rarely was lucky with my black army styled hobnailed boots, but that didn't prevent me from having secret visits to the 'House' cobblers. It was instant rapport on my first visit to the rustic cobblers den and it was the same with the small, lean, but muscular man with the warm but sad looking eyes that appeared to be forever looking down at his small, sharp nose that in later years donned a pair of rimless specs. It was to be an unusual relationship because Jack the cobbler didn't know that for almost two years before we met, I had good reasons to curse him over and over again.

Never known to Jack, this is what happened...

Midway through the first winter of my stay in Nazareth House I had problems with my issued boots. The boots were a size or two too large for me and my feet slipped about in them. On informing the Nuns..of my problem I was told to wear them to school that morning and to see one of them on returning for dinner. At dinner time the Nuns didn't want to know me, so I suffered further agony on the way to and from school.

The ill fitting boots wore holes in my knee length stockings causing the skin from my heels to peel and expose the flesh to the back of the boots. My ankles were also skinned but didn't have the soreness of my red, raw heels. During one of my school lessons the lady teacher noticed I was grimacing with pain and inquired what was the matter. With a bubbly nose,being assisted by a flow of tears into and around my pouched mouth, I managed to tell the teacher my problem. "Why on earth did you not tell one of the Sisters the boots didn't fit properly?" "I did," I said as I wiped away the tears, having blown my nose on the handkerchief provided by the teacher. The teacher then placed a comforting arm across my shoulder then walked away.

Lifting my heavy boots in and out of the deep soft snow was a problem going to school in the morning and the three other Journeys were a much bigger problem, and far more painful, as I trampled the uneven hard ice.

Back in the playroom that afternoon Adelmia instructed me to take off my boots, she then removed my wet grey school stockings, taking with them my skin, flesh and all. The Nun then grabbed me by the shoulder, and the way in which I was spoken to as I was ushered into the washroom, made me feel as if I was a leper. Apart from the obvious pain, I also was in considerable discomfort when the Nun grabbed hold of my leg and plunged my foot into the hot salted water. After going through the same torment with the second foot the Nun, after cruelly drying my feet, then went about swabbing them in the purple liquid antiseptic.

During my first year I was puzzled at why the Nuns always

26

seemed to be punishing me, consequently I nearly always went about with a frown on my face and using my eyes to search the faces of the Nuns for answers, just as I was doing during that treatment. Having cut small pieces of lint into squares, the Nun then put them onto strips of elastoplast that-she had already cut from a roll, the elastoplast was then firmly placed across my heels and ankles.

A year later and a year wiser, I had a similar experience with a pair of those army styled boots.

As well as being a little big the boots were also old, well worn and truly beyond repair. A new piece of leather had been crudely nailed to the foot area of my right boot and added were hobnails that were much larger than the well worn rusty ones on the sole of the left boot. On placing my right foot into the repaired boot I felt the sharpness of the nails used by the cobbler to try and keep the sole and upper together. Screaming her head off and with anger in her voice, the Nun repeatedly slapped me across my head and shoulders reminding me of the sins of my father and mother. wear them Just as everyone else has to," were the words coming from Adelmia as the raging Nun pushed me away and against the hive of empty boot pigeon holes.

Now the frowning and searching were replaced by fear and hatred. It was perfectly clear to me the Nuns didn't like me and fear of them developed along side of the hatred I also had of them. I also feared punishment for situations that of which I had nothing to do with. Whatever Christian feelings I had for the Nuns didn't exist and I had grave doubts about God himself, although at times I found it necessary to pray to him for help.

I had only walked about one hundred yards when the boot in question came apart under the arch of my foot. The nails used by the cobbler failed to hold the decayed leather together. To make matters worse, it was a bitterly cold winters morning with a mixture of snow and ice covering the pavements. I was in sheer agony by the time I reached school, the agonising mile left me with a very painful arch and a terribly sore and bleeding right foot.

Somehow a message was received by the Nuns about my complaining to the teachers about the conditions of my boot and the discomfort it was causing. That dinner time, whilst in the playroom, the Nun Adelmia made a bee line for me and without a word spoken she felled me to the floor. Tears of hatred and anger filled my eyes, but I didn't cry as I got back on the bench having obeyed an order and fearing delay would stir the Nun into using the Cricket Wicket. The mouth of the Nun seemed silent as I watched it move up and down but I could feel her eyes burning into mine. It was my turn to remain silent as fear placed my mouth into a lipless seam

27

refusing to give a reply to Adelmia's silent words.

Taking off my boot was a slow and painful experience and so also was the removal of my stocking as it was sticking to my sore, blistered and skinned foot. Whilst in bed that night my thoughts were mingled with those of the year earlier.

The cobbler wasn't in his rustic cobbled floor den, so I remained cross-legged on the floor of the workroom until the other boys arrived from school. So it was to be the following morning before I had my first encounter with Jack the cobbler. Jack always answered my searching boyish questions and when he had a quiet period he would tell me stories of his past life. Jack nearly always wore the same khaki coloured shirts which were always worn under a dark, shiny, greasy jacket that was partly covered by a well worn leather cobblers apron. Rarely did I see the shoes, boots or trousers worn by my friend, this was because he was forever in a sitting position on a low stool with his heavy leather apron trailing the floor. Whenever Jack wanted anything out of his reach when I was with him, he always knew I would always give him a helping hand.

Now why the friendship between the poorly paid, friendly cobbler and I came to an unexpected and heart aching end. "What's this I hear of you visiting the cobblers?" "Me?" I quizzed. "You know what I am talking about." I shrugged my shoulders, then my lips went into a lipless seam. "One of these days the Lord will surely punish you. You are evil!" Crack! The hand of Adelmia left its mark on the side of my face. I winced before saying, "I've done nothing wrong." "Sister!" Adelmia shouted. "I have done nothing wrong, Sister." Immediately I answered her demand, then the Nun scowled at me. I felt my face flood with anger as I muttered to myself, "I hate you!".

On orders I left the"'Washroom and entered the playroom where I seeked out MacQuirk junior. On finding him playing with his usual friends I pounced on him, sending him crashing to the floor. I wrenched him upwards, then let go of him fearing my younger brother would be bullied if I continued hitting him. I closed my eyes tightly and clenched my teeth as I had the desire to smash his face in on seeing that inviting grin on his sickly looking face. He then stared at me for a moment before saying, "Hit me if you dare."

I suddenly became cold inside, then I threw myself on top of him and threw a volley of punches to his partly covered face and hands as he tried to protect himself. I was aware we had a small group gathering and from that group a voice yelled, "Stop it, stop it!". It was the voice of MacQuirk senior, he pushed his way forward shouting, "Leave him alone, leave him alone." The next minute he and I were wrestling on the floor, trying hard to be the first with a punch to the others face, I had an opportunity to land such a punch but was held back by that fear. Anyway we were parted by an unexpected visitor in the name of Nigel Bruce, another ex boy who was on leave from the Royal Air Force. The hatred burning inside me was so intense it was driving me insane, my mind was in turmoil and I wanted to murder the two Nuns, but with clenched fists it was MacQuirk junior that' I headed for, only to be prevented from getting to by the return of one of the Nuns. Not being an aggressive person made my life most difficult. There I was standing with a cold sweat on my forehead, I felt sick, my heart was thumping and pounding against my ribs. Standing there I was thinking, "If I couldn't kill those Nuns I wish someone else would."

"Perhaps it would be better if we all sat down and were quiet for a while," Adelmia shouted having blown her whistle. Several of the boys, myself included, cast nasty glances in the direction of the Nun. An instant feeling of fear was ebbing its way through my body when Adelmia hauled me away from the rest of the boys. Just inches from the doorway leading to the landing the boys began talking between themselves. "Silence!" bellowed Adelmia as she turned her head in the direction of the noise. We all knew from past experience not to hesitate about obeying an order.

It was out on the landing when I felt the power of Adelmia's hand across the side of my face. It only travelled a few inches, but when it landed I momentarily thought my head had come off my shoulders. And I sensed a hundred pair of eyes peering at me through the stone walls. Picking me up Adelmia angrily whispered into my ear, "You sly little devil, you will burn in hell for all the trouble you have caused." "You are a little liar," Adelmia again spoke in a whisper My answer was given by the shake of my head. "You are a little Liar and I don't know how on earth I can touch you," again Adelmia whispered. My head shook and my body trembled, I raised my painful head from my chest, I drew in air then wearily let it out.

Although I was to pass the cobblers hundreds of times after that ordeal, I only once got a glimpse of the friendly man. Then years later when I had settled in with the new Nuns, I popped in to see Jack and to my essorant joy Jack remembered me.

CHRISTMAS

Christmas time 1942. In the playroom the overhead rows of our hand made colourful paper chains and the Christmas tree brought delight and excitement to all of us, but not to all of us all of the time, during the Christmas period. Probably I was more excited than anyone else that particular Christmas. The tall fresh and well spruced Christmas tree was showing signs of being alive as more and more of our home made decorations and what appeared to be wrapped Christmas gifts were sprouting from the dark green branches.

As customary Mass was an hour earlier than all the other days of the year. This was to allow time for us to receive our presents before going to breakfast.

Prior to every Christmas day, Nuns and a select few from the older boys would spend quite some time sorting out in the workroom the toys collected from the previous Christmas and those which were donated from local outsiders and other resources, a daily National Newspaper I believe was a regular donator of gifts to the 'House of God'. Once the toys, etc. were sorted out it was then the task of deciding which of us got what. That Christmas I was told of the Nuns decision allowing me to have my book, Black Beauty. The book was a present from my father for my birthday earlier in the year, only to be taken from me a short while after receiving it.

On receiving the book from one of the Nuns, I immediately went to sit on the bench where I always sat when in the playroom. Filled with excitement at both receiving a present from my father and at having in my hands my very own book about Black Beauty, had me not knowing the other boys were out of the room. It was the Nun Adelmia who approached me demanding the return of the book when I was excitingly and nervously fingering my way through the pages of my present. Saying to me, "You don't deserve it. You are a little liar." That followed by what I believe were the words spoken by that Nun. "You will receive it at Christmas, providing you behave yourself between now and then." A cold smile frosted her face before ordering me to join the other boys. Spontaneously I wanted to cry and a wave of depression swept through my body. Anger and bitterness whisked with self pity. Then I was thinking how much I hated those Nuns and how much I hated that place.

During the Christmas Morning Mass, the Chapel was buzzing with excitement, I could see it and I could sense it. At the end of the service we waited impatiently for the last of the girls to leave the Chapel; and as one can expect, there was a fair amount of pushing and shoving with the boys as we were leaving the Chapel. The Nuns were well ahead of us and in the playroom before we arrived to form ourselves into numerical order along

30

the corridor outside the closed playroom doors. On opening the doors we were asked to stay in formation and to go quietly up to the Nuns by the Christmas tree where we would receive our presents.

The closer I was to the Nuns and the Christmas tree the more I filled with excitement with the thoughts of receiving MY book Black Beauty. It was as if the Christmas tree was holding out its branches towards me inviting me into its arms to collect MY book. All that time my excitement was inward, my inside was humming like a bee-hive. Then standing in front of the Nuns with my hand stretched out in front of me I couldn't conceal my feelings. I flushed with nervous excitement, my smile that wide I could have easily had lock-jaw. My whole body was trembling with the thought that in a second Black Beauty was again to be mine. With face void of emotion and with her non caring expression from her eyes, Adelmia thrust into my outstretched hand something metal loosely wrapped in green crepe paper.

My skin went like that of a cold, plucked chicken. I felt limp and void of words, the moisture in my mouth dried when something was spoken. I could just about nod my head at the sound of the voice, I being too thunderstruck to say anything. Turning away from the Nuns and that tree stillness and silence seemed to be with me before making my way to sit on the bench that they could also deprive me. I sat fumbling with the flimsy wrapping paper to destroy the No. 78 that was attached to it and wanting to destroy whatever the wrapping paper concealed. It was a motorbike of about six inches in length and made of tin. For what seemed an awful long time I sat in silence twisting and untwisting my fingers with the motorbike on the floor between my feet.

My brain was a whirl with conflicting thoughts, I was not aware of the noise of excitement that was around me until a soft cardboard aeroplane caught my ear disturbing the growing hatred that was building inside of me. Looking around with my eyes on nobody in particular I picked up the piece of tin that lay between my feet. Within seconds of picking it up I was holding the two pieces of the tin motorbike in my hands, having spent no time at all prizing apart the tiny metal tabs that were holding the two sides together. Again my eyes wandered aimlessly that was until being glued to one of the boys sitting almost opposite me with a book in his hands. For some time I sat watching the boy reading what I felt sure was MY book. He was certainly enjoying the reading, his feet tapping the floor in excitement. On raising his head our eyes locked, then the boy faintly smiling more like comic grimace, returned his eyes to the reading of the book. That was too much for me. My heart was hammering in my chest. I wanted to see if that book was really mine. Taking in and letting out a faint tremor of breath I then dashed

31

across to the boy Phelan who was wrapped in the security shawl of the Nuns whilst reading MY book. Yes, it was Black Beauty being read, I having seen the cover when on my way towards Phelan. Snatching the book from the boy I immediately went for the front inside cover, although scribbling had covered most of the hand writing, visible to me was part of the name Andrew. That was enough evidence to satisfy me that the book was that of which was sent by my father. "Listen you rat, this is my book and I am having it," were the words I would have used at that time. Although steeling myself to be calm there was tremor in my body approaching the Nuns who were sitting on a bench in conversation close to the now uninspiring Christmas tree that stood in the corner and inches away from the picture of 'The Sacred Heart of Jesus'.

Screaming threats the boy Phelan chased after me and when we stopped in front of the Nuns he attempted to grab the book from me, almost.. having me in the lap of one of the Nuns when attempting to do so. Instantly I was ordered to return the book to the boy Phelan. For a moment I did not reply, at the same time knowing I dare not refuse the order made by the Nuns. During that moment I gave a gasp of pain when from behind, Phelan cowardly punched me in the centre of my back. Then with book in hand Phelan mingled with the boys who were hovering around the Nuns. "No point in getting annoyed," said a cold and uninterested Nun, then telling me to go and play with whatever present I received. Our eyes met, the exchange lasting only a second, but it was enough of a warning to me.

Leaving the playroom I made my way towards the toilets where I sat with closed eyes and whispered a little prayer for my father and mother to some and take us away. My solitude was startled by the deep voice, "Gorman, come out here!" That was the military trained voice of the 'Hawk'.

The Hawk, as I called him, had a very strange and terrible personality. His irregularities caused great anxiety among us. He was stocky built, spruce looking, his hair dark and short, cut in true military style. There was also something I didn't like about his face, he looked evil at times when at other times I got the impression of a nice man. It wasn't long before the Hawks army training and experience were to be of great value to the Nuns and a scourge to several of the boys. With each visit the Hawk became more and more involved, assisting the Nuns whenever and wherever possible. It was that Christmas I learnt the Hawk was originally one of us. Some months prior to that Christmas I had my first sighting of the man in highly polished, black hobnailed boots and in army uniform. He appeared from out of the playroom doorway accompanied by a Nun, on seeing him I had a mental picture of kilted uniforms seen many times before. Sadness was with me that day because my previous sightings were when I was living in freedom in the city of Edinburgh.

Not expecting a call, I jumped at the demand of the Hawk. My legs were trembling when walking out of the toilet and towards the waiting military man. Standing with the Hawk and close to the washroom door was Alemenia. "Upstairs to the choir room, Sister Adelmia is waiting for you," said Alemenia. On my way up the stairs I met with one of the older boys who was coming towards me. Pushing me against the terrazzo wall and screwing his fist under my chin he said something like, "Hey Gorman, do you believe your stupid sisters also get punished every time you upset the Nuns?" I could have given answers to that question but preferred to remain silent, instead I probably said, "Adelmia is waiting for me." Standing in my way he then said, "Go on, I'm not stopping you," before removing his big carcass.

I noticed on entering the choir room, Adelmia already had the Cricket Wicket in her hand and was tapping it gently against the palm of her other. "Didn't I say to you on your Birthday that it all depends upon how you behave yourself! between now and Christmas if you see your book again?" "What have I done wrong?" I quizzed, rather frightened. Disobeying orders, defiance and the taking of which does not belong to me (reference to the book), was enough to warrant punishment according to Adelmia. She then went on to lecture me about being sent to the 'House of God' to be trained in his eyes to be good and proper Catholics in readiness for the day when we have to face the outside world. And also that I wasn't helping my brothers and sisters by being disruptive and disobedient, I was only playing into the hands of the devil of which will not be tolerated in the 'House of God'. "Now I will give you something to remind you for a long time that you are in the 'House of God' and that you will obey his commands."

I didn't wait to be asked to hold out my hands.

ONE. I was thinking about my brothers and sisters.

TWO. Had me wondering how they will be punished.

THREE. I was hating those Nuns and hating them for what they were.

FOUR. The pain had me secretly cursing the Catholic faith, but happy inside of me because she didn't know what I was thinking.

FIVE. My mind wandered towards my parents, wondering where they were as I badly needed their love and protection.

SIX.

She kept me waiting for the WICKET to fall heavily and painfully on its target then I felt the pain stretch to my heart. The hailstones came on

33

really hard again rattling against the window like gravel on a corrugated cover. "Wait here for two or three minutes, then join the others for breakfast," the Nun said as she left the room. I remained. The strain of pretending to be brave added to that of enduring the pain caused by the Cricket Wicket and of the words spoken by that Nun. I looked at my throbbing red hands and thought unthinkable things before crossing the landing for the dining room. It was whilst waiting for my breakfast I started taking my mind from what had just taken place and pondered over other things such as, "Who told the Nuns I prized open that tin motorbike."

Two days later most of the presents given to us were recovered by the Nuns then stored in cupboards in the workroom until Christmas the following year. This procedure was carried out every Christmas, you can imagine the sorrows, sadness, tears and tantrums of boys of different ages on being parted with what some thought to be rightly theirs, some having been given to them by Father Christmas.

When I say Christmas has no meaning for me, I am sure you will understand my reasons. for feeling that way.

THE CATHEDRAL

My memories of my early years attending St Mary's Junior School are perhaps not much different from those of any other of the boys from the orphanage. But my Sunday visits to the St Mary's Catholic Cathedral built in 1849 and situated in Huntly Street just off the famous, long Union Street and all its grandeur with the Woolworths Store and its "Nothing Over Sixpence" logo pleasantly tucked in the 'Attic of my mind', is a different tale.

On Sundays at approximately 11am, the choir boys went to the Cathedral to sing during the High Mass. This weekly trip was for the most of us a duty rather than a pleasure, we having attended our own Holy ceremony earlier in the morning. It was a love hate relationship that I had with the Cathedral in those days, my feelings would change oh so often. Once inside the doorway of the Cathedral I sensed the freedom it gave to me yet I hated being there because it was another 'House of God'.

We, now and then, used our 'pea shooters' to fire our well chewed pieces of paper at the heads of the bald men at the rear of the congregation and immediately below our balcony. That was great fun if only because of the failure of the bald headed victims and their accomplices to find the culprits. On one occasion a bald headed victim did attempt to find out what was going on and he threatened to inform the Mother Superior if it happened again. We waited for his return to his place in the pew, then as soon as he turned his head forward having looked around and up at us, we gave several blasts of our pea shooters in his direction, not all the little balls landed on target but we were satisfied with the result, the little bald headed man being further annoyed but didn't do anything about it.

Then there was the day when I wanted the organ player to fall from his stool so that he wouldn't be able to sit in his usual pompous glory, moving his arms and body as if he were the centre of a grand audience at the Halle. Then looking around and at the organ player I suddenly took a great dislike of his face and the sickly smile I received from it when our eyes met. Another wave-of depression swept through my body, bringing with it the refusal to join in with the other boys with music for the satisfaction of all below us. Well perhaps I did attempt one note.

Then there was a Christmas in the latter years of my school days, when on hearing I was again selected for the choir to attend the Cathedral, I muttered a few swear words that I had picked up but never before used. Thick snow carpeted the ground so we had to set off sooner than we usually did. I wasn't feeling at all pleased at the thought of trekking the long distance just to please a few bald headed men and ladies in stupid hats, but I soon rid myself of that feeling as I more and more enjoyed ploughing

35

through the deep, soft snow and at the fun of throwing and seeing snowballs flying through the air to be sent into dusty snowflakes on reaching their target.

The atmosphere was alive on entering the Cathedral, I sensed music and happiness in the air, although the only sounds came from those moving about to find a suitable place for their hour or so stay in the Cathedral. My feelings again to change on entering the choir balcony and having noticed the groupings of several outsider boys and girls with their mums and dads. Despair and envy replaced the earlier feelings of joy in my mind I was seeing what could be if I, my brothers and sisters and mum and dad were altogether. I did make a great effort to sing in tune with the other boys only because my thoughts were far away with my mum in a previous life. Soon my moments of dreaming were to come to an abrupt end, the choir master having to tap me on the back of my hand with the knuckles of his, then I was aware of scowling eyes upon me. My spirits sank and again I was thinking unthinkable things, which lasted during much of the return journey through the then disturbed snow, I having the solitude of a rear end gunner.

STICKS

It was Christmas time - 1944 and I was 10 years old. The usual Christmas preparations were going on, although I was convinced Saint Patricks' Day was the big day in the calendar of the two Nuns. It was during that festive period when the 'Nativity Sticks' went missing. Little did I know at that time that those STICKS were to be the ghosts of my life. It was coming up to bedtime and after an intensive search and intensive questioning the STICKS were not found.

I was about to slip between the white cotton sheets when the Hawk approached me and requested I got out of bed and follow him to the-landing between the two dormitories. Adelmia was standing against the bannister seemingly meditating. Her head was drooped and the Rosary Beads were slipping through her fingers. "Why have you not mentioned that you were in the workroom early this morning?" Adelmia asked in a firm voice that demanded an answer. Not having been in the workroom at anytime during the day I couldn't give the answer she was waiting for. With a look of disbelief firmly etched on her face and with the prodding assistance in the middle of my back from the Hawk; the Nun didn't get the answer she wanted after asking the same question. "I am not accusing you of taking anything from the workroom, I only want to know what you were doing there before your breakfast?" It was cunningly put by Adelmia but it only gave her the same answer as given to her before. Looking at the Hawk Adelmia said, "I believe what he has said." To me she gave a glazed look and said I could return to my bed. Mumbling to myself, I made myself comfortable in bed and closed my eyes just as the dormitory lights dimmed. I must have slept the night well as I was feeling wide awake the following morning and none the worse for the enquiries of the night before.

Serving breakfast that morning was Alemenia, and as I approached her with my bowl in my hands for my helping of porridge, she gave me a look that sent a nervous shiver along my spine. .I must have had a look of 'OLIVER' and the feelings of him when my hands that were holding the bowl in front of the Nun began to shake on hearing the Nun calling me a liar. Having scooped the porridge from the urn, Alemenia then plopped the gluey mess into my bowl catching my thumb with the ladle when doing so. I returned to my table muttering to myself that I hated the place and the two Nuns and I wanted to run away.

Unknown to me at that time, Adelmia and the Hawk were in the Choir room questioning a boy called Artist about the missing 'STICKS'. Later we were playing in the playroom, it having rained incessantly for hours. During the time of play, Benny Griffen tugged my arm saying he had something important to tell me so we made our way to the washroom. We were alone during the conversation, he telling me that he was outside the Choir room listening to what was being said and as the door was slightly ajar he could also see what was going on. It wasn't long after Benny and I returned to the playroom that I was SUMMONED to the Choir Room.

Artist scrambled past me on the way downstairs and as I glanced over my shoulder, I saw him vanish into the toilets. In the presence of the Hawk and two of the older boys, Adelmia asked me several searching questions. Not being satisfied with the answers she then called for the return of the boy Artist. "Gorman insists he doesn't know anything about the missing 'STICKS'," Adelmia said to Artist. "He is telling lies Sister. He is always telling lies, isn't he?" Adelmia shook Artist by the shoulder. "Tell me the truth," she shouted at him. "Yes, yes!" Artist frighteningly said to Adelmia, bursting into tears. "I saw Gorman take the 'STICKS ' from the workroom before we had breakfast." "You liar,"I shouted at Artist as I made forward to hit You liar, or shove him, only to be prevented from doing so by the Hawk as he placed his uniformed frame between us. Artist was trembling in every limb. "I did see you take those 'STICKS'. Nobody likes you," he added. "I have never seen them Sister," I replied, when Adelmia turned to me and said, "Well?" Again shaking Artist by the shoulder Adelmia shouted, "Tell the truth. For the last time, when did you see Gorman take those 'STICKS'?" Artist answered as before. I muttered to myself, "Please God tell them I am innocent." The Irish blood in Adelmia was at near boiling point and although she tried to control herself, it was -obviously difficult. With one almighty swoop, her hand caught me a thumping smack across the side of my head, sending me into the arms of the two older boys who were standing close by. I was then left to the mercy of the boys, they having received instructions from Adelmia to get to the 'bottom of it.' The two instantly and pleasurably agreed as soon as we were on our own. After a long and painful period of being shoved from one boy to the other, kicked, punched, arms twisted and verbally abused, it was no joy to see the return of the Nun Adelmia. As she approached me, the Servant of God whispered in my ear, "You are a thief and a liar." When I made no comment, the Nun repeated the words again, this time only a little louder. Pushing me to the floor Adelmia then shouted, "Show me a liar and I will give you a thief." I placed my hands over my ears for I did not want to hear anymore. Pulling away my hands, Adelmia then said, "You will burn in Hell for the trouble you have caused." Ordering me to my feet the Nun continued by saying, "Show me a liar and I will give you a thief," this time the words were directed in the direction of the two onlookers.

For the first time during the period of interrogation the Nun produced the Cricket Wicket, but it was the back of her lethal hand that sent me sprawling to the floor which was the cause of my cheek bone being painful for a long time after. Sweat was now running down my ribs and my vest was clinging to them. All three left the room. My heart began to beat faster. After the lull of anxious waiting I suddenly became cold and petrified. On returning and standing to her height, Adelmia again produced the Cricket Wicket and with a look of anger in her eyes she hurried towards me several times catching me with the Cricket Wicket, leaving my knuckles and wrists the most painful, they being the safer targets for the sadistic pleasure of the Nun. Several of the words that were said before were mentioned again and again. My tongue stayed firmly behind my teeth, my mouth wouldn't open.

"The boys are waiting to be served," said Alemenia as she stood in the doorway. Alemenia smiled a sickly smile, the smile widened as she looked at me. Grimacing with pain and clenched fists pressing one and another between my knees, I made my way across to the dining room where the other boys were impatiently waiting for their dinner. Within seconds of the Nuns entering the dining room the talking ceased and so did all movements. In times such as this, the Nuns only had to present themselves to us to command instant silence.

Standing face towards us Adelmia said, "I only want to know the truth about the missing 'STICKS', so if any one of you saw or knows what happened to the 'STICKS' let me know. Don't be afraid of coming forward, as it will be a secret." The Nun did not have to raise her voice when she spoke, the room being eerily quiet. After the meal and having brought us all to her attention, Alemenia had her say about the 'STICKS'. 'Her words were more or less a repeat of what was mentioned earlier by her partner. Apart from two of the helpers, the rest of us made our way to the playroom. Some time had passed then Adelmia arrived on the scene, again there was that deadly eerie silence. Every one of us waited, breathlessly waiting for the Nun to say or do something. There were about eighty boys suddenly transformed into robots, daring not to move from the positions we were holding, whilst the eyes of the Nun travelled like a searchlight over all of us before returning to a fixed position on me. She then pushed towards me and with one almighty swipe felled me to my knees, then I toppled over having ducked a second swipe. I, returning to my knees, looked Adelmia in the face, she getting the message of my hatred of her without a word being spoken. Grabbing me by the shoulder to lift me to my feet, Adelmia once again told me that I had the eyes of the devil. On the release of her grip, I stumbled into Tom MacQuirk and received a sharp kick on the ankle from him. I wished I had the guts to go for MacQuirk, for inwardly I knew I could batter him, but I would soon be in trouble if I laid a finger on him. It was MacQuirks younger brother Jack that was the one who was spreading rumours that I was the thief that everyone wanted brought to justice. But under constant questioning, Jack MacQuirk admitted he invented the story to get his own back on me for claiming the marbles he found the day before. With the Hawk in charge, the Nuns left the room for their period of prayers or for whatever they had to do. I was greatly relieved during the period the nuns were away, even though I received a great deal of verbal abuse and threats from several of the boys.

My friend Gerry noticed I was a sitting target for a group of boys who found great delight in several attempts to jerk me off the bench on which I was sitting. Having told the group to move away, Gerry then tried to comfort me by saying that he believed I was set up and that the culprit will soon be caught. That uplifting of spirit was soon dampened by the return of one of the Nuns indicating as always that it was nearing tea time. I was ready for my tea, for the happenings of the day had left me cold and hungry. I kept a low profile at tea time, helped of course by having my tea given to me at my table by one of the servers. That incident brought puzzled glances, not only from my table, but from others as well which made me shudder a little. Before tea was over, the Nun Adelmia approached me requesting I went with her to the Choir room, the Hawk followed.

"What were you doing in the playing field early yesterday morning?" The Nun wanted an immediate reply to her question. I couldn't give it as I was momentarily speechless .... then .... "That isn't true, I wasn't there," I replied in anger. "What did you do with those 'STICKS'," Adelmia repeated over and over again as she thumbed the Cricket Wicket. "I have been told you threw them over the railings onto the street," said the Nun with a nerving ring to her voice. "That's a lie!" I shouted. "You will burn in Hell when you die, mark my words," Adelmia was about to repeat herself when Alemenia popped her head through the doorway and beckoned her partner out onto the landing. For a few chilling moments, I was left with the Hawk. I wasn't one of his punch bags, neither was I one of his friends.

On her return, Adelmia looking at the Hawk and pointing a rigid finger in my direction, angrily said, "He is a thief! A liar! and he has the eyes of the devil." Then after a brief pause, "Holy Mary Mother of God," the Nun angrily said to herself as she forced me to arms length, then with her free hand she sent the Cricket Wicket crashing down onto the back of my hand, removing skin from my knuckles, it hurt but I didn't cry, that angered the Nun even more. "Holy Saint Patrick ....," the rest of the words were completed under her breath. "What is the 7th Commandment," I was asked by the nun. "Thou shall not steal, is the 7th Commandment," Adelmia dictated to me. "Say it aloud twenty times," bellowed the Hawk, as his horrible snub nose almost touched mine. I was well aware of what was in store for me if I didn't obey the instructions of the Hawk. I commenced immediately. At the end of the count, both the Hawk and the Nun left the room, I didn't know what to do but I did let out a temporary sigh of relief, which was painful. Time was passing and during that time I didn't know whether to stand, walk, sit on the piano stool or edge my way towards the open door. I made my mind up and edged my way to the doorway with the hope of seeing nobody as I wanted to go to the toilet. Standing there, waiting to be brave and make a move, I was thinking and feeling hatred towards the Nuns and the place I was in.

It wasn't normal hatred, it was a fired hatred, my whole body seemed to be aflame as if the fires of hell were burning inside me. My whole personality seemed to be changing, the change sweeping through my body. No longer was I interested in anyone or anything except my brothers and sisters, and throwing myself over the stair bannister wasn't going to help them.

A call of nature was the only reason for me spotting a boy on his way upstairs as I looked over the bannister, he had come to tell me I was wanted in the playroom. I scrambled down the stairs as fast as I could, the urge of nature overriding all other feelings I had. After relieving myself, I nervously and hesitantly made my way into the playroom where the two Nuns and the other boys were gathered. A handful of boys were sitting around the Nuns, most of whom were darning socks. On being seen, Adelmia beckoned me to sit on the floor dangerously close to Alemenia. Within seconds of my sitting my head was thrust back and a wooden cotton spool thrust into my mouth, and within seconds it began its drying and drawing effects. Also within seconds of placing the wooden spool into my mouth, the Nun said it would prevent me from telling anymore lies. That remark brought a few feeble laughs from the surrounding boys. To add to my humiliation, a sock was tied around my head. With the blindfold, the wooden spool in my mouth and my hands tied behind my back, (knotted with fear), I was an easy target for the cowards, the show-offs and the crawlers, all of which kindled the fire of hatred still burning inside of me. At tea time I was released 'and allowed to join the others for tea. Only my aching limbs and sore swollen mouth gave me an indication of how long I was at the mercy of others, for inchoate thoughts flashed inexorably through my mind, all of which were of a culpable nature.

Nothing out of the ordinary happened until before breakfast the following morning. It was then the wooden spool was again thrust into my mouth by the Nun Alemenia. I was then ordered to place my hands behind my back before being frog marched from the bathroom to the dining room. Not having received my porridge, I found myself sitting looking down at the piece of bacon and a measure of scrambled egg on the plate in front of me. I couldn't remove the spool from my mouth because I was too afraid to release my hands behind my back. The boy next to me quickly acted on the opportunity and scoffed the-lot in a matter of seconds. Making my way down the stairs towards the playroom was another painful experience, as my hands still remained tied, and the wooden spool was still being held firmly in place by my teeth .... being given the occasional nudge didn't help-either. For what reason, I do not know, but soon after arriving in the playroom, the spool was removed and I was ordered into the washroom to get a drink of water. Although being very glad to get a drink, it was painful swallowing, my mouth was that sore and raw in places. My hours before dinner were mostly spent sitting on a bench watching the other boys playing, and a few who couldn't resist, a punch or two when it was safe to do so.

At last it was time for a meal, and I was ready to eat anything not having eaten since the day before. In the dining room I joined the queue to be served a bowl of the usual watery soup, having received mine I returned to my table where one of the Nuns was standing. Fearing to look at her I didn't do so, I just placed my bowl of soup on the table and waited for prayers to be said before lifting my spoon to my mouth. I was glad the soup wasn't too hot, because the inside of my mouth was quite sore and raw in places. That wasn't to be my only problem! The Nun standing close to me made sure of that by again thrusting the wooden spool into my mouth and tried to force me to suck the soup through the small hole of the spool. To prevent too much of a mess, the Nun used one hand to grip the back of my shirt and the other hand to gently force my head down towards the soup. 'With a horrible chilling anger in her voice, the Nun several times ordered me to suck through the hole of the spool. That I found impossible to do, so the Nun forced my-face, spool as well, into the bowl of soup. Immediately I began to cough and splutter, afraid to use my hands to steady the bowl. During that ordeal I was watched by a hundred pair of eyes, all of which were ordered to mind their own business. Breathing rather heavily, the Nun ordered the remainder of the meal to be served. Slowly and painfully I digested what was in front of me, having received permission to remove the spool from my mouth, and also told to replace it when I had finished my cup of tea.

Grace after meal was voiced, then I became a standing exhibition to all who passed me on their way out of the dining room to the playroom. With an unforgettable look of aversion, Alemenia ordered me downstairs to stand in the corner near to the picture of the Sacred Heart of Jesus, and I had to face the corner not to move until told to do so. Within a matter of minutes of doing what I was told, my hands were then placed behind my back and I was forced closer to the corner. The noise in the playroom grew. Paper planes were made and thrown, a few of which landed near me. I began to feel faint and my eyes were heavy and closing. I had to move away from the corner otherwise I would have landed in a pile on the floor. At a later stage I wanted to pee, slowly I began crossing my knees and hoping to catch the eyes of one of the two Nuns when I peered over my shoulder. My knees were crossing more frequently and the glances towards the Nuns more pleading. My eyes met Adelmia's and within a second I was on my way to the toilet. Dribbles were running down the inside of my left leg as I rushed towards the toilet and my willy was in my hand urinating long before I reached the urinal. After shuddering with relief, I dried my wet leg with the sleeve of my shirt, then dried my hands on my pants before returning to the stand in the corner. The trauma of the STICKS was having its affects, my legs were weak and I was feeling tired, it was a sickly tiredness I was experiencing and I was wishing I could float off to somewhere dark and quiet never to be found.

Although one of the Nuns had removed the wooden spool from my mouth, I couldn't face food or drink at tea time, the boy sitting near to me soon pounced on my plate when I nodded to his request. Nothing more was said to me that evening until we were undressing for bed. Having donned my pyjamas I was then ordered to wait near to the Cell of the Nun Adelmia, she and Alemenia soon arrived and having concluded their close conversation Alemenia left to go to her dormitory. Adelmia then was joined by three of the older boys, the group were standing close to me and were discussing the latest information about the STICKS. I stood tensely quiet and deeply frightened at what I overheard. "Where exactly was your brother when you saw him in the workroom?" An edge of steel underlined the question put by Adelmia. Not having been anywhere near the workroom on the day in question and not knowing what the STICKS looked like, I couldn't give the answer the Nun desperately desired. "Well, I believe what I have heard, now you have a last chance to tell the truth before you and your brother are handed over." Without uttering another word, the Nun grabbed me by the arm and pulled me towards the landing just outside the door nearest to us. Maintaining her firm grip and hugging me close to her the Nun injected cold, sickly words of animosity into my ear. You have brought nothing but trouble and sin into the 'House of the Lord' and God will never forgive you unless you change your ways." After a moments pause the Nun continued by saying, "Don't you think you have suffered enough for the sins of your father and mother without further angering our Lord by telling lies and stealing in his holy house?" I stiffened but couldn't answer. Just then the

43

Nun Alemenia returned meeting Adelmia in the middle of the landing well away from where I was standing. Returning together the Nuns told me that my brother Bill had actually admitted to seeing me in possession of the STICKS and that I was running towards the playing field at the time. Although we were rarely in each others company I couldn't believe my brother would say such a thing about me. "Why should I admit to something I know nothing about?" I nervously replied to what my brother had supposedly said. Clout! "Speak up," bellowed Adelmia, then in a different tone of anger she said, "You stole those STICKS, admit it!" More hatred and confusion immediately got tangled in my disrupting and over tired and weary mind. Again I said I knew nothing about the STICKS. Adelmia then opened her mouth to reply, then closed it and stared a peering stare in my direction, her jaw was clenched angrily as she said in a cold, firm voice, "Do you realise what is in store for you if you don't confess?" I shuddered at the thought. Having failed to persuade me, Adelmia handed me over to the three older boys who were waiting in the dormitory. The boys who were not yet in bed were ordered to do so by Alemenia as she parted from Adelmia, both Nuns making their way to their cells.

Almost immediately my legs were attacked from behind. "You liar, show me a liar and I will give you a thief." The words of the Nuns were repeated by one of the boys. A couple of sneezes brought pain to my chest. From behind a boy firmly placed his hand on my shoulder and gave me a shove that had all the strength of a strong person behind it. I stumbled then fell to the floor. As I picked myself up I pleaded I didn't know anything about the missing STICKS. One of the three boys was of senior age to the other two and he was also a regular 'alter boy', and it was he who said to me that I made it perfectly clear during the last few days that I didn't care if the rest of them didn't enjoy their Christmas. And he also said that for a long time he suspected the devil to be behind my shinning-and evil eyes. I had an awful feeling it was to be a long weary night under the blue dim lit night light. I was being a source of entertainment for those boys who were awake and daring enough to be caught.

"You feel tired don't you skinny Gorman," one of the attackers said to me. To answer I could only shake my head. "No," said another with a sly grin on his face, "You are not thirsty either are you?" Again I answered by moving my head slowly from side to side. After a period of silence I asked to go to the toilet. "You can't," came one voice. Then after a short pause; "Tell us what you did with the STICKS then you can go to the toilet," said another voice. Standing there momentarily floating and mustering a little strength I managed to cross my legs, and then, "Go on," said the first voice on hearing the movements of a Nun coming up the stairs towards

44

the dormitory. On passing Alemenia on the stairs I answered her piercing glance by telling her I was going for a 'No. 1' and at the same time ducking my head to avoid a back hander from the Servant of God.

After relieving myself I sat on the first stair of the flight landing to the dormitory, too scared for returning to the 'Kangaroo Court', where I might be beaten up if I continued to plead my innocence. Well after a few short and somewhat weary intakes of breath I clambered my way back to the dormitory. At the end of-another spell of interrogation and being bombarded with the words "Holy Mary Mother of God" before and after every question fired at me by the Nuns, they handed me over to the three boys. That wasn't for long though, it was a reminder of the time by one Nun to the other that saved me from further abuse, all of us being told to return to our beds, the three were thanked for their help. I can't remember sleeping that night, but I do remember it being a night during which I welled private tears, tears for the situation in which I found myself, tears for my brothers and sisters and for being separated from them and they from one another. There were tears for my father and mother and at being parted from them and at not knowing where they were, and there were tears for the memories of the past life.

The following day I was subjected to further torture and ridicule. The moment of that day which I also can never forget was when we were all in line formation on the stairs going to the dining room at tea time. At the dining room doorway Adelmia grabbed hold of me and called out, "Show me a thief and I will give you a liar". It was a deep wound because my five year old brother, (for the pleasure of the Nun), called me a stinking liar and aimed a kick at my ankles on his way past me. To this day that ulcer raises its ugly head.

Today is Saturday and unknown to me at the time, it was to be my final day of punishment over the missing STICKS. Just as every Saturday, it was domestic day. I and about seven others were selected to polish the playroom floor. This time I was given no protection for my knees and after only a few yards of polishing and a few kicks on the backside, my knees started slipping from under me and by the time I reached the end of the floor my knees were burning like hell and looking like crinkled raw tomatoes. The older boys who were supervising seemed to be pleased with our labour and allowed us to put away the tins of polish and the soggy cloths with them. All the chores being done and inspected to the satisfaction of the Nuns, most of the boys made their way to the playing field, I found myself in the company of a bunch of older boys. We were in the washroom when Adelmia grabbed me by the back of the neck with great force. The Nun whispered into my ear, "you little skinny wretch, you horrible son of the

45

devil." And in between almost every word she gave me a clout with her bare hand. Releasing her grip on my neck, Adelmia allowed me to join the other boys in the playing field, but I was not to speak to anyone.

I will not go into the pain I suffered from the scalding hot water and the Jeyes fluid at bath time, neither will I mention the thoughts that were running through my mind when the Nun was applying medication to my skinned and burning knees.

That night after we had said bed prayers, Adelmia approached me instructing' me to stand near to her cell and that I was to place my hands behind my back. The floor polish beneath me began to soften from the heat of my bare feet and I was having slight dizzy spells. My eyes were terribly tired and awfully heavy and my body started to sway a little as a result of standing in one position for what seemed a long time. There was movement behind—the curtained window of Adelmia's cell, the curtains having moved slightly. Closing her cell door behind her, Adelmia then closed in on me holding her Cricket Wicket in her hand, she stuck it under my chin until my head would go no further back. That placed me in further discomfort, engraving in my heart further hatred for the Nuns. The usual holy names and sayings were not having the slightest effect on me and after a while I was allowed to go to bed. I slipped between the bedclothes and had just placed my weary head on the pillow when Adelmia rushed over, half dragging me out of bed, she told me I hadn't said my prayers, having said them for the second time that night I got into bed.

It was an agonising night of tossing and turning, my mind in turmoil. Nun's voices were coming at me from all directions, they were as sharp as a warriors arrow and having the same penetrating effect. I was trapped in an old barn in the middle of a horrific thunder storm, the Nuns sprouted wings and floated around the barn as if they were on a cushion of air. I kicked out at them and missed. Suddenly they changed into devils and insane red lights danced in their eyes. Again I kicked out at them and missed. I was terrified, the Nun's voices were trapped inside my head and threatening to break loose, I felt I was going to explode in all directions. One of the Nuns approached me with a swish in her hand, she was flicking and twisting it as if it were a whip. With the words: "You are going to Hell when you die," echoing in my head I fell into a deep sleep, the sort of sleep that is painful to wake from.

The stench of wet beds seemed stronger than usual that morning and my body and mind were so numb I could hardly muster the energy to think. There was no physical punishment that day and the STICKS were never again mentioned. That may read good to you, but I can assure you the mental scars are still with me to this day.

BATHROOM INCIDENTS

We were assembled in the bathroom for our weekly bath when, there was an outburst of laughter from a group of boys standing a little distance from where I and others were grouped. I didn't see anything that warranted such an outburst of laughter so I assumed it was something that was said within the group. Laughter was rare in the bathroom only because it was forbidden by the Nuns. Laughter in the bathroom incorporated sins according to the Nuns and this usually brought the 'SWISH' into action.

The SWISH!

Growing in the street side of the playing field was an evergreen Holly tree. When removed, the long thin subtle branches were cleanly stripped of their twigs and knots cut to about three feet long leaving an ideal substitute for the Cricket Wicket. To me the SWISH always seemed to be alive, the Nuns used it in the same manner as a cowboy used his whip during a display of skills. As the swish howled, whined and swished through the air it scattered us all in directions causing many of us to lose control of the towel that wrapped around our waist. Unusually, the bath room door was closed preventing anyone escaping what appeared to be a period of sadistic joy for the Nun in charge. Without causing any physical damage and having gained control of her Irish temper, the Nun ordered us into our usual groups outside the bath cubicles. At about that time the other Nun arrived to assist her friend in the bathing of those who had not quite reached a reliable age to bath themselves.

Our heart beats had returned to normal by the time the Nuns had tested the temperature of the bath water and added, as usual, too much Jeyes fluid to the water. As always boys were leaving the bath cubicles with the usual red colouring from the chest downwards, a result of the over hot bath water assisted by over use of the scrubbing brush which the Nuns used to cleanse our bodies; at times I thought they were trying to 'reach our Souls! Those of us who were unfortunate to house sores found the Jeyes fluid as much a weapon as the Cricket Wicket, the swish and the lethal hands of the Nuns.

I was about ten years of age when a further incident took place in the bathroom. Having bathed the younger boys the Nuns surprisingly made their way into our cubicles. We who were waiting to have a bath looked at one another in total amazement. That amazement soon turned into looks of sudden awareness when a Nun shouted, "Next!" The boy who had been in the bath when Adelmia entered the cubicle just shrugged his shoulders when he passed us with a towel around his waist. The Nun Adelmia was in a mean mood, that was obvious by the painful noises coming from the cubicle, then the sudden silence. That boy left the cubicle with a face as red as his lower parts, as he passed us he lowered his head, his eyes staring at the floor in front of him which had several patches of bath water resting on it. Adelmia released some of the bath water adding cleaner, hotter water mixing with it a further dosage of that burning Jeyes fluid. Noises similar to which came from the previous boy echoed the same bath cubicle, this was immediately followed by a disturbance of water and the same eerie silence as before. That boy also had signs of embarrassment covering his face when he appeared at the cubicle entrance, and he also was obviously quite nervous when passing us. It was to be the same for the boy who followed.

My mind was in a whirl. What is she doing? What is she doing? was going through my mind. Myself and the other three boys who were waiting for a bath were fidgety, moving our feet nervously, then trying to jockey for places other than the first. "Next!" Adelmia s unwelcome voice penetrated my ears. On response we continued jockeying to avoid or should I say, delay an e-x-p-e-r-i-e-n-c-e. "Next one!" Again the voice from within the cubicle feverishly echoed between my ears. The unfortunate boy seemed to be struggling, we could hear lots of water being splashed about and a few moans followed by muffled sounds which together added further fear into my fearing body. Although the central heating kindled warmth into our bodies, it was such occasions that that blanket of warmth was penetrated by ice cold fear harpooned by the Nuns. With my mind in turmoil the boy appeared from the cubicle flushed and breathing rather heavily. Standing for a few seconds in front of me my eyes desperately and firmly fixed on his, desirous of an answer I didn't get. The boy moved off leaving my mind strangled with briars and weeds.

"Next one?" The words from the cubicle took longer to penetrate bringing Adelmia out of the cubicle. I was the nearest but the Nun grabbed another boy firmly, placing her witch-like hand around his upper arm causing the boy to wince. Seconds later bath water was slapping the cubicle floor reminding me of sea water being disturbed by whatever disturbs an angry sea. Hardly a voice was heard from the cubicle, but when the boy rushed out of the cubicle he was well flushed holding his towel firmly against his private parts.

A lethal smell of Jeyes fluid penetrated my nostrils as I waited the Order of command, I was sick with fear of what was in store for me. As the messenger of God loomed in front of me, her wet hands in the praying position, I could only stand and look at her riddled with a guilt invidious face. "You can bath yourself," Adelmia said with breathing difficulties, throwing my mind into frightening disbelief. I was in and out of the bath within seconds of my feet touching the bottom. I needn't of worried because one of the boys popped his head through the doorway to tell me the Nuns had left

48

the bathroom. As far as I can remember, there were no complaints from the boys who were bathed by Alemenia. Come to think about it, I can't remember anyone complaining about Adelmia either.

There was an almighty thud when a boys head met the wet terrazzo floor of the bathroom. All eyes were fixed on the figure lying motionless ..... it was my brother Bill. I stood there staring, my life seemed to have stopped, there was no beat in my heart, I felt glued to the floor. Bill looked to be dead. He slipped on the wet terrazzo floor, fell backwards hitting the floor with the back of his head. Adelmia's voice of offer of assistance jerked me to life, I with others, offered to assist the Nun lift my brother to a bed in the nearby dormitory. A bigger and older boy was summoned to assist the Nun, I being rejected. Rushing upstairs was Alemenia, in a state of panic she knocked over two small boys who unhurt, immediately picked themselves up. Obviously the Nun had knowledge of what had happened as she was crossing herself time after time until she entered the bedroom. Before entering the bedroom a voice rang out, "It's Bill Gorman, he... he...he has hit his head on the bathroom floor." The voice of the boy threw a series of cold and uncertain shudders through my body. With both Nuns in the bedroom I crouched by the door peering, stretching my neck and strenuously pricking my ears in desperation eager to find out if my brother was alive. When there was no response to the repeated pleas of "Come on, wake up" the Nuns broke into a muttered and anxious conversation, up," resulting in one of them hurrying along the bedroom and through the door. With a couple of the older boys standing by my brother Alemenia made her way towards where I was painfully crouched. "I want to see my brother," I pleaded in a fragile voice. You can't, was Alemenia's reply. The pleading look on my face as I got to standing position met with a slap on the face from the wiry hand of the Nun. Further pleading received as before followed by, "Get out of my sight." That scowling reply coiled further despair and deeper hatred of the Nuns and the place I was in. "Holy Mary give me strength. Out of my sight," Alemenia demanded when I didn't move from where I was standing. "I...I...I...I want to see my brother." Before I could say more, the Nun grabbed my arm in a vice like grip, shaking me vigorously I was pulled into the bathroom where the Nun bellowed into my ear, "Stay in here and keep quiet." Before leaving the bathroom the Nun checked everyone had had their bath, satisfied she then quickly gave orders for the cleaning of the baths and bathroom. On leaving the room the Nun stared at me as if I was a thorn in her side, I returned a similar stare wanting to jump on her and beat her to the ground until she was dead. That's an awful feeling, but that is exactly how I felt, I could feel the hatred burning inside me. I badly wanted to see my brother. "Why won't they let me see my brother?" those words were racing through my mind .... I edged my way to the bathroom door. "Good," I said to myself, seeing no Nuns in sight, only a few boys of my own age on the landing between the bathroom and the bedroom where my brother was. Cyril was the nearest to me. "Pst...Pst...Pst, Cyril!" I thought he would never hear me, then he turned around, responding to beckoning gestures, Cyril moved towards me. I asked what was going on. "They think Bill is dead," Cyril said in a nervous whisper. The tears wouldn't flow, I wanted them to flow but they wouldn't. "Adelmia has gone to get a Priest and a Doctor," were Cyrils concluding words. That was it! I couldn't stand there any longer. Having hurried my way through the group of boys standing on the landing I entered the bedroom only to be met by the Nun Alemenia. "You little disobedient creature, you were told to stay in the bathroom," 'her hand held high pointing in that direction. I placed myself in front of Alemenia and facing her I looked up into her eyes and pleaded to see my brother. My plea failed. To the bathroom I returned. Every pulse in my body was thumping. In my head I had thoughts of dozens of Nuns with Cricket Wickets pounding away. My arms were dangling by my side and my fists were clenched so tight they ached. How I hated those Nuns. I hated them both for what they really are. Standing in the cold atmosphere of the bathroom I was thinking, "Where is my brother, where is he, what happened to him, where is he? Has the Doctor taken Bill away," also entered my thoughts. The muscles in my stomach began to harden and pains were entering my chest, the Nuns were still there with their Cricket Wickets.

"Where is my brother," echoed around the bathroom as I shouted the words out. My mind was again in turmoil. "Have they taken Bill away, is he dead? Why won't they allow me to see my brother, why?" I dashed quickly out of the bathroom and into the dormitory ... there was no one there! Momentarily my heart stopped, then a hand rested on my shoulder, momentarily again my heart stopped, I turned my head slowly around, it was my friend Gerry. "Bill is o.k. he is in the sick room. The Doctor said he has to be kept quiet and to rest for a few days." My knees wobbled with relief, I shuddered then went cold. The tension drained away from me only to be replaced with a fiery anger at not being allowed to see Bill. My thanks to my friend Gerry for the good news was just a 'Thank You' smile.

On leaving the dormitory I met Adelmia coming downstairs from the sick room where they had taken Bill, I asked the Nun if I could see Bill. The Nun snapped at me saying, "You are the last person in this world your brother needs to see." I pouched my mouth, dropped my head on my chest, took a deep intake of breath and wished fire to flow from my mouth in the direction of the Nuns clothing. It was several days after that I saw Bill, he was sitting in the sunlight close to the swings.

NICK THE PROTAGONIST

Cricket was a game for the sissy's of England, so we were made to believe not only by the Nuns but by the older boys. So as soccer was the name of the game I can't give you the exact time of the year the following incident took place. What I do know is it was a lovely crisp, sunny Saturday morning, either late into summer or very early into autumn.

Twenty or so of the boys were playing soccer, others were either playing at minor games that children of various ages usually play or several, but not all of the others, were passing time away engaging themselves in nature studies, such as searching the soil and crumbling red brick walls for creepy crawlies, or chasing after butterflies. Two of the boys were given the o.k. by the Nun on duty to build a make shift tent on top of the concrete shelter in the corner of the playing field, near to the field entrance.

Unknown to the Nun or to anyone, the two boys had accumulated over a period of time a stock pile of rubbish which they had hidden in the concrete shelter. Well the two boys enjoyed playing with their tent made out of old patched cotton sheets and strong branches from trees growing in the playing field. That particular enjoyment was after a while concluded by the Nun because she feared there could be an accident. The two boys resented being told to dismantle their tent and that they and their tent had to come down. Within seconds of the Nun blowing her whistle, flames and smoke were seen to be coming from the inside of the tent on top of the concrete shelter. They had piled most of their accumulated rubbish into the tent and set it alight. The Nun was scared out of her habit, petrified in case the scene turned nasty. She was throwing her arms all over the place, shouting at, then pleading with the two boys to put to an end their new found enjoyment. When I got closer to the scene I noticed it was Nick and his friend that were entertaining us and scaring the life out of the Nun who had three or perhaps four sympathisers.

Nick and his partner in crime were standing a few feet apart smiling at each other when I joined the jubilant crowd close to the stage. Apparently the smiles were their unspoken answer to the Nuns pleading for them to come down. "Holy Mary Mother of God, will you come down before you are burnt to death," shouted the Nun as she got to within fifteen feet of the shelter. "No Sister," shouted Nick as he danced with joy, his friend repeated and copied everything Nick said and did. "Please come down," pleaded the Nun. Again Nick shouted his refusal and emphasised his feelings by linking arms with his friend and put on a display of Highland Dancing, ignoring the sparks from the fire beside them. Constantly feeding the fire with more rubbish, Nick and his friend had us fused in excitement at the entertainment. It was indeed a rare event and we were making the most

51

of it. We were soon joined by the boys who took advantage of the situation to continue playing their game of soccer until a goal was scored. They also revelled at the, by now hilarious entertainment, put on not only by Nick and his friend, but also by the hysterical Nun. To try and put an end to the situation, the Nun had sent a couple of her friends to the back of the shelter. The plan was to creep up from behind the two boys and grab them forcing a come down. Of course that plan was never on, several of us made sure of that by shouting what was going on to Nick and his friend. As soon as fingers appeared over the edge of the shelter, Nick would either place his foot on them or tickle them, shouting, "Tickle, tickle" several times. This new act added further laughter to my ineffable joy which lasted about thirty to forty minutes. The younger boys were mostly jumping up and down laughing and shouting as they did so at the excitement, a few of them were waving their arms in the air. I was well into my twelfth birthday and surrounded by boys of around the same age who were as equally exuberant as the younger boys displaying in our emotions, but with our feet firmly on the ground.

The air was cold and crisp that sunny Saturday morning in Aberdeen and there was a wind that had caused smoke from the dying fire to bring tears to the eyes of Nick and his friend. They coughed a little but it didn't dampen their spirits. As a matter of fact, Nick took advantage of the situation by overdramatising and exaggerating his cough, and bringing a knee to his chest and his chin down to his knee. Half coughing and part laughing, Nicks friend made it a double act. Now we had two Nuns shouting at Nick and his friend to come down from the shelter. Shouting at the top of her voice the new Nun to the scene, angry at the continued defiance of the two boys, threatened as to what they would get if they didn't immediately obey. By that time the fire was just a mere flicker. Our entertainment at an end we individually, or in groups, slowly filtered our way back to the main building. With one Nun on her way to the main building, the other stayed to continue pleading with Nick and his friend. The two knowing only too well what was in store for them when they did come down, continued to entertain, but only to a diminished audience and a bitterly angry Nun.

Having died of starvation, the cinders and ashes of the fire were swept away by buckets of water handed to the two boys by others. When the last of the boys were leaving the playing field, the Nun was heard to say, "Are you two monsters coming down," in reply the friend of Nick was shouting, "only if you promise not to punish us Sister," ending by both doing a fling on top of the shelter. We were all in the playing room receiving instructions for bath time, when Nick and his friend were seen running upstairs. What an impish, devilish character Nick was. God surely sent him to us. The uncanny look in the Nuns eyes should have warned Nick that he might be taking things a little too far. But it didn't and Nick suffered as a result.

It was a sunny Sunday mid afternoon and morale was unusually high. Nick, as nearly always, was the centre of attraction. This time he was clowning with his selfmade mouse, made out of an old mid grey wool sock. There was childish laughter and crying, screams and giggles from the small group of young boys that were being entertained by Nick. Nick was putting his make believe mouse through the motions of a live one; one moment it was travelling up the pants of one boy, the next it was running down the chest of another and so on. Then Nick was chasing a less sure boy, several others were following ominously thinking it was hilarious; not so Alemenia. "What on earth is going on," shouted the Nun as soon as she entered the playroom at the top end. "Nick had a real mouse," shrieked one of the young highly excited boys. "What!" snapped Alemenia. The much younger new Nun arrived on the scene having made her entrance through the opposite door to Alemenia; Alemenia just dropping her whistle after using it to demand attention. But on seeing the new Nun the boys gathered around her excitingly shouting their delight at her about Nick and his mouse. Instantly the Nun threw her hands into the praying position, then crossed herself with the sign of the cross saying a quick prayer to someone. Nick was sharp to take advantage of the Nun being new, young and frightened, she believing the mouse to be real allowed Nick to chase after her as she hurriedly made her way towards Alemenia, who was coming towards her from the other end of the room. Meeting about half way, red in the face and breathing heavily, they exchanged quick words while the young boys continued to show their excitement. Unsure of what to expect from the Nuns, Nick again turned his attention on the young boys and with a devilish twinkle in his brown eyes, he followed the young boys out to the playing yard, he having forced them to do so with his make-believe mouse. Later when we were all in the playroom, Alemenia sent a message to Nick saying he was wanted by the Nun. The Nun was showing signs of anger, while Nick was trying to clown his way out of being punished for his earlier showbiz act. The angry Nun was having none of it when Nick chuckled as he went on his knees at the feet of the Nun, hands together as in prayer.

Alemenia produced the Cricket Wicket and Nick, fully expecting the blows to be of a gentle nature, (it being Sunday), held out a willing hand, quickly throwing it under his left armpit to nurse the pain from the savage blow on his wrist when Alemenia brought the wicket swiftly down on him. Refusing to obey Alemenials further demands for more torture, Nick with acute anger and great disbelief etched on his face made his way

53

out of the room. On his return Nick walked straight past Adelmia and made his way to where I was sitting. Twenty four hours later Nick was still feeling the result of the Cricket Wicket on his wrist.

Another boy and myself were summoned to the choir room. I was getting anxious as we ascended the stairs. "Wait a minute," I said to the boy, just as we were about to enter the room. He stopped with me outside the room. "What's the matter?" he asked anxiously. "Why are we wanted?" I quizzed. He didn't seem to know. On opening the door I followed him. The adrenalin was on the move making my heart beat faster. I was standing more or less in the centre of the room when the door closed behind me. We turned our heads to see who it was; puzzled we looked at one another and let out an almighty laugh. We were the only people in the room. Someone had played a joke on us. On returning to the playroom I looked across at Nick; he was laughing in his throat and shaking with amusement. He choked off the last of his laughter and wiped his eyes with the inside of his wrists.

Nick had the ability to charm the Nuns - well, nearly always. A thread of character that was to weave continually through the dark days, weeks, months and years ahead. Nick, all smiles, entered the playroom. I asked him if he was crazy. Letting out his 'hee, bee, bee,' and giving a shrug he continued on his way and out of the other door. I could not help admire his nerve. As we moved off, Nick murmured to me, "This is going to be one of those days." He stopped to tie his boot laces. "Get up," shouted the Hawk, prodding Nick with one of his shiny black army boots. Nick rose, one boot untied, was forced to walk with the rest of us. A male teacher from another class, who recently joined the school, was sitting at the teachers desk when we arrived. He was a strange man; tall, dark wavy hair flopping over his forehead just above a strange pair of light blue steel cold eyes. His white, heavily starched collar of his matching tunic shirt was gripping his short, thick, reddish neck that supported a smallish, clean shaven face. I also noticed that his dark blue three piece suit was of a heavy material and it didn't seem to fit awfully well. The teacher also had a strange delivery of words, spoken as if he stepped out of a Dickens novel.

That particular morning we were seated awaiting instructions to stand for our daily morning prayers, when the teacher noticed an empty seat within the boys section. "Who is ...." then Nick walked in. "Who are you?" said the new teacher. "My name Sir," said Nick. "My name is Nick, Sir." "Allow me to ask what is your surname, Nick." "My surname, Sir, is Rogers." It wasn't. Sitting behind our desks we were trying to hide the smiles on our faces by covering them with our hands. Nick must have said something because the teacher shouted to Nick to hold his tongue, with a

54

tone of power in his voice. "I will not, Sir!" replied Nick. "Hold your tongue this instant or I will." At that very moment he brought his thick, hairy hand across the side of Nicks head. Nick, clutching with both hands the left hand side of his head, fell to the floor. That incident instantly caused an uproar in the classroom. Desks were being banged, rulers and pens, etc. were being thrown all over the place. It had taken several minutes and the assistance of the Headmaster to quieten the class. After hearing what the teacher had to say about the incident, the headmaster walked between the rows of girls. One girl was heard to say to the Headmaster, "Some teachers don't like the 'Home Boys'."

In the meantime, Nick was out of the classroom, presumably to receive treatment to the swelling above his left eye. An infuriated Headmaster, after having words with the new school teacher, left the classroom. With a couple of light taps on his desk with a short stick, we were asked by the teacher to bring out a book from our desks and to open it at a certain page and to read from that particular page. At the end of that English period, Nick returned and made his way to his desk amidst several sympathetic gestures from the rest of us. And at the end of the morning session, with very little noise and no one speaking, we left the classroom. As soon as we were out on the street, Nick was surrounded by twenty or so boys and girls. Despite his encounter, Nick was in his usual high spirits; he was a 'Star Attraction'.

The following week we were again receiving the English lesson from the new male teacher. All during the lesson the teacher was showing signs of compassion towards Nick, this was clear in the way he addressed Nick when asking questions on the English lesson. Nick hadn't forgiven the teacher for what happened to him the previous week and he was to show that when, at the end of the English lesson and the ending of the morning session, the teacher asked him if he would like to ring the school bell. Nick gave the brass wooden hand bell a couple of quick dongs when he removed the bell from the small square table near the doorway to the classroom. That act of devilment again sent our hands to our faces to hold back an outburst of laughter. There was a triumphant gleam to Nicks' brown eyes when the embarrassed teacher ordered him to go outside to ring the bell. Seconds later we all heard the distant sound of the bell ringing, instantly yet again covering our faces with our hands, a few peeping at the teacher through wide spread fingers. It was clearly visible that the teacher was very, very angry, as well as being embarrassed. He had every right to be feeling the way he was, Nick had gone on to the street to ring the bell. Taking his ink nibbled pen out of his mouth as Nick re-entered the classroom, the teacher said to Nick, "I wish to speak to you," very gravely. "I am sorry to have to do it, but you leave me no alternative my boy." Nick just stood there looking up at the teachers face. "Your behaviour is far from pleasing, I am anxious that you do well, but you will not if you continue to do as you are." Nick looked at the teacher and said nothing. "Looking at me in that way will not prevent me saying what I am going to say." "But Sir, you told me to go outside." Again we covered our faces with our hands. "I will not be answered, young man. I am not accustomed to being answered. Do you hear me?" "But Sir" and before Nick could finish the teacher sharply said, quiet boy! Nick nodded, quietly saying, "Yes Sir." "I must insist on you immediately altering your ways," said the teacher turning his head in our direction and lifting his head as to look at the sky. "Oh!" said Nick with an impish dazzle in his eyes, and a silly grin on his face. "I will personally write a letter of complaint to the Rev. Mother of Nazareth. The contents of that letter will be of a very grave nature concerning your disruptive attitude to learning." "Thank you most kindly Sir," said Nick, as he bent his left leg in gesture. The teachers lips twitched into a sly smile after he ordered Nick to replace the bell and return to his desk. Before Nick carried out those instructions, the teacher beckoned him saying, "You are too clever for your own good and I will endeavour to dampen your ideas for you." "Alright Sir," said Nick, with a broader grin on his face.

BANANAS

It was one of the days when the banana cart stood unattended in the shopping recess. Ripe the bananas may not have been but ripe they were for a few nimble fingers to take advantage of the opportunity offered to them Immediately the stolen fruit was distributed to the trustworthy few whose job it was to hide, until ripe, the stolen green bananas. Well this was usually done by the individual hiding the fruit somewhere in their clothing cupboard in the playroom. As on previous occasions the holders of the forbidden fruit started to feel insecure with their little holding and began searching for one boy to take the lot and carry the can if caught by one of the Nuns• The separated bananas soon became a bunch of seven again and the boy foolish enough to take on the responsibility to hide the bunch was MacQuirk junior, he probably thought he would be making an impression thus hoping to become 'one of the boys'.

It was Sunday, two days after the bananas were stolen and the day MacQuirk junior found them to be missing from where he had hidden them. Murmurs and unfound rumours soon spread amongst us, accusations were ripe on the day, small gatherings were taking place. From one gathering emerged the plump, dark haired MacQuirk junior and with an outstretched arm and finger pointing, the ten year old shouted, "Who asked you to poke your nose in you little twerp, this is my affair and nothing to do with you." Suddenly the boy MacQuirk sent a boy sprawling across the floor, then pandemonium broke out and pockets of fights were taking place. There was a surge towards MacQuirk junior as he attempted to leave the playroom, only to be prevented from doing so by the arrival of a Nun standing in the doorway. Having given a couple of short blasts with her whistle, the Nun Adelmia then made her way hurriedly towards the tall, lean fair haired Collins and grabbed him by the ear, we all stood waiting for further action from the Nun but there wasn't any. But there was a triumphant gleam in the eyes of Collins as she walked passed me and into the landing. It was said Adelmia had watched Collins land a cracker of a punch to the eye of one boy and a beauty of a punch to the stomach of another. Shortly after a calm period, I heard of a fight going on in the washroom. As I and others entered the washroom we could see on the other side of the double row of washbasins MacClusky and Kirby standing nose to nose, animosity was ripe between the two and had been for some months. Apparently the bananas were found in the clothing of eleven year old MacClusky, so it wasn't a surprise to hear Kirby was the suspect.

"You have nothing on me so buzz off." "I have nothing on you that is a fact, just the same, you are the one that planted those bananas." "Huh."' "I say you are the one that planted those bananas." "Alright, alright, I am

57

the one that did it. Go ahead and prove it," said the equally tall Kirby. "Grab him!" shouted MacClusky to his pals that were closing on Kirby from behind. Wanting no part of what was going on and that I wanted to answer a call of nature I left the room; as I was leaving I was aware that a boy was whispering something to another and for an answer he gave him a light push on the shoulder. I was prevented from going for a 'No. 1', I being ushered into the playroom by both Adelmia and Alemenia; they earlier had been incorrectly informed about the bananas.

All eyes of the boys in the playroom turned towards the two Nuns and myself as we struggled in the corner, with the radio resting on a shelf behind and above us. The Nuns for a while didn't speak to me, they exchanged words with one another, words that had me trembling in my plimsolls. I began silently to pray, and I said, "Our father who art in Heaven, hallowed be.." I was then painfully disturbed as the vice like grip of Alemenia tightened around my wrist causing my fingers to pulsate. I had that dreadful sickness I experienced three months earlier when accused of stealing the Nativity Sticks. Head raised I looked from one Nun to the other and could see their faces were etched with anger. I wanted to die, there and then. "Look Sister, I have to get the truth out of this little devil," said one of the Nuns to the other. It was Alemenia still gripping my wrist that asked me what I did with the bananas. When my answer was not forth coming, she let go of her grip, then knocked me to the floor with a thump to the shoulder. My face screwed as I awaited the next source of punishment. It was not long in arriving, and when it did the back of my head hurt. I didn't protest, I just closed my eyes and shut my mouth tightly. Alemenia grabbed me by my painful wrist and pulled me to my feet and shook me violently, asking over and over again, where are those bananas? and who along with me were responsible for bringing them into the 'House of the Lord'. My mind was in a whirl of doubts and fears, again my legs began to tremble and I had difficulty in controlling them; then my whole body trembled. With my wrist still in the clutches of Alemenia, she slowly and slyly forced me back onto my knees, words were still flowing between the two Nuns and very little was said to me during this ordeal. Alemenia decided to release her grip on my wrist and transferred her hand to my quill of hair, raising me to a standing position. My arms stiffened and my fists clenched tightly as the Nun stretched me to my limit, my toes hardly able to take the weight of my body. Although the Nuns were talking to each other, I couldn't hear or didn't want to hear what they were saying Until Alemenia let go of her hold on me and told me to go and join the others.

Within seconds of my release I spotted MacQuirk junior, he was with a group of others on their hands and knees playing marbles. I pulled

58

MacQuirk junior upwards and made him stand in front of me, staring at him I said, "You have done it again, haven't you?" "What are you talking about?" he pretentiously replied. "You know!" "What, me." "Yes you. You have been telling lies again." "I've not, I swear I've not," he said. I didn't believe him. He wrestled free of the grip I had on his arm and made off to seek sanctuary with his older brother and his brothers friends, he didn't get very far as I had followed and when catching up with him, grabbed hold of his shoulder and punched him in the back. Again he got free, this time I was unable to get my hands on the blighter, he seeking sanctuary beside the two Nuns who were, at that time, standing outside the washroom telling fantasy stories about their Saint Patrick and of the beauty of Gods Emerald Isle.

Saint Patricks day wasn't very far off. To me it became one of the most hated days of my life. Luckily for me I was unseen by the Nuns so I returned to relax in the playroom. It was shortly after my relaxation period that I was summoned to the choir room. "Do not be afraid," said a male voice when I closed the door behind me, having been quietly instructed to do so by that same male voice, it being the voice of the Hawk. "We know you are not guilty of bringing the stolen bananas into the 'House of the Lord'," said Adelmia, her eyes then lifted and she stared at the ceiling for a while, her hands linking together as if in prayer. The Nun then turned her gaze on me and the look in her eyes made me want to scarper. I looked down at my fingers that were nervously plucking at my grey woollen slipover. There was that feeling running through my body when the Nun and the Hawk put their heads together and talking in a voice too quiet for me to hear. At a time during the secret conversation, I was beckoned to sit on the piano stool. "We do believe you know who broke the 7th Commandment and wrongfully brought those bananas into this Holy House." "N. .... No," I stammered. "I d.....don't know anything," I replied to Adelmia's cleverly put question. The Hawk fumbled with the buttons on his army jacket and grinning happily to himself made his way towards me, then lifted the lid of the piano and began to play the tune of 'Hail Glorious Saint Patrick,' then he attempted a shorter version of 'Over the Sea to Skye,' he and the Nun then left the room closing the door behind them. I stood watching the rain-drops falling from the frame of the partly open window, and at that moment I had a nice feeling of isolation that was to be short lived, when the Hawk opened the door saying I have to go and join the other boys in the playroom.

I couldn't understand why the Nun wanted me in the choir room to answer so few questions. I can only suppose it was a part of the mental torture, imposed on us by the Brutal Regime.

RELIGIOUS EXAM

I was into my seventh year of my stay in the orphanage when the Nun Adelmia scathingly demanded better religious exam results than the previous year. That demand included top marks from one boy in each class. Sitting at my desk knowing what was in store for all of us if we failed the Nuns demands, I decided if I was to be top of the class I had to cheat, so every opportunity that came my way I sneaked my hand under the lid of my desk and nervously and disgustingly removed the Holy Book and placed it on my lap flicking through the pages' until finding the answer to the question required. My head was buzzing, my body cold and trembling, not at the thought of being caught, you see I occupied a desk in the back row of the class and the desk to the right of me was vacant. The nauseating situation was brought about by the indelible words of the two Nuns, "Show me a thief and I will give you a liar," rumbling about in my mind and I saying in my mind, "You now are what the Nuns branded a thief and a liar." With the exam over I began to feel ill, my stomach was churning, the back of my neck was so taut, my legs so weak my feet wouldn't move. I wanted to yawn but couldn't muster enough strength to unlock the grip of my teeth. I felt ashamed, so terribly ashamed, I asked God to forgive me for the only mortal sin I had ever committed. Back at the orphanage the Nuns were of the impression that good Religious exam results were soon to be on their way to them. The Nuns were certainly highly optimistic that they were to be pleased, the mood and the atmosphere in the 'House of the Lord' conveyed that optimism to me.

Back at school the late exam results were late in coming, this was doing me no good whatsoever. I was a bundle of nerves sitting at my desk oblivious as to what was going on around me. I was so ashamed at not only branding myself a thief and a liar, but on cheating on my class mates, so much so I had great difficulty preventing my head dropping onto the lid of my desk. It was the banging of desk lids that brought me back to life with a jolt at that. The results of the long awaited exam were read to us, sending several cold waves. .... travelling along my spine and down to the tip of my toes, when hearing I had gained equal top marks with my class girlfriend. Then my body warmed a little having been told a mark had been deducted for my appalling handwriting.

The Nuns were hopping mad on learning the religious exam results and try as I did, they didn't want to hear what I had to say. Extra domestics were enforced and our leisure time was to be taken over by answering questions from the Holy Book. With Saturday out of the way and in Chapel on Sunday morning I occupied the position directly in front of the Nun Adelmia, having held that place for about two weeks for a reason or reasons unknown to me. Not as many boys as usual attended Holy Communion that morning and the two Nuns were showing signs of anger and embarrassment which sent warning whirls amongst us. Steelingly I set myself fully expecting an arrow like pierce in the middle of my back from the fingers of the Nun immediately behind me. Instead, Adelmia brought her hand swooping across the side of my face... Crack! Everyone in the Chapel looked directly at where the sound came from. Grimacing from pain and with clenched fists pressing against my legs, I embarrassingly and reluctantly made my way to the alter, then with guilt added to my other feelings I somehow returned to from where I left. Within seconds of my arrival my thoughts were back at the alter where I couldn't prevent my tongue from trembling when I stuck it out to receive 'The Bread of Heaven'. At that time I was remembering the frightening words from one of the Nuns that it was a sacrilege to allow the Holy Bread touch any part of your mouth other than your tongue and you will be dammed forever and after death you will banish in the fires of Hell. Those were the fearful words clouding my mind, and with the fear of punishment from God and from the two Nuns, plus added thoughts of receiving Holy Communion without attending the Confessional to confess my cheating of the exam, my spirit was at a low ebb.

Apart from meal times, most of that day was spent in the crossed legged position in our usual three row sittings, listening or pretending to listen to the words from the Holy book which were spoken by one of the Nuns. Questions were asked .... answers were given of which I had no need to answer. Amidst dense and painful thoughts, I was thinking, "Do they know about my exam result?" All that day I was loaded with the burden of fear and guilt and with the tortured mind I had previously inherited I found it difficult to bear.

The sweet nauseating odour from the swinging crucible during Benediction that evening curled its way along the isle of the Chapel filling my lungs and penetrating my mind to mix with the thickening clouds of earlier hours. That latest burning intruder, having mixed with the other, sent my head into a slow uncontrollable orbit, forcing me to cling firmly to the wood in front of me.

Later that evening, self pity got hold of me and I was in need of total isolation which I almost found in one of the toilet cubicles. Sitting there my thoughts were with another reason for cheating the exam, you see I also was of the hopeful opinion that if I did succeed in fulfilling the wishes of the Nuns I might just might be in favour with them and God and perhaps there would be an end to the brutal treatment I was receiving and of the hatred I was bearing towards the two of them.

HAIR OIL

An aroma floated through the air of the toilets, washroom, the landing and the playroom.

I had been in the playroom for several minutes before Adelmia unexpectedly made an appearance. Flustered, I began to fumble about in my cupboard, but soon it became obvious the Nun wasn't going to leave. "What have you got on your hair?" asked Adelmia, standing just inside the main entrance of the playroom as I passed her. "God forbid!" "Ouch! I yelled as the Nun grabbed the back of my shirt collar and yanked me back to her. "Holy Mary Mother of God! What on earth have you got on your hair?" Her voice was firm and decisive, systematically sniffing as she spoke.

I couldn't resist the temptation to apply to my hair the perfumed hair oil given to me by Paul Gregson; when it was on offer by Paul to several of us as we were outside the school at the end of school for the day. Having applied the oil to my hair, I began to feel excited ..... nervously excited, and by the time I reached the mansion I was trembling in every limb.

A great look of horror and surprise appeared on the face of Adelmia as our eyes met when I turned my head to look at her. Taking a deep intake of breath and raising her head to gaze at the high ceiling, then .... eyes closed, Adelmia said, "Oh my God!" Her inhaled breath was released with the power of a stem engine, when she lowered her head and stared at me. She drew another long breath and let it out again. In a sepulchral voice, Adelmia said to me, "Go into the washroom, strip to the waist and wait until I arrive." Nervously I obeyed. "Sissy!" shouted the two boys who were in the playroom at that time. They were immediately ordered out by the Nun. "You fool" Gerry followed by saying, "Why did you put that stuff on your hair? You knew what lay ahead when you got back here." With a little sympathetic smile on his face and a few quick shakes of his head, then slowly releasing the small amount of breath he had earlier inhaled, Gerry left on hearing the voice of Adelmia. Now I was alone with Adelmia, the washroom being vacated by a handful of boys who scarpered when they were aware of the presence of the Nun. Our eyes met again and my chilled body was now feeling as if I had been placed in a refrigerator, only to be thawed again as my head was plunged into the sink of hot water.

"Ouch! ..... Ow! ..... Ooh! ..... Ouch! ....." The hot soapy water running into my eyes added to the pain I was enduring at the hands of Adelmia, as she tore into my scalp with her strong fat hands. Unaware of the silent footsteps behind me, Alemenia took over from Adelmia after an exchange of words. "Ouch!" etc. etc. I continued to yell during my ordeal. Whenever I attempted to use my hands to clear away the hot soapy water from my eyes, I was told in no uncertain manner to return my hands to my sides.

Dark greasy rings clung to the otherwise snow white sink, the greasy water having been released down the plug hole. Several streams of dirty water cascaded down my body when the angry Nun yanked my head upwards by grabbing my wet and soapy hair. The similar sepulchral voice commanded my uncomfortably wet legs to take several steps backwards to give enough room to allow the owner of that sepulchral voice space to clean the oil stained sink before she plunged my head into the clear cold water, rinsing thoroughly my dripping wet soapy hair. Again water cascaded down my body as I was yanked upwards. Dripping wet I willingly headed to my 'No. 78' peg from which I quickly removed my towel.

I was on my way to the bathroom, having been told to do so by the Nun Adelmia when she returned to the washroom. "If you stood sideways nobody would see you," remarked one of the older boys as we passed on the stairway. "Pay no attention to him," said another. "Hi Ya Andrew! I bet you have no nits in YOUR hair,"wisecracked another boy on his way down-stairs. That remark brought a consolation smile to my face.

Of course I didn't have a bath. With two inches of water in the bath I turned off the taps, then I removed my scuffed school shoes and wet, grey, knee length socks, that were crumpled around my ankles. I stepped into the ankle deep water and immediately stepped out. Before releasing the bath water, I wet the soap and face cloth that were beside the bath taps and splashed water onto the blue/grey terrazzo walls and floor. Then it was into the wash area where I removed my wet pants and underpants, and with a towel from a rail under one of the sinks, I dried my feet and my already dry-ing other parts. Replacing the towel, I then donned my pants and slipped into my sculled school shoes. To waste a few minutes, I sat on the bench near to the door entrance.

Soon I was deep into a past experience. Sister Luke was in charge of the vegetable plot and of the dozen or so hens that provide food for, for I don't know who! The Nun had been in charge that long she got into the habit of talking to the hens as if they were humans. The hens were a mixture of white leghorns and red. On my day for working with the hens I arrived at about 8 am. A red hen was attacking a white one and stripping it of its feathers. The poor hen was running round in circles making an awful squawking noise. By late morning that white hen had its head and bottom bare, and looking terribly sore, she was also stripped of most of her feath-ers. There wasn't anything I or Sister Luke could do for that hen because we were time tabled to collect the eggs, clean the pens and feed the hens. Sister Luke also had to kill and prepare two chickens for someones table. I wasn't around when the execution of the birds took place. I chickened out and went into the cobblers shop across from the pens. At that time in life, I couldn't understand why a nice person like Sister Luke could kill a hen.

Thinking one of the Nuns might be sending for me I decided to make my way downstairs. With head on chest and my lips pouted, I slowly descended the stairs until I saw a Lady Bird resting between two bannister rails halfway on the second flight of stairs. I sat down, picking up the lady Bird I placed it in the palm of my hand, gently stroking it with the fingers of my left. After about two minutes, the brown coloured Lady Bird flew off. What a shame, I was thinking to myself, it was good company.

On my way downstairs I suddenly remembered it was 'Goodies' time, but by the time I arrived, the 'goodies' were all gone. on closer examination of the tray there wasn't even a crumb in it. "Hell!" I said to myself as I made my way back into the washroom-where the others were preparing for Benediction ..... it being Wednesday.

Adelmia was in her usual place, attending to the cuts and bruises of those who wanted meditation. Alemenia was doing what she seemed to enjoy ..... screwing the edge of a towel hard into the ear of one of the boys. That act always brought us to our toes, clinging to the Nun and tugging at her arm with the slender hope of easing the pain. Alemenia was screwing hard into the ear of another boy, sending a cold shudder down my spine as I watched and felt the suffering that boy was enduring. Adelmia was in the process of removing a small brown bottle from the 2' x 3' free standing medicine cupboard, when our eyes met. For a split second, I froze. Instant hatred for one another electrified. Hell, I was thinking, I have left my socks and underpants in the bathroom! "Come here!" Adelmia demanded. When I got to within arms length, Adelmia reached out and grabbed my arm in that vice like grip. Squeezing my arm as firmly as she dared, Adelmia queried the were abouts of my socks and underpants. Sickened at the thought of me not wearing underpants, the Nun sent me to the bathroom then to the work-room where I was to be given a clean shirt, vest, pants, underpants and socks.

On my return to the washroom an almighty roar of laughter let loose. I noticed a group of lads flicking water at one another, Nick being one of them. It was a good feeling to see and feel happiness. It didn't come very often and when it did, happiness was enjoyed to the full. Later that afternoon I learnt that the outburst of laughter was when Nick splashed a little water on the face of Alemenia, having been dared to do so by a couple of the boys.

On the Saturday afternoon following that Wednesday, we were out in the yard playing. It was around three o'clock, the sky was clear and the air crisp and dry after the heavy rainfall of the earlier hours. It was then that

I heard that I was not the only boy to be caught with perfumed hair oil that Wednesday. The supplier, Paul Gregson, was the one to be caught, and 'Boy-oh-Boy' wasn't he punished! Paul was two years my senior, he being thirteen years of age and he was to hold the limelight for that afternoon.

Dressed in a full length emerald green dress, waisted with a two inch broad gold coloured ribbon and an emerald green bow in his hair, Paul was presented to us as we played, and a few fought in the yard. He must have been in the girls playing yard because he made his entrance from that direction. I, and I am sure many of the others, had the feeling of deep sympathy for Paul as he was well liked by almost all of the boys; he also appeared to be on friendly terms with the two Nuns. I just had a fleeting glance at Paul because I was too sickened at the thought of the humiliation Paul was enduring. Trembling with fear and with a lump in my throat, I headed for refuge in one of the toilet cubicles.

I selected the end cubicle, not because it was the cleanest, but because psychologically it was the safest. On the other side of the toilet wall I could hear the girls also playing. Simmering inside me was the wish to go and have a sneak look to find out if my sisters were playing. Then my mind transferred to the large imposing wooden gates at the bottom of the yard. Beyond those large imposing wooden gates lies a whole new world thought I, as I sat on the toilet seat. A world that I desperately need to be a part of. And yet I am doomed to this sordid way of life for three more years. Ugh! How sick I felt at the thought and I was only eleven years old. I felt I didn't belong. I wanted to get away. I yearned to get away. Yet I knew that running away wasn't the answer.

Later information reached me that Paul Gregson was paraded around the boys and the girls playing yards. It was also said that a handful of the Nuns crawlers laughed and shouted sissy at Paul when he, embarrassed and humiliated, walked around the yard, hugging the walls as he did so. How could Nuns, supposedly messengers of God, humiliate a child of God in that manner. It only added to my feelings of animosity towards them.

Did they believe that whatever they did to us, however brutal or sadistic their sins were, if they confessed in the confessional box their sins would be forgiven?

MY SISTER BETSY

ɪ For the first time in seven years of entering the orphanage, I was to get a close look at my sister Betsy. Until then, at the age of thirteen, I only had distant and fleeting glances at my baby sister. And all during that time I wasn't a hundred per cent sure that the face I had been looking at was really my youngest sister.

We were playing in our yard and the girls were playing in theirs, when I received a message. One of the boys who was playing at the top end of the yard told me that my sister Yvonne wanted to see me. He also said Yvonne was waiting at the corner of the air raid shelter at the girls yard. Hurriedly, but with the greatest of caution, I made my way past the swing area farthest from where the Nun was sitting. When I arrived at the end of our building I took the necessary glances over my shoulder before slipping round the corner to where Yvonne was anxiously waiting.

Yvonne appeared to be less nervous than I as we talked. On a previous visit to the Chapel, Yvonne had the senior girl in charge of the junior girls point me out to Betsy. Yvonne was also telling me that Betsy had earlier in the week been transferred from the juniors to the senior girls. Nervous excitement was slowly intruding my body as Yvonne was talking to me and that excitement was the cause of me to shiver as it filled my body. Yvonne and others had made arrangements for our little sister to be seated to the rear of the senior girls when we attended Benediction that evening. Betsy deeply wanted me to look for her as she was to be looking out for me. Seeing, talking with and being with Yvonne was in itself an exciting experience, but knowing that I was soon to be having a close look at my baby sister for the first time in seven years of her life, sent me light headed and gave me the feeling of floating on air.

Yvonnes 'lookout' hissed and beckoned her to return to the play area as the coast was clear to do so. Standing erect with her back to the wall of the concrete air raid shelter, Yvonne slowly edged her way along the few inches to the corner of the shelter then slipped out of my sight to join in play with the other girls. Yvonne was eleven years of age at that time and that was the first time we had been together alone for seven years, or since the day we entered the orphanage. I then placed myself erect. Standing against the cold silver granite toilet building I also edged my way into play with my friends. On returning to the boys yard I, with my back against the toilet wall, slipped down to the crouched position. I looked up into the sky. The white puffs of clouds were high and resting against a warm blue sky and I was wishing from the bottom of my heart that I could be up there alone, away from all the unpleasantries of life.

Two shrieking ear piercing blasts from Alemenia's silver steel whistle brought my thoughts back to reality. Apparently two young boys were attempting to climb the wrought iron railing at the bottom of the yard. The disturbance saw me slowly making my way towards the swings area to play with my friends, only to be diverted into sanctuary of the toilets by the hard resentful look in the eyes of Alemenia as our eyes met. And as I closed to her she said, "You have the eyes of the devil. You will go to Hell when you die, mark my words". She smiled nervously, the corners of her mouth twitching as she did. A wave of fear and the feeling of loneliness swept through my body and I began to tremble.

I selected the cleanest of the toilet cubicles and snibbed the door behind me before resting on the toilet seat. Crossing my arms then resting my elbows on my knees, I slowly rocked myself backwards and forwards almost into a deep sleep. Again I was disturbed by instant noise. This time it was the sudden and noisy burst of boys through the doorway from the yard into the square for 'Goodies'. On unsnibbing the cubicle door, I ran out of the toilet and joined the scramble to grab what and as much as I could before being caught by an older boy or a Nun. We washed, changed our clothing and made our final preparations before forming an orderly line to proceed to the Chapel for Benediction.

Daringly, I chose the pew directly behind the junior boys and where Adelmia always occupied. Having chosen my pew, I then selected to occupy the position nearest the aisle and directly behind where Alemenia always occupied. To my utter horror, Alemenia forced me off the position I selected when she entered the pew, saying to me, "What are you up to in the 'House of the Lord', you evil little monster." Her voice was in anger and fearing to me. Raising the tone of her voice, Alemenia said that I would be dealt with after the service. Still in the kneeling position and facing the alter, Alemenia removed her head from the side of my face then settled into her usual praying position. With my ears burning and my inside burning I found it difficult to pray. I was so full of hatred of Alemenia and the place she represented that I could only wish.

I wished with everything within me that something nasty and horrible would happen to that Nun. Immediately the service was over, Alemenia got up and made her way out of the Chapel, stopping only to have a few words with Adelmia, who hadn't moved from her position at the rear of the Chapel. In the meantime, I, after a few seconds delay, also got out and followed Alemenia. It was then my eyes and the sparkling light blue warming eyes of a pale, freckled, angelic face of a girl met. A small Mona Lisa smile touched the corners of her delicate mouth, then a broad smile of high delight engulfed her face when I winked. My heart began to pound. My blood began flooding my face and my head. My arms, my legs, every part of my body pounded with ecstasy. I couldn't hide my feelings, they were written all over my broad smiling face. As I was leaving the Chapel, I passionately repeated to myself "my sister, my sister!"

As I was leaving the Chapel I didn't notice the tall thin figure of Alemenia standing in the corner of the Chapel entrance. Crack! I stumbled, my smiling face was now grimacing with pain from the effect of the ferocious hand of the Nun across my face. "Be in the playroom when I get there," she said to me in a quiet but raging voice. With my hands firmly pressed against the left hand side of my face, I with further fear and hatred made my way to the playroom, where on entering I said to myself, "the bloody torture chamber." I then hurriedly made my way to sanctuary in the toilets, thinking and hoping the Nun would forget.

My name echoed through the toilet chamber, it being released from the mouths of three boys and that of Alemenia. Shocked at the sight of the Nun when the toilet door burst open, I quickly grabbed my vest and covered my private parts, tugging several times at my vest in the space of a few seconds to ensure complete coverage from the eyes of Alemenia. "Get up!" was the order of the fuming Nun, not knowing I was midway in doing a 'No. 2'. I was so frightened I quickly closed the cubicle door just as the Nun turned to walk away. Moments after I had finished my 'No. 2', a sickness swept through my body and I shuddered a cold shudder when I noticed there was no paper to wipe my bottom. I looked at the walls and the inside of the door and saw the results of other boys who had found themselves in the same position. Again I shuddered, then thought to myself, "I couldn't do that." With both hands I hauled my trousers to just above the knees. Then on opening the door I noticed Alemenia was standing in the toilet doorway with her back to me. I slipped into the next cubicle and wiped my bottom with pieces of newspaper that were lying on the floor. Having done that, I then closed the cubicle door and rested on the toilet to allow myself time to settle my nerves. Not for long though, because again my name was released from the mouth of Alemenia, demanding me to come out of the toilet, her terrifying voice penetrated my system with the ease of a surgeons knife. Huge waves of fear pounded every inch of that nervous system as I made my way out of the cubicle and towards the Nun.

The middle of the Cricket Wicket bounced from the top of my head as I was ushered into the playroom where the other boys were changing their clothes. According to both Nuns I had cardinally sinned and also brought shame on the 'House of God'. I had to be punished. And I had to be punished in view of all the boys as a example as to what will happen if that incident in the Chapel ever happened again. Forced by Adelmia, I was made to stand with my back to the wall below the painting of the Sacred Heart.

68

With my hands firmly clasped, (with fear), behind my back, the boys were invited to show their anger and disgust by punishing me, either physically or verbally, or both if they desired.

As always, the boys were in single file in numerical order down the middle of the room waiting for the order to proceed to the dining room. with Adelmia and Alemenia in position to the right of the doorway, I to the left below the painting of the Sacred Heart, one of the Nuns beckoned the boys mobile. As they filed past, a few boys said their I"Most Sacred Heart of Jesus' before they either threw their verbal or physical onslaught, or both. A few said theirs after they displayed their feelings towards me. I have to say, that it was mostly the under ten year olds that pleased the Nuns. The older boys just looked at me and registered their disapproval at what was happening; this was displayed by facial or body movements. My two brothers walked past with their chins resting on their chests. Adelmia followed the last of the boys to leave the room, leaving me alone with Alemenia. Now I had no thoughts or feelings for anyone, except for my brothers and sisters, and through-fear, I had to separate myself from them.

I hadn't heard Alemenia's first demand for me to go to the washroom to wipe away the trickle of blood from my nose, that I inadvertently spread over my face. Grabbing me and violently shaking me by my arm, she was shouting angrily, "Do you hear me, you evil little creature. I'll be glad when all you Gormans are away from here, you are nothing but trouble." I was too saddened and humiliated to respond to the outbursts of the Nun, and even the prods, slaps, punches, the kicks and foot stamping from the young boys had no effect on me.

Having carried out the instructions of the Nun, I, automatically placing my hands behind my back, made my way to join the others in the dining room. With fear still raging in my empty but fear congested stomach, I proceeded to my place at my usual table. No sooner was I there when a plate of food was dumped in front of me. Try as I may, I couldn't release my hands from behind me. I seemed to be tugging and tugging but still they wouldn't part. Noticing I wasn't eating, the boy next to me asked, "Do you want it?" My reply was a quick shake of my head. One little boy approached me and stuck out his tongue and said, "Sissy!" then he scarpered like a scared rabbit. He was soon followed by one of the Nuns who, towering over me, ordered my return to the previous position I held in the playroom. As I hadn't consumed neither food or drink, the Nun said there was no need to thank the Lord for his thanksgiving. Cold, hungry and sulking, I made my way to the playroom, soon to be joined by the others.

Not a lot happened during my hour stance in the playroom, except that I was told by Alemenia that I was an evil little monster and that I gave the impression that butter wouldn't melt in my mouth. She also said that I would burn in Hell if I didn't change my ways. Later into that hour Adelmia approached me saying, "You might as well look down at Hell because you may never see Heaven". After a short pause the Nun also said "You will confess your sins at the next confessional. Do you hear me?" Her words were harpoon sharp.

Lying in bed that night, those same words were echoing in my head as if my head were an empty metal drum. There was a wind that night and as I looked out of the window before going into a turbulent sleep, that wind drove the angry looking clouds fast past the window. Although I was lying in bed watching, I was alone out there on one of those clouds. A vision of my little sister Betsy appeared in front of me, her light blue eyes widened and her warming Mona Lisa smile was there to be loved. Betsy was standing there, elegant and beautiful, taller than I expected. Suddenly ..... fear swept me away, fear of the Nuns, fear of God. Fear that if caught I would be punished by the Nuns. Fear that if caught I would be punished by God. A second later I was seeing my little sister, now a dark solid wooden door was looming in front of me and I was thumping it with what little strength I had "Let me in, let me in!" I 'repeated as I thumped on the doorway to Heaven. But before there was an answer I was disturbed by rows of Nuns in mass prayer. Suddenly there were only two, and they, Alemenia and Adelmia, were praying to God because they believed he was the complete answer to unanswerable things.

Although I was on one of those clouds, I was now lying in a disturbed bed awake from a turbulent sleep. Lying in bed I was wishing I could disappear or be swallowed. I felt the solid ice around my heart solidifying even more. How I hated that place. How I hated the Nuns and how I hated God. And at that moment I began to hate myself. Hating myself for not being strong enough to stand up and defend myself against all that was fearful to me.

On the Saturday morning I was sent to the confessional. On the way to the confessional and in the confessional box every vein and every muscle in my body were pulsating. "What have you done?" came the words from the other side of the small coloured divider. "I...I...ha...have...I have winked at my sister," I answered in a frightened and hushed voice and rushing the 'I have winked at my sister' in fear of being heard by the priest. "Is that all?" asked the pious voice. "Yes Father," I replied. "That isn't a sin, my child," allowing me time to sigh a quick sigh of relief before adding, "Who sent you to me?" After my answer I was given three hail Mary's to say for someone or something, which, I don't know. Although feeling a little more relaxed I shuddered a cold shudder as I passed the statue of St.

Anthony of Padua, on my way out of the Chapel and on my way to the playroom.

On opening the playroom door, I closed it again having noticed the floor was in the process of being waxed and polished. Relieved that I wasn't one of the applicants, I took the route to the toilet via the playing ward. On entering the toilet I saw a little boy crying. "Why are you crying?" I asked, approaching and putting my hands on his shoulders. "You mustn't cry, because other boys will think you are a sissy and they will bully you." Some of the older boys got a few ideas in their head and thought they were God, Hitler or Churchill.

Having relieved myself of a 'No. 1', I was met by Alemenia when I set foot on the square. After a brief exchange of words about the confessional, Alemenia sent me to assist in the workroom. Later I and other boys were playing on the playing field.

THE BEACH OUTING

It was during a very hot summers day that we were privileged to go to the local beach. My excitement and enjoyment of that scorching hot day was marred by a mischievous tongue.

Under close supervision of the Nuns we were all enjoying ourselves, running in and out of the cooling salt sea water. Castles were being made with the warm sand and we were doing what all children do when at the seaside. After a while, over the horizon raced a black swirl of clouds. The calm sea began to get rough, then it began to thunder. At first it sounded like a distant rumble but it soon swelled into a thunderous roar and people started leaving the sands. I shivered and felt a little scared and to add to my fear, seagulls were above me swooping and crying. One of the gulls screamed and fluttered its way down to land on a weathered stump of wood slightly to the right of me. Then the gull turned its head in robotic style. Before I made an attempt to move away I watched the gull tugging at something, stretching it as if it were a piece of elastic. It looked like a worm, my stomach knotted, I wanted to be sick but couldn't. The gull seemed to be looking at me sending ripples down my spine.

The rain came...... but it didn't, scattering boys and Nuns all over the place. Having organised a gathering the Nuns then began a count. Having completed a double count the Nuns found a boy to be missing. At the time none of us had any idea who was missing, so the Nuns quickly and in a state of panic ordered us into numerical order. Minutes past when, without uttering a word Adelmia grabbed me by the ear from behind and cracked me hard with her other hand across the side of the face. The slap was brutal and I let out a yell. "Where is he, where is he?" Adelmia shouted angrily. "I don't know what you are talking about?" I spluttered. The rumour circulating was that I had seen the boy being carried off on a huge wave. Steve Wane was the missing boy and having failed to find him the Nuns reluctantly agreed to inform the police. On the way to the tram stop I was kicked, punched, sneered at, pushed and verbally threatened both by the boys surrounding me and later by the Nuns immediately behind me, having been dragged to the rear by two older boys. During our wait for the tram a few of the young boys were saying the Devil has taken the missing boy and carried him off on a wave.

The blood of the Irish Nuns was boiling and the atmosphere in the playroom was, to say the least, tense. The rustle of the Rosary Beads was upon me and in her usual aggressive manner, the Nun Adelmia asked me why I didn't mention to her or Sister Alemenia that I saw the boy being carried off on a wave. With great difficulty in answering, I told the Nun I didn't see or know of anything about the missing boy and that someone must have made up the story. With a frightening look of great disgust in her eyes Adelmia scathingly said I had brought further sin into the 'House of the Lord' and that I had the look of the devil and the eyes of the devil. I was then ordered to the Confessional where a Priest was waiting for me. "In this one," came a voice from behind a curtain. My whole body went into vibration on entering the confessional. "Take your time my Son, take your time," were the other words from the hidden face. I spluttered several I...I...I...I's, then on a calmer note I managed to tell the faceless priest I had no sins to confess. On leaving the Confessional I was puzzled at being given three Hail Marys for having a clean soul.

Later that evening the missing boy turned up, with him were two relations, an Aunt and an Uncle. Apparently the boy was spotted by his Aunt and Uncle while on the beach, the excitement of the meeting blotting out any thought of contact with any of us, when they went to the Fair close to the sea front. The two Nuns left the playroom with the Hawk in charge, he held out a handful of wrapped sweets. "Can I have one of them," shouted Nick, causing an outburst of laughter from all of us, relieving the tension we all endured. Later the Nuns returned with the boy who went missing.. Grinning like a Cheshire Cat on rejoining us, the boy was soon surrounded by a dozen or so inquisitive faces. At one time between then and going to bed, one of the Nuns pulled me close to her saying, I was a very lucky boy and I deserved what I got because I was surely being punished for the sins of my parents.

For days after, several of the boys were more than usually friendly towards me, a few of them were either saying, shouting or singing the words 'Over the sea to Skye' when they approached or passed me wherever I was in the building. Whether this had something to do with the two Nuns being on edge I'll never know, nor will I ever know if they received a 'dressing down' from the Mother Superior, if so, was this the reason, or added reason, for their uncanny behaviour.

I had more or less 'fitted in' with all of the boys by the time I was of age to attend Saint Peters Secondary School in St. Clairs Street at the other end of town. Having also made a few close friends, all in my class included, I was soon to be given the answer as to why several of the boys who were entitled to get a tram to school always held back from the main group. This was because they were waiting for an empty tram on its way to a pick up spot for its conductor. When the tram slowed on entering Union Street from Holburn Street, the boys dashed on board and immediately set about searching the tram seats and under them for any money that was lying in wait for those searching fingers. There was to be rich pickings for the lucky ones and it was this Gerald and I were talking about, Gerald being one of a few who believed that the tram findings were sinful, he being of the opinion the coins were lost property. We were alone and somewhere in the playroom when Alemenia walked in just as Gerald removed his hand from my shoulder. "What are you two up to?" the Nun said in a low but firm voice. "You can go," the Nun said looking at Gerald. "I want words with this one," sounded Alemenia in a more determined voice. The witch then grabbed hold of my ear, twisting it she pulled me close to her. Talking between her teeth she made my heart pump with hatred, the blood in my veins stuttered when hearing again; "There is something I don't like about you, you shouldn't be here in the first place; none of you." The Nun let go of my ear which was burning hot with the twisting it received. My neck was the next feeding point for the powerful witch like hand of the Nun, the fingers of which closed around my neck squeezing the living daylights out of me. The evil witch squeezed and squeezed, then releasing her grip, aloud and firmly she said "Go and join the others in the washroom." I felt my legs wobble as I made my way out of the playroom to the washroom via the toilet for a pee.

On entering the washroom I quickly stripped to the waist having noticed an unused wash basin at this side of me, that was good because the Nuns were at the other side. I was soon to be applying cool water to my hot and painful neck using my face flannel to absorb as much of the cool water a possible. I was just about to move away from the wash basin when I realised I had left my towel on my peg. Oh God I thought, when suddenly I felt a cold trickle of water running down my back only to be stopped by the rim of my underpants. I dashed to remove my towel from my peg and facing the wall began to dry myself when my heart jumped as I was ushered back to the washbasin by that Nun Alemenia.

"I've been watching you, you didn't use soap and you didn't touch your ears either! Afraid of water are we? Boys get carried off on waves do they?"Those were the words I was greeted with when the Nun plunged my hands and then almost my head, into a basin full of hottish water. Looking towards a group of boys the Nun demanded one of them get a face cloth for her. Using her left hand the Nun grabbed me by the quill of hair, yanked up my head with arms following then plunged me back into the water. This exercise was carried out three or four times with a well soaped face cloth being used in between. To ensure I would be the cleanest to leave the washroom, down went my face and head into the water with the force of Alemenia's right hand at the back of my neck ... that was a rinse. Tugging at my hair my head was jerked up and back bringing me to an almost upright position so the Nun could begin an attack on my body. "Carried off on a wave was he?" the Nun said as we struggled, when she painfully

74

entered my ear with the corner of the towel in her hand. Twisting and turning the corner of the towel with all her evil strength into one ear, then the other, had me struggling for my life. For one terrifying moment I had the feeling of being at the mercy of a lunatic tarantula, the Nuns long, spider like arms drawing me into her web of yards of dark blue material almost smothering me and her Rosary Beads almost strangling me. I surrendered the thirty second silent struggle, the spider and the web having me trapped. At one time during that period of cruel sadistic brutality, the Nun had me standing on the tip of my toes and gritting my teeth, struggling to ease the pain inflicted when the towel screwed into my ears with all the strength the Nun could muster. Letting go of me, the Nun with a ring of cynicism to her voice said, "You wont be in a hurry to see any more waves."

RUNAWAYS

The new boy, so called because he was fortunate enough to have stayed with us for a mere couple of days, nobody got to know his name. I have a feeling he was English and about 8 years of age, hence the reasons for his behaviour. All of us were enjoying a period of relaxation when we were joined by the Nun Adelmia and a new face. The new face never left the side of Adelmia following her wherever she moved in and around the playroom. For a while the new boy was shedding tears, watched and listened to what was going on in his new and somewhat strange surroundings. I watched him screw a couple of fingers into each of his eyes, rub his face with his hands as if to stem the flow of tears. Snot mingled with his tears as he began sobbing, not being able to control his emotions. "For Gods sake stop your crying," Adelmia said when she knelt down beside her new captive. "I want my mummy and daddy," spluttered the new boy. Pulling out a clean white handkerchief the Nun firmly wiped away the existing tears and snot from the boys face. Returning the handkerchief to the slot in her robe, the Nun then mentioned to the new boy that we were all laughing at him. As he continued to flow tears and cry out for his parents, the Nun turned to the new boy and said, "Keep this up and the other boys will not want you to play with you. Now you don't want that to happen, do you?" The new boy shook his head, drew first one arm and then the other across his eyes then under his nose, further spreading the tears and snot to his ears.

Having had enough of the little sorry, Adelmia ushered the new boy to join a group of his own age. The boy was not having any of this and made a dash towards the closed playroom door. Unfortunately Alemenia was just about to enter the room and the two collided. The Nuns strongly objected to being called 'Lady' by the new boy, but he persisted in doing so even after receiving a few verbal warnings from both Nuns. At bed time the new boy refused to get undressed and was forcibly stripped of his arrival clothing by Alemenia and one of the older boys. The lights were then dimmed to the night light and on awaking the following morning the new boy had gone.

Later that day the new boy was caught and returned to us. On instructions from the two Nuns the runaway was taken to the workroom where he was firmly held and his head shaved and at bedtime the boy was firmly tied to his bed, so he again wouldn't disgrace the Holy House. In the morning he was again found to be missing, again escaping during the time of darkness. When caught the boy was not returned to us, we being told he was sent to a more secure 'Home'.

Instead of going to school my brother Bill and three others put their escape into operation. Well not quite, one boy decided to go his own route to freedom.

On returning for our afternoon meal I and several others were questioned about the whereabouts of the four missing boys. Nobody at that time suspected a runaway, it was a close secret between the three boys and my brother. What went on for the search of the runaways whilst we were attending the afternoon session at school I don't know. What I do remember is being approached by one of the Nuns and being told I had something to do with the four runaways. I stood where I was, trembling from head to foot, I trembled that much I felt a sickness in my stomach. "Why involve me," I repeated to myself, we, (that is my brother and I), don't even talk to one another. No one was allowed to leave the playroom except to go to the toilet, and then those that had to, reported to the Nun on returning. With rumours circulating that the runaways were on to a hiding to nothing, no one dared attempt an escape.

Late that night, my brother and his two companions were caught and returned, later that same night the fourth runaway was also returned, after being caught on a train station somewhere outside Aberdeen. It wasn't until the following morning did I hear the story of my brother and his partners in crime. They were driven back in a police car which was very small, probably an Austin 10 or 12, and it was driven by an enormously fat policeman. I am also informed that the three runaways wondered how on earth that enormously fat policeman got in and out of such a small matchbox size car!

My brother and his friends were caught by an A.A. patrol officer, whom they encountered earlier that day when he stopped his yellow motorbike and sidecar and took a long backward look at them whilst they were walking along a quiet road in the country. At that point all three bolted into the woodlands which stood tall and directly to their left. It seemed to get dark rather quickly whilst they were in the dense woodland through which they ran aimlessly. Eventually they came across a house where a light shone from what was to them a very small window. There was no way around the house because it was so dark, they simply couldn't see. But they did see a face at the window, though not looking out of it, but peering into a small square mirror which the man was using to shave. The man spotted the faces outside the window and was outside in seconds, the man being the very same A.A. patrol man the three had seen earlier that day.

WORLD WAR TWO

Before being allowed to listen to the radio for news of how the war was going, our main source of information came from outsiders when we attended school and from newspapers brought into the orphanage by male ex-inmate visitors.

Good or bad, the war news always had me excited, at times that excitement had to be kept inwards. To me the war was my secret fantasy adventure taking my thoughts away from internal regime and my internal battle to keep control of my senses. Winston Churchill, portrayed to us as a war monger and an English pig by the two Irish Nuns, was one of several names such as Hitler, Rommel and Montgomery to be etched foremost in my mind as my personal heroes. And alongside those names are those flying machines: Hurricanes, Spitfires, Lancaster Bombers and Messerschmitts.

My memory is being unwillingly dragged to the radio reports of the heavy bombing and heavy air fighting in the south of England coastal towns of Weymouth, Harwich, Portsmouth, Southampton, Dover and all the airfields in the south of England. My excitement on hearing over the radio of those attacks was mainly because, believing at that time English people were pigs, I wanted them wiped off the earth so as we Scots could then take over the country after the Germans had bombed it. What had me excited more than anything else, was the single raids from Norway on Aberdeen and other places in the north of Scotland. Those were single raids and most certainly nearly all German invaders were shot down by fighter aircraft from nearby airfield Dyce and from other small airfields in the area before the bombers reached our shores. Also getting the adrenalin flowing, were the stories about German spies being hunted in the Grampian Mountains and in the streets and lanes of the Highland towns and villages. That news certainly sent my imagination running wild, sending me out of the building in the early morning to go and have a look up at the branches of the half dozen trees that lined the boys entrance to the orphanage. Seeing nothing, I then ran towards the playing field and glanced searchingly at all corners of the field. Disappointed at finding nothing and failing to become a hero, I quickly returned to join the others before being missed by the Nuns.

Of course there were other exciting times for me during the war; the Battle of Dunkirk, the sinking of the Bismark, the Dambusters raid and the Germans scattering in all directions in the cruel winter conditions of a Russian winter. One of the German bombers from Norway that got through our defences dropped a single bomb and that bomb hit the building of the 'House of God'.

The sirens went off, as on previous occasions, in an orderly manner we left our dormitories to go to the playroom. There was an ear piercing whistle as we all were on our downward journey. Suddenly their was an almighty thud, a bomb hit the top right hand corner of the building, (our side), it shook the solid granite 'House of God' spreading panic everywhere. Within seconds of the 'Hit', there was an almighty blast as the bomb exploded a short distance away, causing the swing doors that separated sections of the building to swing open with such force they sent boy crashing against boy and lifting some off their feet as we tumbled down the stairs, most of us finishing up in a pile on the bottom of the stairway. Amidst the yells and screams were the unheard voices from the Nuns trying and failing to convince us we were to keep calm as we were safe in the 'House of God'. Once in the playroom, faithful ones prayed on their knees in front of the picture of the 'Sacred Heart of Jesus'. The not so faithful were either on benches or fighting for places inside cupboards. The two Nuns had a hopeless task trying to calm us, as a matter of fact they made matters worse by chasing after the young and hysterical. The all clear siren ended and the punishment began. All of us paid the price via the Cricket Wicket for our yells and screams and for our lack of faith in God.

The war was closing to an end and one of Hitlers Generals committed suicide. The Nuns had the jitters. One could sense the unrest amongst us. We all were waiting for something to happen. It did; on May 8 1945. Sadly there were no Highland Flings danced on the table tops in the 'House of God'. Gradually the Nuns were losing control, and they dare not use their offensive weapon they used to try and destroy us. The ending of the war gradually brought the Brutal Regime to its knees, then, all were replaced by kinder and more gentle Nuns who appeared to understand the position we all were in.

There were changes, some gradual, some swift and all for the better. One of the first changes was the degrading and terrible task of waxing and polishing of the wooden floors on our hands and knees. Hence no more scabs! That ordeal was to be carried out with the use of rags tied onto the heads of long handled, soft bristled brooms. The unenvious task of scrubbing the stairs and other stone floors were to be done with the use of long handled mops, which also brought laughter among us when used for fun tactics. The abolishment of those two chores brought a little sanity into the place and perhaps a little willingness to co-operate with the Nuns. Pocket money was available to spend as we wished, I preferring to use mine to visit a local cinema, mainly to watch Movieton Newsreel. Never did I want those newsreels to end, I could have sat from morning to night, my eyes glued to the screen.

They had to get rid of several of us, and fast. This is where the

'Emigration Scheme' came in useful. Those of us who were eligible to leave, that had no known relatives, were the chosen ones who had their destination planned for them. Casually sitting about the playroom, the three line regimental ordeal being done away with, we were called, by voice, to pay attention and listen to the names, (not numbers), that were to be called out. Most of us already had learnt who those names were, but none of us had any information who was going where and when they were to go. About thirty names were read out, most of whom were either going to Australia and Canada, with a tiny minority bound for New Zealand. It was an emotional period for all of us, especially for those of us on the emigration list. And, although there were mixed feelings about our future we, who were old enough and capable of understanding, couldn't put blame on the Nuns at floor level, the orders coming from the heartless powers from above. That was our feelings at that time. Gerry, one of my close friends, said to me on learning he was due for Canada, "Andy, my brain is shell shocked." Gerry was so mixed up he didn't know whether he was on his head or his feet.

Whatever they had been given in the form of luggage, had previously been put aboard the black Maria van. One by one they turned and waved as they place their first foot into the jaws of the van. From the smouldering ashes the Brutal Regime raised its ugly head. With us were two boys by the name of Steve and Hugh MacDonald, but only one of them boarded the van for the journey to the railway station. Both boys had their name called on the list read out two weeks earlier. Cunningly, on departure day they were separated by the new Nuns. Our deathly silence on seeing only one brother go into the van and on seeing the van doors about to be closed, our attention was interrupted by screams coming from the area of our main door entrance. The other MacDonald boy was running towards us and the by now closed Maria van door. Screaming his head off and crying, Hugh MacDonald hammered his fists against the bodywork of. the black van, calling and pleading to see and be with Steve who was about to be taken from him, when the driver of the van received his instructions to get into first gear. Frantically Hugh hammered his fists against the vehicle before being dragged away by a Nun assisted by other boys. It wasn't a pretty sight seeing the van and the Nuns cargo aboard drive out and to the left of the large double, heavy wooden gates. For years both Hugh and Steve believed they were brothers and so did all of us. But that was not the case, the Nuns made it up for reasons we will never know. Hugh, always regarded as a tough guy, was on his knees on the cold hard concrete ground and he was crying his eyes out as he was being comforted by his close pals. "Come back! Come back! Steve come back!" Hugh was shouting as he was

80

restrained from taking off after his Steve.

Whoever wrote the following could not possibly believe it would be used to describe other than what it was intended.

> Cold in blood and in mind,
> Inscrutable as stone,
> They are beyond my empathy.

In the past I was never allowed to play soccer on the self made soccer pitch in the playing field, however at times I could and did play with a small ball when a kick about was organised during playtime in the playing yard. So when on a bright and warm late summers day, when watching a game of soccer being played by the usual select, I was grinning all over my face when asked by Sister Osman if I would like to take part in the sport I was watching. On the blast of the Nuns whistle the game stopped, seconds later I, full of tremor and excitement, was taking part in my very first game of soccer. The excitement got the better of me, a great delight to the opposition for sure. I missed almost every ball that came my way and miskicked most of the others.

Under the care of the new Nuns I was treated like a human being, given lots of kindness I responded eagerly and was given responsibilities that I believed to be just. During the opportune moment when we were alone in the playing yard, Sister Osman placed her arm around my shoulder, telling me she heard about me from the Brutal Regime. Finding what she had heard as disturbing and that she was sorry it all happened, I was to try and put it all behind me and to look forward to a better life. My heart was stuttering. I could hear it beat inside my chest and felt it choking my throat. Taking deep intakes of breath, I tried to calm my nervousness as I was released on the sighting of another Nun. Fearing no retaliation I said, "I hate it in this place", when the approaching Nun asked what was the matter with me. "There are worse places than this," replied one of the new Nuns. Nodding my agreement, but with the scars of yesterday I left to join the other boys.

On the morning of the first emigration day, there was an uneasy atmosphere in the building, several of those leaving us on that day were in tears, one or two not wanting to leave despite being abused during their day under those cruel Nuns. For the first time the black Maria van was allowed to park on the concrete of the playing yard, with its rear doors open, like a crab shell it was after its prey.

The changes within the 'House of God' were getting to me. At the age of thirteen years I was beginning to realise I was a live human being, several times having to pinch myself to believe it. My head felt light as if all what had been inside was drained away leaving a vacuum. From the powers who organised the sailing on the high seas came the arrangements for everyone within the granite wall to assemble in the girls playroom, (much larger than ours), to watch silent movies, courtesy of one of our priests. Months later a dance was organised for the boys and girls. The Brutal Regime again raised its ugly head from the smouldering ashes; at the dance I was too frightened to touch the hand of my sisters and my knees wobbled as I stood near them, too scared in case we even rubbed shoulders.

A few months later and into the month of April 1948, I was at school leaving age, that meant the Nuns were not duty bound to keep me in the orphanage. On a morning shortly after breakfast and only minutes before a prearranged outing, Sister Osman approached me saying, "Andrew, you will not be going with the other boys. Will you please go to the workroom and I will explain why to you in a few minutes." Puzzled but not afraid, I made my way to the workroom as requested. A few minutes the Nun said and a few minutes it was, when she entered through the door of the workroom where another Nun was busy on one of the sewing machines.

"Andrew, " the Nun said, "You are leaving us today. You are going to live with your father in Birmingham." I can't remember my exact feelings at that time, but I do remember thinking to myself, "Birmingham? I have never heard of it." Handing to me a neatly folded pile of new clothing with a pair of black laced shoes resting on top, I was asked to go across the landing to the dining room to change... no long trousers! Minutes after my return to the workroom, Sister Osman then told me Mother Superior thought it better for me not to say goodbye to my brothers and sisters as it would upset all of us. The news of my departure and an explanation as to why we couldn't say our farewells was to be given to my brothers and sisters on their separate day outings. With a kiss on top of my head and with words not to abandon God and I will be alright, Sister Osman handed me over to two other Nuns who were waiting for me outside in the playing yard, by the van that was to take me on my return journey to the railway station where we first met all those years ago. On pulling away from that imposing solid granite building, tears were in my eyes and I found myself with rain in my heart.

SCRATCHINGS

Scratchings of happy memories under the Brutal Regime are found behind the layers of darkness in 'The Attic Of My Mind'.

By the main door entrance into the boys part of the building was a gathering of several younger boys up to about seven years of age, a few of them had not been with us very long. I and two or three others silently crept up unnoticed by the Nun sitting on the bench with her small gathering. To one of the questions being put to the gathering a very virtuous and innocent young boy spluttered out, "Sister, I want to grow up to be a priest in Ireland so I can preach to everyone how Holy God is and how nice you are." "God Bless your little soul," came the Nuns reply. Laughter was waiting to burst out of my ribs, I had the feeling my cheeks were being pumped hard and that they were going red. My nose was itching, my lips tingling at the effort to remain silent. It was looking the same for the others of my age. Two of them did giggle, the effort to remain silent was too much for them.

The film, 'The Bells of Saint Marys', was showing at a local cinema. At a time when we were all in the playroom a Nun blew her whistle, "All those who wish to go to see 'The Bells of Saint Mary's' put up your hands." Having had swallowed a Threepenny Bit and been given a mouthful of cotton wool covered in jam to ease the swallowing and the passing through my back passage, I couldn't go to the cinema. In a strange sort of a way I felt very happy about having to stay behind and I certainly enjoyed the unusual opportunity to play football with a handful of older boys who ¢hose not to see the film.

Sitting on a bench in the playroom, legs stretched out in front of him, wearing his kilted uniform, including steel-studded highly polished black boots and sitting behind his newspaper was ... the Hawk. It was a day when we all were in the playroom with most of the running about being done by the younger boys with a new boy joining those that were throwing paper aeroplanes and other objects of soft material. Such an object I believe, fell on the lap of the Hawk. The new boy was about to retrieve the fallen object but hesitated in doing so when the military man presented himself over the top of his paper. Predictably, the voice behind the newspaper said, "I suppose you are the new boy, are you?" "Yes sir," replied the new boy. "How long have you been here?" inquired the voice behind the newspaper. "Three weeks, sir," replied the boy. "Three weeks, eh! How old are you boy?" "Six, sir" the boy said "Then kiss my boots six times," said the voice behind the newspaper.

"I wonder why we don't murder them," was going through my mind as I was sitting reading a murder story from a piece of newspaper. 'Them' meaning the Nuns. "I would if I could," also passed through my mind at that time. I heard Alemenia's voice echo through the toilets before she opened the door of the cubicle where I had been sitting. She gave a sardonic smile, I was caught with my pants down.

Standing in front of my class was my Geography teacher Miss Marshal, who to me at that time was the most wonderful person in the world. I hoped and prayed the impossible to happen ... that she would be my class teacher for ever and ever. Miss Marshal made my Geography lessons a real adventure. One hour each week I had the rivers and mountains of the world all to myself. I fell in love with nature, with the animals, the air, the winds, the trees, the smells. The bracken covered Grampian mountains belonged to me.

Window alcoves in the dormitories were many times used as safe places to read the banned 'works of the Devil' (comics). Desperate Dan ... sent to turn us against God. My! Keyhole Kate ... a spy devil in disguise - honestly, where did those Nuns get those ideas? It was during one of those secretive times when Bruce and I, from the prostrate position we were in and the protection from the rows of beds first of all heard two sets of footsteps ascending the stone stairs leading to our dormitory, one set muffled, the other set heavier. Then we watched the black shoes and dark trouser bottoms worn by a man accompanied by the skirt of a Nuns garment enter the dormitory. Instantly we stuffed our comics under the mattress of the bed immediately above us. Then we drew back into the window alcove behind us. From our worms eye view under the rows of beds we both watched two pairs of feet slowly make their way along the dormitory to stop at the door of the Nuns Cell (bedroom). They hesitated for a moment on reaching the door of the Cell, then entered closing the- door behind them. Bruce and I looked at each other in puzzled astonishment. then as we turned our heads towards the direction of the main doorway Bruce gave me a nudge with his elbow and said in a whisper, "Lets go before we are caught." Then, we heard the noise of a key turning in a keyhole. Quickly, both petrified at the thought of being caught, we remained motionless. ..... Both our hearts were pounding as we lay there in silence at for what seemed a very long time. Also I remember feeling scared, terribly scared as the adrenalin pumped into my body and my heart was beating fast and heavy as I made my way in a sprawling position under the beds, along the landing, then to run as fast as my legs would go down the stairway when, on reaching the bottom Bruce and I looked at each other, a burst of laughter evaporated from both of us, then we separated.

The only time I can recall 'being at a bonfire was with my only weekend with the Scouts, or was it the Cubs? No; it was the Scouts.' I suppose that comes to my mind because when the bonfire was at its height, it let out an awful lot of heat, I feeling like a roasted chestnut at the time. It was a good feeling being out in the free and open spaces and actually feeling a belonging to it. And seeing everyone enjoying the spirit of the occasion, that was a gift from God. As there was a strong wind approaching, no more wood was added to the bonfire, that didn't dampen my spirits as I equally enjoyed the freedom of the night. The arrival of the wind caused sparks to fly and the acrid smell of smoke made my eyes smart and tear ducks overflow. Later that night George Crombie, our Scout Master, allowed us to gather round the dying bonfire when there were only white embers glowing red in the then slightly swirling wind. I and others crouched close to the ashes of the dying. bonfire blowing with all our might but couldn't rekindle what was to me a symbol of freedom. That, at the age of about thirteen years was my first 'free' weekend since being admitted to the Orphanage. I often wonder if that kind local farmer who allowed us the use of one of his fields realised what happiness he brought to all of us that weekend.

The playing fields at Hazlehead were at times visited by us but only on one occasion do I remember being there. I was bored and tense at having to sit on the rough grass close to the black mountain of a Nun, she having a stool to sit on. Somehow I managed to slip away from her and forty or so other boys who at that time were absorbed in watching (outsiders) groups of Scouts, Cubs and boys of the Boys Brigade all of whom were thoroughly enjoying whatever they were enjoying. Under no circumstances were we allowed to speak to any of the 'outsiders' not even if they spoke to us. The playing area of Hazlehead of which we were guests was about 250 metres by about 150 metres in size and was partly hidden by woodland of densely populated trees and shrubs with a screening of a metre high stone built wall stretching the full length of the area we occupied. With my back to that hand laid and embedded wall I eased myself up and onto the earth of the woodland. After picking my way through the brambles I found a tree to climb. Trees clustered everywhere in all shapes and sizes and in dense clumps where birds were chirping away and to each other. Having found a good branch or branches to sit on, sadness and loneliness again was with me, but in saying that, I was glad to be on my own. From where I was sitting parted branches allowed warm rays of sunshine to help in drying the tears that were trickling down my cheeks. Soon I was feeling free, assisted by the warm sunshine I was a million miles away and in another world where the sunlight, warmth and freedom and colours were so different from anything I had ever seen. I wasn't alone I had the birds and the trees singing to me and to each other. Suddenly I was brought back to earth when, below me a dry twig snapped. Momentarily I was scared and climbed down the tree. When I reached the bottom I looked around and saw nobody. Then my heart went into a nervous jitter, I feeling I was alone and that everyone had gone and left me behind. Nervously I hurried along the path whence I came and was delighted to see the Nuns and the other boys grouping to set off on the return journey.

As with the visits to Hazlehead I can only recall a single visit to the banks of the luring fresh crystal clear water of the River Dee. The reason I remember that bright, warm and sunny day is because after several hours of heavenly freedom I had a slight accident having placed my hand on broken glass when on the embankment I sat to towel myself after a great time in the river. From the arches of the old stone historical bridge, we allowed the gentle flowing river carry us down stream on our backs. I enjoyed that so much that I did it time and time again, equally enjoying the 200 yards or so wading about knee length back to the starting point at the bridge. Occasionally I joined in with others watching fish skulking in the shadow of the historical bridge and to join in throwing flat and suitably weighted stones to skim across the waters of the river trying to bounce them as far as we could towards the other embankment. I also vividly remember enjoying younger boys dancing about and splashing in the cool water of the river pointing and gesticulating and getting all excited at their freedom of the day.As the first of the boys were collecting to put behind them the joys of the day I paused at the rivers edge, looking along at the cool, clear smoothly flowing river water. Gradually my painful thoughts were being carried away with every ripple that passed me by. It was as if I was sending a message of help to somebody. Then I was thinking, all I had to do was strip to my underpants, go into the river, take a deep intake of breath, face the sky and paddle like hell and with the help from the down flow of the river I would be free. Well, we all have our dreams!

Duthie Park with its acres of green carpet like lawns, razor cut garden areas with colourful flowers that always seemed to be in full bloom gave me the feeling of being on a desert island every time we visited that lovely park. Probably I got that feeling because of the beauty and vastness of it.

ANOTHER EXPERIENCE

At the end of a long and tiresome journey by train from Aberdeen to New Street Station in gritty Birmingham, I was met by my father. I didn't like the feel of his hand nor did I like the uncertainty of his company. As we walked through Birmingham town centre heaving with people walking and travelling in all directions and the heavy industrial transport churning up the dust and grime adding further discomfort to the heat of the day another form of isolation swept through me. And I had new and unwelcome company ... fear and anguish. I felt as if I were a walking corpse inside a jacket and shirt and trousers. I was so tired, sticky with dusty heat of the day, and also bewildered I couldn't muster the strength to reply to my fathers voice when he offered to buy me an ice cream. "Didn't the Nuns teach you manners?" the voice, obviously angry and demanding of a reply. I did reply, but not verbally, I couldn't open my mouth (or didn't want to), instead I gave several quick shakes—of my head. Quick with a reply my father said, "I hope you are not going to be a problem." He received a second refusal on the offer of an ice cream, I having said, "No thanks." Now the fear of the busy and noisy traffic was having an effect on me, especially when we were standing on the pavements edge and the heavy industrial vehicles rumbled past barely an inch from my nose throwing on to me and into my nostrils the dirty industrial dust from the old and terribly worn streets. At one waiting point I gave a tremendous tremble which was felt by my father as his voice had a sympathetic tone to it when saying, "Of course you are not used to all this traffic, are you?" I looked away and said, "no." My clean handkerchief was neatly folded in the left hand pocket of my trousers and I badly wanted the use of it to wipe off the mucky sweat from my hands, face and around my aching neck. Fear of being separated from my father and getting lost made me suffer a little until we arrived at the other side of the road, then I slipped my sweaty hand from the hold it had on me and having quickly and somewhat nervously wiped my face, neck and arms. I replaced the now not so clean handkerchief in my pocket and renewed links with my father.

A few hundred yards from where I was to be taken stood a working mens care that belonged to an aunt, so we stopped there for an introduction, a free mug of tea and for me an awaited rest. It was only when I sat down at one of the empty tables that I realised that the heat of the day fouled by petrol and diesel exhaust fumes mingled with the dust and grit had me feeling sick. That mug of tea was welcome, it washed away the horrible fouling taste that was in my mouth and edging towards my throat. I was alone at the table, actually apart from my aunt and her brother, I was the only other person in the care at that time. That suited me fine, being alone was relaxing and I was in no mood for answering questions. Having cooled a little I decided to give myself another wipe with my handkerchief and on removing it from my pocket I found it to be mostly filthy from the previous use. Having found a clean part it was used not so much to wipe away the sweat but to remove the dirt that had mingled with it. "Feeling better son," the words from my father were met by a feeble but never the less verbal reply which was agreeably accepted by my father. I waved goodbye to my aunt, having been told to do so.

Nothing more was said to me until we reached the doorsteps of what appeared to me to be an old unoccupied derelict building. Decades of industrial dust and grime embedded the walls and windows, the windows showing grubby worn lace curtains. "This is your new 'home' Andrew." The sickness and all that was washed away with the mug of tea immediately returned to my mouth and my knees wobbled as I stood and momentarily stared at what was presented to me. Then glancing to my right I noticed a small arched with stone railway bridge was attached to the building. On the way from the care I was thinking and wondering why my aunt and my father were talking in a low and heated voice, now my mind was blank.

The old and faded brown lino which ran along side a mufti coloured dark hessian looking well trodden carpet that ran along the dark hallway and up the first flight of stairs was highly polished. And to the bottom left hand of the hallway were several well worn sandy coloured stone steps leading to a cobbled floor kitchen-meal room. To the immediate left of the kitchen stood a lady in a bright red suit peeling potatoes in the two tone brown coloured stone sink. That lady was introduced to me as my mother. Further dislike for my father and hatred for that woman were instantly installed into my heart. Inwardly I was crying for help and with self pity. Turning in my direction and with a hand held out to greet me her smile left her face, it being replaced by sadness and understanding on receiving no response from me. But from that moment I felt Kathy was a nice person so I responded by the offer of my hand, hers felt nice. With hatred for Kathy no longer with me I willingly accepted her invitation to sit at the kitchen table that was to the right of me and against the green oil painted brick wall. At that time my father said he would take my small suitcase into his bedroom.

It was when alone and at the table that Kathy apologised to me for the introduction and saying also that it was the way my father wanted it. "When we have finished our tea I will show you your bedroom and the bathroom where you can have a wash then you will feel better." It was obvious the old badly chipped and stained white enamel painted bath had not served its purpose for several years so I had to settle for a wash down at the wash basin. I used the newly laundered bath towel not knowing or thinking if it was for my use or not. Anyway I had noted how it was folded and returned it in that way to the rail on the inside of the bathroom door. "Andrew, your clean clothing is on the table in the hallway," Kathy shouted up to me. I dressed, ran downstairs, grabbed my clothes, ran back to the washroom, closed the door behind me, undressed and dressed again all within two minutes. Having done all that I then didn't know what next to do so I nervously sat on the edge of the old iron bath and hoped to hear a voice asking me to come downstairs. It wasn't long in coming, the evening paper was delivered and Kathy asked me to join her when she collected the paper from the porch. With my changed clothes in my hand I made my way to the kitchen where a meat sandwich and. another mug of tea were waiting for me.

Kathy was reading the evening paper when she suddenly lowered it to the table and said to me, "Did your dad tell you what sort of house this is?" I was startled but managed to shake my head. "Well we take in lodgers, mostly Irish labourers." Kathy immediately knew by the expression on my face that I didn't know what she was talking about. Shortly after hearing footsteps going upstairs Kathy said, "That's two of them going to their rooms." Kathy could see I was still puzzled so she explained everything to me then handed the evening paper to me saying I wouldn't understand the local news but there is sport in the back pages. I was soon to be joined at the table by two red faced burly Irishmen and their Irish accent amused me, unfortunately both were of the impression that I was laughing at them. I wasn't really laughing at them, it was just that I had never before heard such an accent as theirs. "Ah! You must be Tony's (my fathers name) son, he told us you would be arriving today from Scotland where you have been attending a convent school." He is lying I wanted to shout. Although the cooking smelt good I didn't really pay much attention to it with my mind being on other things. In a way I resented sharing the table with the two burly Irishmen but with a full stomach that feeling ebbed a little. The meal served by Kathy was very good, the best I had ever tasted. No sooner had Patrick and Shaun left the table I was joined by a small but stockily built man and by his appearance it was obvious to me he worked in an engineering factory of some description. He was called Brummie being the only Birmingham born person in the house. Unlike the two Irishmen Brummie didn't have any manners, he not being able to get his food into his mouth quick enough.

Kathy was furious at the 'Old Man' being late for his meal. "He will blame me if his dinner is all dried up when he does decide to come over from the club." That was the first time I heard my father being called an

'Old Man' but I liked it. Some time had passed and Kathy was really annoyed, so she decided she wasn't waiting any longer so she took her own meal out of the oven and joined with me at the table. Eventually the 'Old Man' did turn up and the smell from his mouth was vile and I didn't like the way he moved or talked. Sitting at the opposite end of the table I saw the old man had great difficulty with his knife and fork and that he found my presence an embarrassment. Giving up the struggle with the knife and fork the old man relied on the fork only to feed himself. All during his meal the old man was churning away to himself, I catching an odd word now and then. The whisky had got the better of him and I was frightened and I tried my best not to show any signs of fear. I hadn't realised until the old man had left the kitchen that I had removed the Rosary Beads from my pocket and that I had them held tightly in my hands between my knees. Was I praying? I don't really know, my mind was in such a whirl. With my face being distorted with pain and disgust at seeing my father in a drunken stupor Kathy came over to me. Drawing her chair close to mine then placing a hand on my shoulder Kathy looked me in the eye and began apologising at me seeing the old man in a drunken condition on my first day with him. Then Kathy went to say I would be seeing a lot more of it but not to be thinking too badly about my father because he is a very lonely man. that sent shudders of horror and disbelief along my spine down to my heels, that triggered off the resentment of being brought into 'Another Experience'.

Later at about six o'clock Brummie returned with the local Saturday sports paper (I hadn't noticed he had gone) and after checking his football coupon he handed the paper to me. Immediately I looked at the football results of Hearts and Aberdeen, then my interest was with the other Scottish teams, At that time I wanted to be back in Scotland with my brothers and sisters. With Brummie gone I was on my own so on finished reading the sports paper I drew my chair closer to the open coal fire that Kathy lit a few minutes earlier before leaving to make a phone call.

I was looking in the direction of the slowly burning coal fire when the old man returned looking quite sober and wearing a satisfied smile on his unpredictable face. "I've got a wee surprise for you son," then he said, "Are you feeling in the mood for a wee drive to see your Grandma in Leamington Spa. She will be very annoyed if I don't take you to see her." I was silent not knowing what to say, then I saw the first signs of anger from the old man when he said, "Put a bloody smile on your face Andrew." Although he almost succeeded in covering that anger I took it as a signpost into the future especially at remembering the earlier words from Kathy. The old man and I hardly spoke on the drive to see my Grandma, the only words I could hear were that Grandma was his mother and that she has been dying for a long time and that the priest has been visiting her on a regular basis. I wasn't concerned that Auntie Annie wasn't mentioned until we approached the house in Leamington.

With my Grandmother being bedridden it was difficult for her to get her arms around me for the hug she dearly wanted. After that was over it was the turn of Auntie Annie to show her delight in seeing me. Well we all had cups of tea and biscuits and a lot of words were exchanged some of which I found over dramatic and others of no interest to me whatsoever. With the promise to come back the following day, my mind being made up for me, we set off on the return journey to Birmingham. Again not many words were spoken and the journey didn't take as long as the first and I was soon to know why. Pulling to a stop outside my new 'home' in Islington Row the old man opened the door at my side of the car and explained why he wasn't allowed to park outside the house and that he had to leave it somewhere else. In the kitchen was Kathy and she was dressed and looking different ... ready to go to the club when the old man was ready. With the old man already knowing I preferred going to bed rather than the club he had taken my suitcase into my bedroom and when he came down to the kitchen I was asked to say good night to Kathy, she in turn said she will see me in the morning. You are in the bedroom next to mine and as the old man approached the bedroom and I behind him I noticed the door to the bedroom was of a dirty brown colour with a badly worn and dented brass door knob that rattled when the door was opened. And once the door was ajar I went sick. There was a chair behind the bedroom door and as my father placed my suitcase on it he turned round to me and said, "Son, you are fortunate at having this room for yourself, usually I have three paying lodgers in here! I'm going for a 'wee dram,' I'll pop in and look at you when I come back. Sleep well son."

Within minutes of being left alone, I heard a rumbling and it was getting closer and louder. The noise was nearing the house then on remembering seeing the railway bridge attached to the property, my fear left me. When the coal train with several wagons of coal dust reached the house the windows rattled bringing to my notice the appalling state they were in. The dirty brownish window glass and the blistered dark brown woodwork were kept in place with years old browning newspaper. Then my eyes were drawn to the very, very old brass 4ft bed that was standing against and close to the left hand corner of the room. A couple of army styled blankets covered the bare, sagging pee stained mattress, the prison like stripes matching those of the pillow which rested against the distorted brass strips that were a part of the other brass fittings constituting a headrest. For a while I remained slumped on the stand chair at the bottom of the bed, I was feeling cold, tired, dejected and although I had washed earlier I still felt dirty and was unable to control my nervous twitch of my head that always sent my quill of hair out of control. And I couldn't believe or understand what was going on around me or within me. I closed my eyes and painfully raising my head towards the heavens I prayed and prayed and prayed for help. To whom I was praying I do not know, I just wanted someone from the heavens to be with me. The brass knob came off in my hand when I climbed onto the bed and I couldn't get it back so I left it on the floor at the side of the bed leg. With the pee stained mattress sagging in the middle I decided it would be safer for me to keep as near to the pillow end as possible. With the feeling the mattress could also be full of bugs I slipped off the bed and changed into my cotton striped pyjamas that were still in my suitcase. only then did I notice the bare floor boards and the carpet strip that was alongside the bed. Back on the bed and sitting with my arms wrapped around my legs and close to my chin I remember thinking it would be great if I lifted my arms and flew like a bird to a place of a far and isolated destination. I didn't hear anyone open the front door but when the brass door knob of the bedroom door rattled I quickly slipped between the two dark grey blankets giving the old man the impression I was asleep. "Good morning Andrew, did you sleep well?" was the cynicism that left the old man. "Your breakfast is ready. There is no need to wash, you can do that later," were his following words. I struggled a little on attempting to get out of bed, when I moved one way the mattress moved another. Well I did wash when I visited the bathroom not in defiance of the old man but to rid myself of the nauseating smell of the bed I was sleeping in. I was hungry and the smell from the kitchen made me feel better ... smell that bacon! Within me raged anger when a bowl of cornflakes was placed in front of me when I sat at the table. Having noticed the redness of my face and neck the old man inquired as to what was the matter. Even having explained that cornflakes were for Englishmen and that I was hungry the old man insisted I ate the cornflakes or do without. On hearing what was said I pushed away the bowl, the old man then instructed Kathy to serve me with my bacon, egg, sausage and skinned tomatoes and a slice of fried bread with it The mug of tea that followed was also good. Now I was ready for the journey by road to Leamington Spa. I was to stay there for a full week. My shirt and underwear worn by me the previous day had been washed, dried and ironed and placed in my suitcase by Kathy, so all I had to do was add my toothpaste and toothbrush then get into the car that was waiting for me outside. Before removing the handbrake the old man apologised about the cornflakes saga saying he too rejected cornflakes when first he arrived in England. Then as he set off he assured me that it would only be porridge at Leamington Spa.

Nothing much was said whilst we were in Birmingham, concentration of the busy traffic was more important than words. But once we were in the country the old man talked about his poor relationships between himself and his sister Annie and his mother (Grandma), they blaming him- for my brothers and sisters and I being put into an orphanage. At the end of the journey I was left in no doubt that little as possible had to be said about the life in Aberdeen.

During my stay I was treated like I was never treated before, the kindness mingled with sympathy was overwhelming and during my stay I was introduced to a very attractive female with beautiful black shoulder length hair, she being my niece and she was with her playboy boyfriend when we were first introduced. On leaving to return to Birmingham I was again left in no doubt that the feelings between the old man and my auntie and grandma were mutual. What a family!

During my three and a half years stay in Birmingham I frequently visited Leamington Spa but only on flying daytime visits. During the car journey back to Birmingham the old man startled me when saying there was a surprise waiting for me when I got to Islington Row. He didn't say anything more about it but I didn't like the tone of his voice. Neither did I care for his reckless driving. He sure was in a strange mood that had me gripping the sides of my seat.

My towels and clothes had been laundered before leaving Leamington so all I had to do was unpack them and place them on the chair in my bedroom. On top of the pile I placed my toothpaste and toothbrush, then I noticed a difference to the bed, the old mattress had been replaced by a newer and cleaner one, there also were sheets and clean ones at that. Pillow slips were added later that evening. With time to spare before being called by the old man I sat on the edge of the bed and glanced through the comics that were given to me at Leamington and that were branded the works of the devil by the Nuns in Aberdeen. "Andrew," echoed from the kitchen, throwing my heart into pulsating beats. Was' it to be my surprise? It wasn't, there was a slice of fruit cake and a mug of tea waiting for me on the table. The old man didn't say anything he just sat behind a newspaper until disturbed by the opening of the front door followed by footsteps along the hallway then down into the kitchen. During that time my heart was again pounding. It was Brummie wearing that same dirty, oily, dark jacket of which his hands were searching for something in its inside pockets. Apparently there was some money owing by Brummie to the old man on rent arrears and that was why Brummie was making a feeble attempt to find some of it. Knowing he was wasting time the old man told Brummie to forget about it until his next pay day. Then the old man began to introduce

93

Brummie to me not knowing we had previously met. Having repeatingly thanked the boss (my father), for his generosity of spirit, Brummie sat with me at the table rambling on and on about how good the boss had been to him. It was obvious Brummie was afraid of his boss, the way he was 'showing off' indicated that to me. Kathy was next to enter the kitchen and she was wearing another suit which was brown in colour. On entering the kitchen Kathy and the old man threw themselves into a hushed and somewhat hurried conversation. In the meantime Brummie was rambling on at me about the job he does and about where he worked.

Unnoticed by Kathy and the old man I left the kitchen and headed for my bedroom, on entering I was shocked and angry to see a seven year old 'boy squeezing my toothpaste between the bare floorboards and at the sight of used matchsticks sticking in a rowstretch he had completed. On my asking who he was and what he thought he was up to, the boy got up from his knees and ran passed me shouting, "Help! Help! That new man is hitting me." I was met at the top of the kitchen steps by the old man, the boy having disappeared down into the kitchen. I was grabbed by the shoulder and heaved into the bedroom where the old man pulled me towards him saying in a low stern voice that had me frightened and puzzled, "You lay a finger on John I will tan the hide off you. Do you hear me?"

I was trembling all over. My thoughts were in a mincing machine. Then I thought I was hearing voices. I wasn't hearing voices but one voice and it was that of my father and it was saying to me ... "John is your new brother......I'm sorry you have met your brother under these circumstances...... John was to be the surprise I was telling you about. I'm Johns dad and Kathy is his mother."

The tension within me was terrible, in fact so terrible I thought I was about to burst into pieces. What, if anything, was going through my mind during the minutes that followed I'll never know.

I had heard enough but the old man went on to apologise for not telling me of John saying he didn't know how to go about it. I didn't believe him. Unknown to me the old man had acquired his sisters house just a few minutes walk from his house and that was where he, Kathy and John had spent the night. I never saw John again.

Before the old man had left the bedroom he placed his hand on the top of my head and said, "I'm sorry son. I will see you tomorrow when I get back from work." These words added more disgust and nauseation to what I was already feeling.

Still sitting on the edge of the bed I managed to muster enough strength to again raise my head towards the heavens and with heavy eyes that were closed and with what little energy I had I prayed for someone up

94

there to be with me. The shock of what I'd just experienced took some time to ease and when it did I made my way down to the kitchen for material warmth from the heat of the coal fire and the warmth from a mug of hot sweet tea.

I was somewhat surprised to see Kathy in the kitchen and her presence turned out to be to my advantage. Kathy did her best to explain the situation between her and the old man and her son John. It was then I learnt that John was also born on the date April 8th ... That makes three and a half sharing that birthdate. Kathy also explained the way in which the old man got his sister into the care of the Salvation Army so he could get his hands on her house. It was a awful story of which both Kathy and I didn't like. On hearing from Kathy that the old man had decided I was to join him at his new purchase I decided there and then that I was staying where I am. John was with his father in the club across the road and Kathy had to get over there to collect John and take him back to live with his grandparents in Warwick. Although I was most grateful for the information received from Kathy I was still in a land of whirlpools. The mug of tea and roast beef sandwich made for me was good and with having washed and dried both mug and plate I returned to my bedroom.

With Kathy and John out of the way the old man called for me, knocking on the bedroom door before entering he requested I go for a wash then he will take me over to the club rather than have me sitting here on my own. To me his request was more like a demand so I obeyed.

I'm in the club and the eyes of all except of the snooker players were either upon me or aiming in my direction making me feel as if I were a subject out of the novel Scrooge. The owners of those eyes then had their heads together in silent whispers or in voices meant not for my ears or of those of the person who brought me.. After being introduced to a married middle aged couple it was the turn of the short, plump and red of face jovial man behind the small bar to say hello and welcome. With a glass of shandy in my had I turned around to notice the talking and nodding were still going on and again I sensed a thousand eyes upon me. The club was filling with people and consequently tobacco smoke, also I was being pushed about a little with the bar being close to the door. And with the old man at the snooker table I got out into fresher air as I made my way across the road to bed. Soon the unpredictable old man was in my bedroom cursing me for my bad manners and for embarrassing him in front of his friends (mostly pretentious) and for feeding fuel for fire to his arch enemies. He didn't stop to hear I couldn't accept the packed conditions of the club.

Little did the old man know that that night was the beginning of the end of our father/son relationship.

95

The following morning after breakfast I was introduced to my first football coupon, it was William Hills fixed odds coupon. Not knowing a great deal about Scottish football and nothing about English or Welsh teams I just sat and pondered. Having decided how much I was going to invest from the few shillings received from different relations I then made my mind to go for the 'Eight Results'. My choice of eight matches were chased by my feelings when running my fingers up and down the 'Eight Results' column stopping at certain matches. With my coupon completed I held on to it for a couple of days until giving it to the Irishman who gave it to me who later on gave me the postal order counterfoil. The old man didn't go to work that day instead about mid morning I was taken for an interview at a local bakery for a vacancy the old man had seen in a local newspaper. This interview was part one of a brain wave of the old man. He had plans for my three sisters and two brothers to be a part of his scheme to own a famous restaurant and we were to be his underpaid staff. It was all up to me to toe the line and obey the old mans wishes then he will arrange for all of us to be together in business making a lot of money.

That was not to be because my stay at the bakery was to be short lived, I not caring much for those I was working with and their dirty habits during their making of cakes and bread etc. My father was furious when he heard of my sack from the bakery, his dream in ruins before it got off the ground. "If you bloody well think you are going to sit about all day and do nothing and get fed and roofed for nothing you have another thing coming!" The old man hammered at me in a very angry controlled voice as we met in the kitchen. "You will get tonights papers and look for the apprentice engineering job you have always wanted." Realising he had been lecturing me for the best part of half an hour and saying so after looking at his watch. The old man changed his personality when using a pale blue voice suggesting I looked through the Situations vacant section of the evening paper for a job that appealed to me. And if I circled those jobs of interest I would receive help in sorting them out.

Although letters were requested by a few of the companies the old man wasn't having anything or anyone preventing him from getting a quick reply so phone calls were made to all advertisers. As a result of his determination we had an interview with a toolmaking company two days later. The directors of the small engineering company agreed a six months supervisory period at which time I would again be interviewed. Six months later and on my birthday I, the old man a director and a witness signed Apprentice papers for the company in Hylton Street in the heart of the Jewellery Centre of Birmingham. Sadly my happy days with that company were to last just over three years.

It was my first Christmas in Birmingham and I was politely ordered to the festive party at the club across the road. I hated it. At first there were only a few of us but that rapidly changed to a full house of merrymaking drunken people most of whom didn't know what they were doing or what was going on around them I didn't 'fit in' and I was ashamed and disgusted at the appalling behaviour of the old man, so well into the celebrations I left and went across the road for a cup of tea. Sometime during the following day I was accused of being a spoilt little brat and a little snob and that I again had embarrassed the old man.

It was during that Christmas period that I began my interest in the four legged animals. With all the lodgers, bar Brummie, over in Ireland and with you know who on the booze day and night I had time on my hands to get my head into the racing sections of a couple of the morning newspapers. I always preferred the newspapers to the racing ones because I was a news addict as well as being a racing fanatic.

Because of my knack for finding winners I was soon to become popular with everyone at the factory; yes I mean everyone. Not all employees gambled but everyone took an interest in the Epsom Derby and the Liverpool Grand National. It wasn't only the hardened experienced gamblers that were interested in my knack for finding winners and what system I had at finding those often high priced winners.

I was well into my second year at the factory when one day I thought I was going to get the sack for my interest in gambling. It was a Saturday morning and unusual for an apprentice I was working overtime when one of the big bosses approached me saying, "I believe you have got an unusual and profitable hobby for a young man?" "God," I thought, "I'm going to get the sack." That wasn't to be. The boss surprised me to the point my knees were trembling when on hearing him say to me, "Have you a winner for today?" I hadn't but on request I promised the boss I would have a look at my paper at breaktime. There was a three horse race at one of the countrys big flat meetings, I think it was either Ascot or Epsom. The winner was the 25/1 outsider and that was what I gave to the boss. Respecting the wish of the boss I didn't say a word about the event to anyone. And all the boss said to me after finding out he had rich pickings was, "How do you do it?" I didn't verbally reply, I couldn't, because I didn't-have the answer myself, a shrug of the shoulders and a smile was acceptable to the boss. Although I selected my horse winners solely from the newspapers finding winners, from dog racing was during race meeting only. Kings Heath, Perry Barr and Hall Green were three dog tracks I attended the last two mentioned were only visited by myself on one occasion.

At Kings Heath I felt relaxed and that is where I was to find my

97

regular winners. Although I only missed the first race at a meeting at Kings Heath on one occasion I didn't always have a bet at each attendance, neither did I always back winners but more often than not I would finish up with money in my pocket.

It was Easter Saturday and the old man delayed my getting to the dog track for the first of the special Easter programme, we were having a hell of an argument, (at this time in life I was standing up for myself) about what I can't remember. By the time I got down among the bookies the dogs were just about all in their traps and I was frantically searching my programme for that race winner. I was too late, the hare was off and the dogs were running that is all except the one I had selected. I needed to settle down so I gave the next race a miss, again my selection was a tail ender. That wasn't the case with the following four selections, they all being winners, and I collected from all four. Although I stayed for the other races I had no interest in them the feeling just was not there.

Then there was that other Easter race meeting again at my favourite Dog track when the dogs ran in appalling conditions. I wakened that morning to torrential rain and I put the idea of going to the track out of my mind, firstly I was thinking it would surely be cancelled. Then having counted my money I felt there wasn't enough to encourage me to take part in any form of gambling. Well, I was terribly bored and isolated and the thought to be missing out if the dogs did run was all I could think about. The thoughts of Kings Heath Dog Track were strong in my mind and wouldn't go away, this had an unsettling affect on me and I didn't settle until I had paid my fare on the bus that was to take me to that lovely stadium.

The track was like a quagmire and I was thinking there would be a change in the programme; there wasn't. I was feeling good despite the heavy rainfall. I gave the first two races a miss, collected a little on the third and fourth races, then there was a dog named 'Sunless Sunday' running in another race. The rain had eased a little, then it came down 'cats and dogs' scattering people into the stands, and of course out of the reach of the bookies, myself included. But the dog 'Sunless Sunday' wouldn't leave my mind and at the odds of 25/1 I wanted it to because I thought I would be on a loser if I wagered on it. The announcement was, "The dogs are going into their traps." I was out in the torrential rain running from one bookmaker to the other holding a 'Ten Bob' note in my hand which was getting so wet it was almost coming apart. "They're Off," and I was holding out my by now soggy 'Ten Bob' note to a bookie saying, "Ten Bob to win Sunless Sunday."

Sunless Sunday 'skated in' on the boggy surface and I was in efferent joy with my outstretched hands and fingers joining my eyes towards the heavens and I silently saying, "Thank you." I noticed my soaking wet Ten Bob note draped over the top of the bookies board when I collected my winnings. On handing out my winnings the bookie said something like, "You deserve your 'pick up' for having the guts to back that stupid dog, I've backed it several times and it owes me." With the money safely in my wallet I again turned to the heavens and silently said another thank you.

Being an apprentice I didn't earn big wages and by the time I had paid the 'Landlord' I was left little to myself. Never the less I was always able to keep my head above water and when I needed money it was always there to be collected. At a time during my stay in Birmingham I joined a local Boxing Club that was turning out good boxers on a regular basis. I was still skin and bones at that time so I decided to join a local Health and Fitness Club with the hope of putting on weight. "You have put half an inch on your biceps," said one of the trainers after my third night of exercising. I didn't believe him and I didn't go back. But as I was doing well at the Boxing Club I decided it was for me to make the effort to succeed. It didn't take long before I caught the eye of one of the trainers and shortly after I was winning my first contest. On winning several of my other contests I thought I was going places.

The old man heard of my gambling and of my boxing and he didn't like what he heard. He had the absurd idea that I took up boxing so as one day I would be able to knock his head off his shoulders. And as for my gambling he was convinced, believing what he was told, I had a little nest egg growing so he had me out of my bedroom and into another sharing with two of the Irishmen and Brummie. That move didn't go down well with my new room mates for one thing they thought I was sent to spy on them as I was the son of the 'Landlord', the 'Boss' Brummie always called him. I wasn't too pleased either. Although I repeated what the 'Landlord' had said to me the three were not for believing.

The two Irishmen often asked questions about my life in Nazareth House and I foolishly gave them a true account of what happened. With both Irishmen being Roman Catholics and practising ones at that, most of what I had told them was difficult for them to accept, even having mentioned that I had nothing to gain by the answers they received to their inquisitive questions. Then there was Brummie, I found out to my horror he was the reason the old man knew so much about what I was saying and talking about. Brummie was acting childishly during one of the rare nights none of us went out, I think that was because of the weather conditions that severe winter. One of the two Irishmen left the room to go upstairs to play

99

the board game 'Crown and Anchor' (now illegal), minutes later the other Irishman went to the bathroom to wash some of his soiled clothing to get away from the temptation to land one on Brummie. With two others out of the room Brummie turned his attention on me. Gradually his childish taunts were getting the better of me and .after several unheeded warnings I threw myself at the idiot. Within seconds Brummie was pleading for his life, I having punched him on to the floor in a corner of the room. Luckily for Brummie one of our room mates returned saving Brummie further punishment.

With Brummie freely telling the 'Boss' how he came about getting the swollen cheekbone and his black eye, etc., the 'Old Man' left a written message for me and left it on the kitchen table available for anyone to read. A further two days later I was having another of the old mans scathing verbal attacks. Drunk of course; I was at the receiving end of a raving lunatic who ranted and raved at me having several times missing my head and face with his flying fists. A great dislike for me was clear throughout his actions and a protectiveness for Brummie was also in evidence. Some weeks or months later I was to find out the reason why the Boss had a soft spot for Brummie, and that was because Brummie .... has no family life.

"You are back in your old bedroom as from now, those were the final words fired at me as the 'Old Man' left the kitchen. I was pleased to have a room to myself again but that delight was somewhat erased on learning from Kathy the 'Landlord' had increased my rent. There was a large and heavy suitcase in the bedroom and had been there for just over a week until the owner returned to collect it. The caller for the suitcase explained to me the reason for his and his friends short stay and that was because they had been sent to another part of the country by their construction company. These short stays by the lodgers infuriated the 'Landlord', empty beds didn't bring in his booze and gambling money and also they were a stumbling block to his determination for a luxurious life.

My brother Bill was a thorn in the side of the nuns in charge of the boys section in Nazareth House, Aberdeen and they wanted him out of the orphanage. On hearing of the problem the 'Old Man' went wild. Bill still had a few weeks left before he reached school leaving age and the nuns were not allowing this to stand in their way of seeing the back of my brother, they wanted and demanded Bill was taken away. Apart from the fact the 'Old Man' didn't want Bill, my brother was to be a non paying lodger.

Bill arrived in Birmingham and behind a charade of a smile he was made welcome by the 'Old Man' who immediately took Bill to Wheeleys Road from New Street Station, I at that time being at work. There was no love lost between Bill and I but I did want to be at the station to meet him hence the resentment when I was told it was best all round if I obeyed and didn't take time off from work. From the minute they arrived at Wheeleys Road the 'Old Man' was to find Bill a handful. After all the years of being 'cooped up' Bill wasn't to sit back and take orders from his father lightly and being an outspoken and somewhat aggressive person he was to be rid of as soon as the 'Old Man' found the opportunity. Bill demanded new and different clothing and the 'Old Man' had problems hiding dislike of having to part with his money. All three of us went to a clothes shop on the first Saturday in the week Bill was with 'us'. I was pleased with my purchase, Bill wasn't with what his father had spent. I can't exactly remember what the circumstances were but I do remember the look of disgust on the face of my brother as we stood outside that outfitters shop. Apparently the 'Old Man' was saying there was no more money for clothing and that Bill was to wait until there was money available. Again I can't remember the circumstances but I will never forget going into the nearby bookies and selecting and betting on two horses running at the same time at two of the meetings that day. I also can't remember how much money I received from the two winners but it was enough to buy my brother whatever it was he wanted.

Bills stay in Birmingham was of short duration and he was soon on his way to famous Horse Racing Stables to train as a jockey. Whether there is any truth in it or not I do not know but it was circulated that the 'Old Man' was expecting 'inside information' from the racing world and keeping his fingers crossed that Bill would be a good jockey therefore giving the 'Old Man' an opportunity of easy money. Neither was to be the case. As we were living apart I didn't see much of Bill, this was mainly due to the old man wanting it that way than anything else. It was rumoured the old man and Bill having several bare fist fights and that chairs etc. were not left out either. I not wanting any part of physical violence preferred to keep a quiet house.

I got to like going to the club across the road mainly because I was there most of the times when the old man would be somewhere else. Not liking my popularity with the club members and also fearing they were hearing about my life the old man didn't honestly talk about, also feeling embarrassed the old man had plans for me.

One day whilst I was in my bedroom with neither Kathy or the old man aware I was off work with an ailment, I over heard their conversation and to get a clearer understanding I pressed my ear against the bedroom door. It was then I heard, "He is a stuck up little bastard." That was followed by a muffled sound from Kathy, then the old man said something like I'll bring his bloody pride down. "What are you going to do, you are not going to hit him are you?" were the words from Kathy. My body began to tremble on hearing the last few words then on hearing the old man saying, "No, I'll bring him to Wheeleys Road." On hearing that last remark I firmly clenched my fists and gripped my teeth both in anger and resentment, thinking to myself if he attempts to force me to live in Wheeleys Road I will be off to somewhere else.

With the footsteps going silent as they reached the kitchen steps I slowly and very carefully opened and closed my bedroom door and again slowly and carefully made my way up to the attic bedroom of an Irishman with an English name whom I often confided in and he, always willing to listen and give good advice. He was unlike the other lodgers in as much as he was always smartly dressed, well spoken and had a very good job with a great deal of responsibility for his 'on the site' colleagues. That pleasant Irishman and friend made his small attic room like a 'home from home', and when the Landlord got to hear about the home comforts up went the rent of that cosy attic room.

I was also able to avoid the old man for several days that followed. Bill Jones an elderly gentleman and a father figure, as well as a friend to me, lived in a two up two down terraced house in the heart of Birminghams Industrial Area and not that far from our work place. It was with Bill that I often sought sanctuary from the perils of home life and living on his own he also enjoyed and valued my company. I wouldn't be far wrong in saying all my visits to Bills house were immediately after work hours in the evenings, that would give me time to spare until the old man was well"On his way 'down the bottle.'

It was always going to be a matter of time before the old man caught up with me and so he did one Saturday morning when I least expected to see him. It was rumoured that he had been in a foul mood for weeks and with or without a drink the old man beat Kathy and that he on a couple of occasions was on the receiving end of someones fists and boots outside his other 'local.' It was as the role of my father that the old man was desperately in need of seeing me. I hadn't been going to the club across the road for a while so the locals were asking questions that certainly had the old man embarrassed, so much was the embarrassment it brought anger to the boil within and that sent him on the war path.

Smashing open the bedroom door my father came towards me, I was being attacked by an irrational animal whose fury was fuelled by the drink consumed. I was up against the bedroom wall of my own choosing and he just inches from my nose. It was only then I noticed the bruising of his face, how he managed to keep his hands off me God only knows. "You stuck up little bastard. You have shown me up too long in front of those other bastards over there," my father managed to splutter out taking several attempts to get it right. "You will pack your things and get down to Wheeleys Road and you have until I get back from the club to be there. If you are not there I will come up and drag you down after beating the hell out of you." Those words were spoken with much difficulty but I didn't doubt their meaning.

Within seconds of that onslaught I was looking and listening to a different person. He was as sober as a judge and smiling pleasantly all over his face then he broke into a nervous little laughter before saying to me, "Son, I don't want to hurt you but you have been asking for a hiding for a long time and you have been lucky not to get one. And I have done little boxing in my time so get any ideas you might have out of your head, O.K. Son?" With having said that my father left me with my thoughts.

For a while I was scared, terribly scared and something was pumping inside me, my heart was beating faster than ever and my headache was getting worse and was sending red hot pain through my head and neck with every heart beat. Inwardly I began praying to God. Then when settled I packed my things, leaving them behind me I then went to my Aunty's care.

The care was busy so I spent my time upstairs in the flat just pondering through magazines and newspapers allowing time to rethink over my earlier thoughts of my future. My cousin was the first to join me when the care closed for the weekend. Her mum stayed behind to_Wash and clean everything for reopening on Monday morning. When she did join us my cousin mentioned what had happened between the old man and myself. When it was time for me to leave we said our goodbyes, they not knowing of my plan to return to Aberdeen. That was one reason for leaving my suitcase in my bedroom, the other reason was because if the old man had called at the house before going to the club he would see my packed suitcase and think his problems were over. Knowing the old man enjoyed a game or two of snooker before he found his singing voice and not daring to take anything for granted I popped across to the club for a sneak view. There he was, cue in hand and his pride bursting out all over him. Quickly I crossed the road into the house and with suitcase in hand I dashed out into the darkness of the night and headed for the railway station on foot, part of the way, then by bus. I was in luck, there was an overnight train to Aberdeen changing at Perth. Having purchased my single ticket I then looked for and found an unoccupied corner seat on the train standing at the directed platform. Just as the guard blew his whistle a woman entered the compartment and sat in the corner opposite me. I didn't much like her presence as I was hoping for a compartment to myself. Nevertheless I didn't allow her to interfere with my painful concentration of the platform outside. The final blow of the guards whistle and the sound of the steam from the enormous steam locomotive followed by that wonderful 'Puff! Puff!' and the movement of the train filled me with a relief so unique, momentarily I was floating. "Are you in trouble with the police, is that what is the matter?" were the first words I heard from the woman opposite. I didn't answer, instead I gave two or three quick shakes of my weary head.

As the city lights were getting dimmer and dimmer the further the train travelled the more tired and relaxed I became until eventually heeding the earlier words of the woman opposite I removed my shoes and stretched out on the welcome and comfortable upholstered seat. The train stopped at at least one railway station because I was alone when I arrived at Perth in the early hours of the morning. It wasn't mentioned that after my three hours wait in the bitterly cold December winds I would be travelling the rest of my journey in an old wooden railway carriage tucked behind a row of milk and cattle trucks with no real protection from the biting winds from the guards van attached to the rear of the carriage.

Arriving at Aberdeens shuttered railway station at seven o' clock on any Sunday morning is not the best of welcomes one would expect from that wonderful friendly city, but that arrival was heavenly. Now it was only my stomach that was crying out for help, it being deprived of solids and liquids for twelve hours it was in need of fulfilment. Luckily there was a night watchman on duty at the station who directed me to the only place open- in Aberdeen for food and that was the Fishermans Market Care, not too far from the station. I was allowed to leave my suitcase with the night watchman so the journey to the care wasn't that tiresome. And when I arrived at the care I could have easily been entering the Hilton Hotel in London by the welcome I received by the local fisherman and the woman behind the care counter. And that breakfast and mug of hot tea, WOW! What a difference both the full breakfast and the friendly welcome and company made to me. I was feeling great.'

With my short lived luxurious life behind me I made my way back to the railway station to collect my suitcase and close the chapter on ....

ANOTHER EXPERIENCE.

104

HERE TODAY BUT NOT TOMORROW

I decided to make the journey on foot to Nazareth House that Sunday morning, feeling the fresh morning air would be therapy after my years in grimy Birmingham. The journey along the empty but belonging city High Street was a journey of calming pleasantness stirred only by a trifle of emotional excitement on entering Union Grove which sign posted me in the direction of Claremont Street and Nazareth House.

Having arrived at the Lodge uninvited it took me some explaining as to who I was and why I arrived. Minutes after the departure of the Nun to the main building, I was being escorted by that same Nun along the garden path to the reception room of the building. My childhood shudders I experienced during my years in the orphanage returned as soon as I entered that building flooding my mind with some of the incidents of the past. Luckily I wasn't waiting long before being received by another Nun who politely explained why it wasn't the right time. for me to see or talk with my brother and sisters. That same Nun also couldn't help me with an accommodation address but did mention the address of an ex boy now married and living in a one roomed flat around the corner.

The double size bed took up most of the room space leaving little room between it and the electric cooker, that I thought dangerous and apparently so did the occupants but it was the best they could afford. There were no chairs to sit on so we sat on the edge of the bed, I didn't have the nerve not to accept the tea offered in a dirty and chipped mug. Feeling nauseated after a few sips of the very strong tea I apologised to the occupants saying I must leave just in case the accommodation address they gave me would not be to my advantage. "Och, I dinna ken if we can pit ya up on a permanent basis," were the lovely words spoken in the local dialect. There is one thing about Aberdeen and its surrounding towns and villages and that is a total guarantee of warmth and friendship. Although the winter months can be bitter and severe one can always feel that warmth and friendship of the city of Aberdeen, and the towns of Keith, Elgin, Banff, Peterhead and all the other places situated in and around the 'sound of music' highland countryside. I was allowed to stay in my new found digs until somewhere more convenient could be found. The two spinsters were very apologetic over there being no meal for me as they had only minutes earlier put away the dishes, pots and pans etc. from their own meal and that of their two young men guests.

John and Jack were in Nazareth House during the time I was an inmate and they would also be about the same age as myself. Neither of them really appreciated my sharing their cramped bedroom at the weekends, I mention weekends because Jack worked away during the weekdays and returned on a Friday evening. I have always been grateful to them for their understanding of the situation I was in and the extra money going to the two very kind and understanding landladies.

The following morning I was in luck again. The new landladies had directed me to a nearby Toolmaking Factory who on inquiring about the chances of employment and as an apprentice said I could begin the following morning. In the meantime they would be getting in contact with my ex employers in Birmingham to see if they would be prepared to transfer my Apprentice papers to them.

For the first time in my life I had Aberdeen all to myself and I made the best of the day familiarising with my new surroundings. I loved every minute of my new found freedom by strolling along King Street taking mental note as if I were a tourist. Then it was into that long and straight famous New Street, the heart of that friendly and warm city of Aberdeen. The winter conditions in Aberdeen always gets its own way so after about six hours of strolling and taking in I, or should I say, the severe cold conditions decided it would be better if I made the return to warmer surroundings. The Silver City Care in King Street were advertising Espresso Coffee so, never before having had one I decided now was the time to have a sample. I was shocked at the asking price but the coffee and the free rock music from the Juke box made me feel I wasn't all together ripped off. Having left the warm and alive care I went passed my lodgings in George Street and got the local evening paper not thinking if there would be one in the lodgings or not.

After reading through the paper there was a call for my presence at the table for the evening meal and very-good it was. Shortly after my meal I made my way to the St. Kathryn's Boxing Club and paid my membership in advance for the year beginning in the month of January 1953. I was however er allowed to use the clubs facilities for the three weeks until then but wasn't allowed to box for them until the commencement date on my membership card.

To make sure I wasn't late for my first day at the Bon Accord Tool Company one of the landladies wakened earlier than was necessary. Porridge and a cup of tea isn't my ideal breakfast but I enjoyed both, especially the Scots Porridge. On my way to the factory I was delighted to see open a home made cake and bread shop. Take a deep breath and allow the smell of those freshly made hot salted Scottish morning rolls to fill your lungs, it's breakfast in itself.

It was always colder inside the factory than it was outside that is until around dinner time on Wednesdays. And I wasn't too keen on using the old fashioned vertical wide belt driven machinery even though they

106

gave a good end product through the acute skills of their operators.

The following Sunday I attended Benediction in Nazareth House only because I thought that by attending there would be a good chance of meeting my youngest brother and my two youngest sisters. Well I was seated at the back of the Chapel so as I wouldn't be noticed and I left the Chapel immediately the service was over for the same reason. Then I proceeded to the Reception Room where I was kept waiting for a considerable length of time before the returning Nun informed me that arrangements were being made to see my two sisters, there was no mention of my brother. I was allowed to view my two sisters through the serving hatch of the boys kitchen. During the few moments of the 'peep Show' it was clear my sisters were delighted on seeing me and I at seeing them. They were at a safe distance from a normal speaking voice so we were only able to exchange smiles then they were led away by their Nun companion and I was asked to leave the 'House of God' because it was everyones tea time.

On my way back to my lodgings I was thinking ... so that is Catholicism. And then I was saying to myself ... "I don't want any part of it anymore." I, John and Jack were invited to an 'Old Boys Reunion' at Nazareth House on New Years Eve but I didn't have the heart to go.

I enjoyed my training evenings at the boxing club and more so the several boxing contests I had when representing the club. One contest I will never forget took place in Inverurie a few miles along the coast from Aberdeen. The boxing fans in the tiny hall were on their feet in amazement and excitement at the speed and accuracy of my left hand punches to my opponents face during almost every second of the second round of that contest. Unfortunately for me my opponent kneed me in the private parts when I was up against it in one of the corners of the ring during the third and final round.

Another wonderful memory for me was the visit to Pittodrie Park, Aberdeens football ground, when their opponents were the team of my dreams, Hearts of Midlothian. Until that match I had never seen Hearts..Football Team except on paper and as one can expect I was quite excited on that day. It was a fantastic match to watch and I would have liked to remember the result, never mind I will always remember the captain of the Hearts Team kick an Aberdeen player up the backside when that player was already on the ground nursing a previous injury.

It was during one of the later days of the month of February when it was brought to my attention by one of my landladies of my outstayed welcome as a lodger. It wasn't that they wanted me out but John and Jack. I couldn't really blame them for wanting things as they were before my doorstep arrival, the tiny flat WAS overcrowded especially when the inclement weather conditions kept Jack at home he not being able to work on the building site. Although the news of having to find another roof for my head didn't come as a shock, it did unsettle me bringing back the terrible feelings of loneliness and' sorrow. I was still carrying my brothers and sisters on my shoulders and the shackles of Catholicism were gripping tightly around me and once again I turned to the heavens for help and guidance.

It was no benefit looking at the accommodation column in the Evening Post, that had already been done for me. With the knowledge of their wait for a suitable corporation house I visited the overcrowded rented house of my friends the Finney family taking with me the news I was given. My friends couldn't help me in any way, they explaining the difficulties of the housing problem in Aberdeen at that time. In my heart there will always be a strong link with the Finney family especially when they looked after myself and my family during our stay with them in that beautiful market town of Keith just a few miles north of Aberdeen. I have no apologies for repeating my heart will always have a strong link with the Finney Family during our stay with them prior to going into the orphanage.

I soon found out my small apprentice earnings couldn't afford board and lodgings within reasonable travelling distance to my place of employment and that began to have me at sixes and sevens as to what I was to do. Time was running out and I was beginning to be made an outcast, so with everything in mind I applied to join the Royal Air Force. Days went by before I received the news that the R.A.F. had accepted me. And on my final day in that dismal factory I said to myself ...

"HERE TODAY BUT NOT TOMORROW".

GLORIOUS YEARS

Enlisted 26th March 1953 then I was on my way by train to the south of England and to R.A.F. Station Cardington in Bedfordshire where, apart from receiving my introduction to life in the forces, I was also given the numbers 4125773 of which I will take with me to my last day on this earth.

It was sad to have to leave the Silver City with the golden sands and sadder still to leave behind my flesh and blood, especially at not being allowed to say farewell. It is strange to me as to why the Mother Superior of Nazareth House gave to me my mothers address on my last day of visiting.

As everyone connected with the Forces knows the military don't waste time in issuing uniform, kitbag and hobbed nail boots, etc. once you have arrived on ones square bashing camp. It was during that period that I wrote my first ever letter to my mother and acknowledgement was received that same week. We who had been given inoculations were allowed a 48 hour pass to get over the ill effects and I and an Airman who lived in London decided to save our money and hitch our way to the big city.

A canvas covered plumbers van pulled up just ahead of us only a few yards outside of the camp gates and on approaching it the driver popped his head out and asked if we wanted a lift and that he was heading for Fulham in London. Well I couldn't believe my luck, a lift right to my doorstep. My companion was also pleased at the offer of a lift so soon after leaving the camp gates and that the driver was heading close to where he wanted dropping off. Pleased we were at receiving a lift but can you imagine how we felt having travelled from Bedford to London sitting on two loose loos on top of and surrounded by a pile of plumbers pipes of varied sizes and lengths, plus all the other metal odds and ends a plumber uses. How we both refrained from being sick I will never know. It was a painfully amusing journey for the first couple of miles then the longer we travelled the worse we felt. My Airman companion was the first to be dropped off he barely able to say his, "Best of luck," when his feet met solid ground.

I also felt the relief of solid ground beneath me and on thanking the driver for his kindness on giving me a lift and he not accepting any payment, I made my way along the narrow terraced street to the house where I was to meet my mother for the first time, in the true sense. It was a hyper emotional meeting with neither of us embracing, Why? Well that was the way it was meant to be or so I instinctively thought. But was it because my mother didn't tell me in her letter that she had another son and daughter aged four and six years of age and that they would soon be coming home? Well I met Alan and Pauline and shortly after I was also introduced to their father who has the surname of Pearce. My mum sensed I had no feelings of animosity against any of them that I know because of the pleasant atmosphere that prevailed.

Perhaps there is no ill feelings coming from me in that direction because I am grateful and happy that someone is loving and looking after my mum.

Having booked in at the Union Jack Club I said my thanks to my mum for the offer of overnight stay and returned the following morning to be with them all duration of the day. At first mum and I talked or should I say my mum was using almost outlet of breath to apologise for the past and the present especially for the position in life in which I found her. It wasn't until I was able to talk with my mums husband that my mum really accepted that I was satisfied with what she had told me and that I was just happy she was alive, well and being cared for. With all the unpleasantness out of the way the day ahead was a good one. Alan and Pauline were taken by their dad to stay the day at one of their relations whilst their dad, my mum and I visited a Social Club which I think overlooked either Fulham or Chelsea Football Club. Anyway the main reason for us going there was for me to be introduced to two of my mums husbands family and a few other of their friends. Later in the afternoon we dined at a classy restaurant before going on to meet three of my relations on my mothers side of the family. My Uncle was pleasant and delighted at seeing me whilst his wife appeared to resent the presence of the three of us. Later their charming daughter arrived only minutes before having finished her day at the local library. Her name was linked with the film actor Lon Chaney, whether they got married or not I do not know, but this I do know, she had a warm and pleasant manner with a good disposition and obviously quite intelligent.

I can't remember the mileage between my uncles home and that of which my mother lived but I do remember feeling the affects of the inoculations as I travelled on the back of his motorbike. And I often wondered how my mum really felt sitting in the sidecar. Again, having booked at the Union Jack Club I thanked my mum and her husband for their hospitality and said my goodbyes to them and Alan and Pauline saying, I will be looking forward to my return invite during my next weekend leave from the camp. I loved being with my mum that weekend and when I slept under the same roof on my second and last visit a few weeks later. The only upset I took with me on returning to the camp was that one of my sisters who lived with our mum for a short period of time found it difficult to gel a relationship with mum and she with my sister. Well my sister found herself went to troubled waters when she went to live with her father in Birmingham.

All in all 1953 was a good year for me as I entered into the month of May. And the month of May was the continuation of the previous months I having been selected for special training to 'Line the Route' during the Coronation of the Queen. The month of June saw me on the 'Passing Out Parade' and the information that I was to be on my way to R.A.F. Weeton

110

near the sea resort of Blackpool for my training as a Motor Mechanic. I also remember the Corporal and the Sergeant who had been with us from day one cracking jokes about Blackpool and one of them went something like this: "If there are any of you here in this room who had not had a sex education or if there are those who think they have, just you wait, you are in for a pleasant surprise. In Blackpool sex is plentiful and it is on offer where ever you go and in places you would least expect to find it." Naturally there was outbursts of laughter from the audience and a few sarcastic remarks were flying around from those not fortunate to be going to Weeton Camp. For my few days leave before travelling north, I hooked in again at the Union Jack Club in London. It wasn't that I didn't want to stay those days with my mother and her family, it was simply because I didn't want to see the heart break returning to the face of my mum. I had a strong feeling she was suffering emotionally and I didn't want to upset her further.

The Union Jack Club was full to capacity, it had to be, we were into the second week of the month of June, and it was hot. The different uniforms of all the armed forces with their multitude of colours, designs and ornamentation was truly a sight to see on entering that forces club. Many had not 'booked in' consequently they had to sleep either in their uniforms or if they had pyjamas they were used if the owners desired. There were men of all ages and of all non commissioned ranks sleeping or just resting in an orderly manner anywhere that didn't cause a restriction. I was glad I had a bed. I spent my few leave days either playing snooker and darts in the club or seeing the life by day and night of the Capital City. Apart from the greater variety of pubs, restaurants and overseas visitors and residents and of course those hotels London didn't have much more to offer me than that other great city, Birmingham.

16th June 1953 and I was the closest I have ever been to the sea town of Blackpool. But it wasn't until the evening after did I actually see the greatest holiday resort in the United Kingdom. My arrival by train ticket was stamped Kirkham Railway Station, that being six miles outside of Blackpool and more inland looking towards Preston rather than Blackpool. A pre organised R.A.F. coach collected about eighteen of us from Kirkham station and drove us the three miles to R.A.F. Weeton and three miles closer to the sea front of Blackpool. I was impressed with the countryside whilst on my way in the coach and the the fresh gentle breeze sent my mind for a moment or two in the direction of that other seaside town where I spent all my school days.

Having unloaded our kitbags from the boot of the coach we then paraded in front of the guard room for identification purposes and to be given our billet numbers and following that we were told, there was a hot meal waiting for us in the cook house, the latter pleased all of us. The wooden billets were identical to those I left behind at R.A.F. Cardington. My Aberdeen friend Donald who was with me from day one was allocated the billet next to mine and during our five month stay at R.A.F. Weeton we became good friends. There was only one hiccup, Donald was faithful to his girlfriend back in Aberdeen. Wherever you are Donald, I hope you are doing well and that life had been good for you.

It was the following evening and we were excited about the news that we could all go to Blackpool for the evening, but we had to wear our No. 1 uniforms. I never did like those shiny peeked caps. Well not all of us did go to town that night, but those of us who did made a bee-line for the magical Tower and the Tower Ballroom. I had never before seen such splendour when I entered the actual dancing arena. The atmosphere was staggeringly electric, the whole arena was like something out of Disneyland and, I couldn't dance. But my dancing problems were soon to be over when, later in the month I joined the Lido School of Dancing beginners class. And it was during one of my beginners classes that my lady tutor introduced me to my very first girl-friend.

We all had to be in our billets before 'Lights Out' and those of us, and I was one of them, who didn't have a girl for the night made our way to wherever it was to get the Ribble Bus back to camp. Not only did I visit the Tower Ballroom, oh no, there was that other world famous Empress Ballroom in the equally famous Winter Gardens waiting for my still two left feet. And when the ballrooms at the Tower and the Winter Gardens were over crowded, and they quite often were, I would then go to the smaller but equally exciting Palace Ballroom. I sometimes preferred the Palace Ballroom, now unfortunately demolished for the terrible Lewis's Departmental Store. The place was certainly more elegant and comfortable than its two bigger rivals and its special lighting effect always blended with the tune that was being played by the band. I can remember not being allowed into the three ballrooms I have mentioned because they were overflowing, so I and a couple of my friends decided to see what was going on at one of the other lesser known ballrooms in the town and that was Burtons Ballroom situated in Burtons Buildings on the promenade, just a couple of minutes walk from the others. We paid our admission price before opening the doors to the ballroom and on entering all three of us decided on the spot that it wasn't for us. Talk about snobbery and old fashioned people, music and boring dancing, nowhere could hold a candle to that place, or was I just too young and ill-appreciative of boring old fashioned styled costumes and music? Of course there were other places in which to find a female but one of those places had never been visited by me and that is the Tower itself and all its 518 feet. Mind you I have made several excuses in other high places such as those entertainment units at the fantastic Pleasure

Beach.

October saw me pass my Motor Mechanics exam and it gave me my first permanent camp and that was to be in West Germany. I spent as much time as possible with my girlfriend while I was a guest at her parents home in Preston New Road in Blackpool and on route to camp. Those happy, enjoyable and loving days were with me on the journey by train to the port of Harwich where I was to be ferried across the channel to the Hook of Holland. I enjoyed the sea journey whilst others didn't, many of them being seasick and several of those vomiting all over the place. My thoughts were always with my girlfriend from the minute we said goodbye until boarding the train at the Hook, then I concentrated on my pocket size German phrase book which I purchased in Blackpool.

On arriving in Germany from Holland I was able to shout out of the carriage windows to the German railway men and woman such as, "Guten morgen" and "Ubber alles Deutchland". That made me feel good but by the look on the faces of those German workers who did look at us I was wondering if our greetings were in vain. Not all my Airmen associates were destined for Cologne railway station, a few were already off the train and heading by military transport to their new life, whilst others travelled further afield than the four of us who were destined for R.A.F. Butzweilerhof in the village bearing the same name and only about seven miles from that historical city Cologne. Missing my girlfriend aside, I was feeling great. What little I saw of Germany I liked and the camp also gave me that same welcome vibes. Before I settled down for the night it was a long and emotional letter to my girlfriend many miles away in 'Blighty' (England).

1953 ended as it begun, I was back in Blackpool celebrating a quiet but unforgettable Christmas with my girlfriend and her family. They were all delighted with the presents I bought while shopping in the town centre of Cologne during my many Saturday afternoon visits to the shops and those fantastic departmental stores. Just going from shop window to shop window was an unforgettably wonderful experience in itself, but entering those stores made me feel poor. When it comes to Christmas displays the shops and stores in Germany take some beating. It wasn't only the magnificent displays that stirred me it was the quality and the variety of goods on offer to the public, and I was thinking, "And we won the war."

Now we are at the beginning of 1954 and I am hoping for another year of excitement and enjoyable happenings. I thought the winters in Scotland were severe, well I can assure you my first winter in Germany was so cold every time I touched bare steel I got a shock identical to an electric shock in every way. It would be an exaggeration on my part if I said I was at times a walking ice cold stainless steel zombie, but I am sure that is how I felt during the month of January until the snow arrived in the early days of February.

Rose Montag is a great festival day in Germany and my first experience of that day will never be forgotten. We at the camp were allowed out of respect to the German people allowed to join in with their big occasion. Well we arrived in time to witness a carnival spectacular and to receive the warmth and welcome unique only to the German people. Drinks of every make were freely handed out by the bottle and the barrel, 'Schnapps' was the word of the day. Well the singing and the dancing and the drinking and whatever else that goes on during such a festival went on into .the next day only to ease off later that night. Nothing prevented me writing my passionate letters to my girlfriend, not even a black headache.

I was short of roadwork for my boxing training because of the severity of the weather so I was confined to the gymnasium on the camp to keep in good shape for my first boxing contest of my life in Germany. I started with the flue on the morning of that boxing night held on our own camp; and when it was time for a medical I was feeling like a raging fire and the Medical Officer past me fit to box barely half an hour of me entering the ring. Hand on my heart I wanted an unfit to box from that Medical Officer but as I didn't get it I went straight to my whiskey bottle and had a few sips from it hoping I would feel better. All I could see on entering the hall was the boxing ring and the glare of searchlights onto the ring area. Once inside the ring everything and everyone was a blur.

D..O...I....N.....G it was round one and all I could hear was one solitary voice shouting "Get your hands up" during the short period when my opponent enjoyed his unbelievable luck at the human defenceless punch bag that was in front of him. I was taking whatever leather was thrown from the chest upwards but the solitary blow to the stomach had my legs like two strings of spaghetti and down I went amidst an echo of boo's. My body from the waist down felt like a lump of lead, as I lay sprawled on the canvas and it had taken two men as well as the referee to assist me to my corner at the opposite side of the ring.

I am pleased to write better results for my other contests during the rest of the year. When not boxing I took part in other sporting interests, with soccer and athletics receiving most interest. Although small in stature I made a good goalkeeper without ever being risked in competitive matches. Now that I have mentioned soccer it takes me to the name of Joe, his real Christian name being Robert, so it was Joe who said to me during a friendly soccer match that I wasn't playing for Scotland. Joe worked as a 'Chippy' in a section of the enormous hanger that housed all the camps motor transport. There was something special about Joe in as much as he didn't have a special pal because we were all pals of Joe.

Just as everyone who visits a country for the first time I made use of most of my spare days getting to view that great country without ever finding the time to step onto bordering countries and that was a pity. Of course my annual 'Blighty' leave was spent with my girlfriend and sleeping under the same roof with her parents. It was during one of those days when the British actor Bonner Collino invited me to join and to think about making the film industry my future. My girlfriends parents entertained other famous stage and film stars such as Ruby Murray, Alma Cogan, a French trapeze couple and others who remain nameless to me. My girlfriend and I continued exchanging letters on my return to my camp, and I continued where I left off being with my camp mates and my social pals.

1955 was similar in many ways to the previous year and it was glorious as well. I seemed to be given more spare time than usual after the New Year celebrations of 1956 and it was then I first experienced an emptiness within me although I was not always aware of its presence. Being a motor mechanic was by now extremely boring and the notice on the hanger notice board advertising for personnel to fill the acute shortage of General Fitters within the R.A.F. couldn't have come at a better time for me. Having explained to my camp C.O. that I was an apprentice toolmaker in civvy street he approved the request to transfer for training at Weeton Camp. This brought resentment and anger amongst a few of my camp friends and several other Airman on the camp, all of whom were desperate to return to their loved ones in 'Blighty'. The acceptance of my transfer further angered two of my work colleagues to the point that one of them and I finished up having a bare listed set to inside one of the lorries that we were working on. I didn't like the look of the blood that was pouring out of both nostrils but he insisted he wanted to be a camp hero. There was only two ways of really ending the fight and that was to turn away and get branded a coward or put an end to it properly and a hard right hand to the pit of his stomach was the answer. As I mentioned earlier, I was given too much spare time and that night of the bare listed farce found me in yet another punch up. Several of us were passing time lying on top of our beds either reading or writing and during that time I was being annoyed by the remarks from a larger than large red headed and fiery tempered Airman who occupied the bed to my left. This annoyance gradually developed into unacceptable harassment which was being keenly noticed by the other Airman in the billet, they all noticing how restless I was becoming and wondering if I was brave enough or stupid enough to take on someone just more than double his size. It was the smugness on his red freckled face that had me punching the hell out of his face as he tried to get off his bed. The speed in which I moved from my bed surprised the onlookers and myself and it brought shock to that other Airman who finished up a sorry state on the floor at the top end of the room. Charges were brought against me but not the perpetrator, this I was told because the Corporal in charge of our billet was carrying out orders from a person of a higher rank. Fourteen days confined to camp then a couple of days later I was saying farewell to Joe and the rest of his pals.

Before leaving the camp that morning, I was received by the Station Commanding Officer who during his farewell talk explained my boxing was the reason for the severity of my punishment and I only had myself to blame, he also saying I angered Airmen by constantly reminding them that I was returning not only to Blighty' but to live with my girlfriend. That was grossly exaggerated to say the least but I wasn't heard. Although I was an unlucky 'runner up' in the 2nd T.A.F. (R.A.F. Forces stationed in Germany) Boxing Championships it wasn't a reason for me wanting to get stationed in the U.K. so as I could challenge the best amateur Lightweight Boxer in the world Dick McTaggart for his R.A.F. Title. As it happened I did have a couple of tries but I shouldn't have wasted my time. Before meeting Dick I had the great pleasure of being with and training with another world famous boxer and that was the gentle, kind hearted and likable Brian London. At the time of our first meeting Brian was training in the Weeton Camp gymnasium for his revenge fight against one of the also famous boxing brothers, the Coopers. Apparently one of the Cooper brothers licked Brians brother Jack and Brian wasn't pleased about it. Now I am talking about the days when they were all respected amateurs in the field of boxing. Brian had a gift of being able to pace himself and it showed well during his miles of running along the narrow winding country lanes that engulfed the camp. After two attempts to run with Brian I gave up to concentrate my training to within the walls of the camp gymnasium. On occasions Brian would ask if I minded sparing with him, this was to be of great advantage to Brian as I was about five stone lighter than he and very fast with my punches and feet movement.

My engineering course was disrupted with only a couple of weeks left for training. It was a revenge return soccer match with the Army Squadron based on the camp. Because of the bog like conditions of the rain sodden ground it was decided by the rest of the team that I would be an advantage to the team if I played up front, right half if I remember correctly. Anyway the match hadn't long started when this big hunk of about sixteen stone of flab came ploughing through the mud towards me. He took one massive swipe and his mud clad hob nailed size eleven boot flew over the ball and fractured the tibia and fibula of my left leg, sending me with an almighty yell to writhing in agony in the soggy mud for minutes until the ambulance arrived to take me to the R.A.F. hospital across the road. That was my first

116

ever experience of being an 'In' patient at a hospital and in many ways I enjoyed it although the fourth week was a little boring. If it wasn't for the attention I was receiving from those lovely and attractive 'Sisters' (all qualified nurses in the Air Force were given Officer ranking and were addressed as 'Sister').

I got on extremely well with one of the 'Sisters' and I am convinced that one night whilst I was asleep it was she who drew an arrow along my plaster coast with the words 'Heaven Above' written alongside of it. I use the word convinced for a very good reason. It was that nurse who days after the 'Logo' requested I stayed behind when the other four or five ward patients went to the camp cinema that evening. As well as being able to play a good game of cards she also was able and free with her ability to rid me of my discomforts when I became uncomfortable whilst in a stationary position in bed. I was also given her 'home' telephone number before leaving the hospital, but for some unknown reason I didn't follow it up. I was at my wits end whilst the others on the ward veranda were in hysterics at the sight of me tossing and turning and writhing in humorous actions when a spider dropped down the space between my plaster east and the sole of my foot. It was a glorious day with the sun beaming into the ward of the timber built hospital, allowing the patrons of the ward the privilege of resting out in the fresh air and warming to the sun of the day. It was when I was sitting in a wicker chair unable to freely move my plaster cast leg when I noticed a spider slowly dropping from the veranda beam. With wooden crutch in hand I was ready to give the dropping spider a swipe if it came within striking distance. Well I didn't have a cat in hells chance, the spider plummeted directly into the space mentioned and soon had me the centre of attraction while it was driving me mad with its crawling about on the sole of my foot. Unable to help myself in any way, someone tried to remove the spider with the aid of a twig from one of the trees in the hospital grounds. That having failed, one bright spark got hold of the fire extinguisher before releasing the foam into the open space. There was a hell of a mess but it did the trick.

Before returning to complete the course, I was further to enjoy myself at the R.A.F. Rehabilitation Centre in Chessington. What a holiday that turned out to be. Free and easy with everything and everyone moving about as if there was all the time in the world to get things done. What a happy and lucky three weeks I had in the constant sunshine and it never got to an unbearable heat. Apart from what had to be done indoors everything else was under blue skies and that included a trip to the races at Epsom with the highlights being the Oaks and the richest of all races, The Epsom Derby. Not all of our new and luxurious life was on firm ground, a trip along the River Thames commencing at the beauty of Kingston and all those beautiful homes with the timeless views brought a new world into my life. Oh, how I envied those people living in such a haven and thought, "Do they really know how fortunate they are to afford such a beautiful part of England". Then there was the day when we were virtually given the freedom of that part of the River Thames when the R.A.F's own speedboats were at our command for a few hours. Although unable to sit back and take in everything that that part of the country offered, when on the Paddle Steamer the week before the opportunity of the freedom of the great river was an experience of its own. I returned to Weeton Camp to complete my course after my three weeks of high living which included early morning and daily volley ball and casual get fit exercises, both of which took place in the morning sunshine.

My training course lasted five months because of my three weeks holiday ending with an expected pass, but if I had spent less time measuring the girlfriend and more time measuring the variety of metals I would have received a better pass mark. My next camp was R.A.F. Halton in leafy Aylesbury in Buckinghamshire. And it was the result of my sparring sessions I got a match against a local civvy, up and coming blue eyed boy. The unofficial betting odds were stacked heavily in my favour, why I will never know. You see I wasn't allowed to box during my course at Weeton Camp and that being the case of my few rounds sparring with Dick McTaggart did not do a lot for me even though I was reasonably fit.

Once again I found myself suffering with the flue on the morning of a boxing contest and once again I was passed fit to box by a Medical Officer. And again I feared backing down. Well I took Beecham powder after Beecham powder and wrapped myself in as many towels I could get my hands on and as many blankets, I even had a hot water can between my feet as I lay in bed before the fight. The highly talked about lightweight boxer from R.A.F. Halton was floored in the second round from a series of 'Love Pat Punches' were the heavy print in the boxing column of the Aylesbury evening paper that following evening. Well my special meals with Dick didn't stop and neither did other privileges that I was glad of but I didn't much like the sarcastic remarks from a few Airmen who didn't even know me. But I had plenty of wins for them to talk about and forget the past. My sparring sessions with Dick soon were at an end and he was on his way to Australia where he was to win an OLYMPIC GOLD MEDAL making him the champion of the world. The powers that be wouldn't allow me to have my photograph taken with the OLYMPIC GOLD WINNER on his return to our camp, so Dick did the next best thing and gave me two signed photographs of himself, one holding the World Boxing Trophy he brought back from Australia and the other with him in the sparring stance. Both photographs are autographed for me by that great ambassador for boxing.

118

It was during those great days at R.A.F. Halton that I accepted to go on an NCO's training course at the Air Forces Camp in Hereford. No, it wasn't all administration and square bashing leadership, the firing range was frequented, I finishing up with a 'Marksmans Badge' which I hurriedly and proudly stitched onto the lower forearm of my uniform jacket before the end of course photograph was taken. Recently I looked at that now framed photograph and noticed how well that badge complimented the Junior Technician stripe further above it. Well I was physically fit on arriving at R.A.F. Hereford and super fit on completion of the four week course and that stood me in good stead for my return to R.A.F. Halton and my next boxing competition held at the R.A.F. Camp at Melksham. It was the finals of the Command Individual Boxing Championships (under I.S.B.A. rules); I thought it was going to be a walkover for me, after all I was super fit. I paid the price for my egotism by losing the competition in the final contest of the Lightweight Division.

My next and final posting was to me 'The Appleyard' of the British Forces stationed in the U.K. Essex itself is a beautiful county, I doubt if any will dispute that whether they live there or visited the county; and it is to the tiny village of Debden that I now bring you and to the R.A.F. Technical College which was where I lived until 9 January 1959. First of all I would like to say that the camp was the most modern of all military camps in the U.K. being arranged in its own country setting just like luxury flats in a secluded holiday establishment. There was greenery everywhere and I could not believe my eyes as I walked along the neatly cut grass areas and past the rows of apple and other trees that were obviously planted after serious thought had been given to their positions. Neither was I informed of the ultra modern dining room and the place mats and conduits that were on all the modern tables. The latest in stainless steel kitchenware and quality cooks were responsible for the high quality help yourself range of food presented to us.

As I wondered through different villages and towns in that beautiful county of Essex on my free days I was aware of a great change within myself but I didn't understand what it was. The town of Saffron Walden and its mystical environment, the beauty and warmth of its neighbouring villages of Braintree, Thaxted, Great Dunmow, Wimbish Green and of course the village of Debden and many others had me in a sort of spiritual trance every time I was with them. Golden Bullocks was my nick name and I wasn't complaining, not even when it was called to me in anger. The Midas touch that had rested for a couple years had more gradually returned, soon my magical feelings were finding winners again as my fingers travelled the horse race meetings in my daily newspaper. There were several veterans and I don't mean just in age because I am bringing you into long hours of card playing when at times the stakes got out of hand, especially in my later months when a brigade from the Army arrived. Not having the experience and the wisdom of several of the veteran card players I relied on those magical feelings within me. And at times those feelings got me into hot water especially when I angered players when I would go several hands without playing a card in certain games we played.

I was 'resting' on the bows of one of those delightful apple trees one night when I was on Mobile Guard Duty and I got the shock of my life when the Station Duty Officer decided to stop below me and flicked his lighter at his watch. It was rumoured that Dick McTaggart was unfit to defend his R.A.F. Lightweight Title and the order given to me was 'Stand By'. In the meantime one of my fellow camp mates was on 'sick leave' or 'compassionate leave' because of the death of either his mum or dad. As he was on standby for action in Cyprus none of us expected him to return to the camp in time to prepare for his expected move. Well he did return and on his stamped returned date and he did go to Cyprus only to be shot dead as soon as he left the aircraft on the runway at Niccosia Airport. It was rumoured within the camp that I was to take his place but was excused because of my boxing arrangements. There was no boxing equipment on the camp so I had to keep fit by using the roads; and during that time pain in my right leg added to the pain of training. I was informed by the Station Commanding Officer of the interest the Imperial Boxing Association had for me to box as a Featherweight and would I get myself down to that fighting weight. I did, but my by now painful leg prevented me from doing any serious training. On Wednesday 11 December 1957 the Inter Command Boxing Semi Finals were held at R.A.F. Stanmore Park and it was there the eyes of the R.A.F. Boxing bodies watched me lose in an arranged 'Special Featherweight Contest'.

My gambling 'luck' spread to the green of the camp snooker table, the wires of the dart boards and anything or everything that one placed their money. I'm taking you along to the month of December of that amazing year. My pockets were heavier than usual so I decided to increase and spread my gambling 'luck' by increasing my usual stakes on the horses and including the 'Homes' and 'Aways' on the Football Pools. My amazing 'luck' was having me a little nervous and I needed all my self discipline and something extra to keep my feet on the ground. Don't get me wrong, I never made big profits out of my gambling investments that is until the Saturday before Christmas.

Nearly all of the Army and my R.A.F. colleagues had taken their weekend off to be with their parents, sweethearts and friends for the Christmas arrangements. A handful of us who were left on the camp decided to spend that day in the town of Saffron Walden where I picked up my winnings and invested some of it on four horses whilst I was in the local

120

Bookmakers. On handing my bet to the owner of the betting shop he said to me something like, "Even you can't expect to win with a bet like this" That was about one o' clock in the afternoon, then I joined the others in the pubs in between window gazing and shopping for Christmas presents. By the end of the afternoon we were all skint and ready for the footslog back to the camp. So they waited for me to call at the Bookies to find out how my horses got on. One curious associate accompanied me into the Bookmakers Shop and he turned away in disbelief when the not too pleased Bookie said, "You have done it again. You have bloody done it again." Well words to that effect.

Eighty three pounds I think it was that I picked up for my £1 wager and I only received it there and then, for the Bookie asked me if I would mind collecting it on the Monday; I didn't trust him so I asked for it there and then. Halfway down the brow walking towards the centre point of town were the others who were just about to be joined by the excited winnings witness. When I caught up with them heads had already began to shake in disbelief and that gesture was soon complimented by the pleasant, enjoyable quizzing and other remarks all of which were in good humour. "You haven't got one Guardian Angel, you've got dozens," were the remarks from on of the lads in the group as he ruffled my hair. To that I replied, "That's alright, I've won the Pools." "Nobody can be that lucky, not even you Golden Bullocks." I believe those were the only words spoken from an otherwise silent group.

Two of the lads preferred to foot it along the three or so miles of the lovely countryside winding lanes to the camp whilst the other two accepted my offer to pay their taxi fare to the camp entrance. We three arrived at the camp in time for me to listen to the Football results on the portable radio on the table in the Airmans room in which I was in charge. At the end of the broadcasted results I remained sitting looking at the coupon with fourteen draws on it and I had eight of them in one line. When my senses returned I quietly and positively told the lads I had won the Pools! That first mention just brought a motion of disbelief from one Airman, a couple of cynical laughs from another and five lettered words from another. I wasn't convincing anyone when one Airman asked another, "Go and have a look," more to shut me up than believing what he was hearing. "He has!" "The jammy bastard has won!" Were I believe the words used after he checked the coupon. But one of the Airmen in the room didn't feel convinced and said he would check the coupon when the results were read out on another wave length later in the evening. That disbeliever checked the coupon and I was right, I had a first dividend due to me from 'The Pools!'. In no time at all all three Airmen in the room were on their way to broadcast their news live to others sharing the same building. Before long the few who were on the camp that weekend were also to learn of the news. Now it was a matter of waiting to get my hands on the Sunday newspapers for their Dividend Forecasts. I and a couple of others were forecasting a very low payout and the following morning the Sunday papers agreed with us, all of them forecast the Treble Chance First Dividend to be less than £3,000 and we were all to be proved correct.

For a moment I am taking you back a couple of days, to be precise, to Thursday night. I could not get to sleep that night and I couldn't understand the reason for it. It has always been known that I could sleep on a clothes line. Into the early hours of the morning I tossed and turned, tossed and turned until my bedclothes were in an unbearable tangle around me. By about three o'clock I had enough so decided to go look for a couple of Aspros or Asprins for my tired headache. It was during the search for the tablets that I came across a 2/6p (22.5p) Postal Order in a breast pocket of my uniform jacket hanging on the hook of my bedroom door. Because all the coupon syndicate members told me they were giving the 'Pools' a miss that week I didn't get a Postal Order for the coupon that week. Looking at my bedside cabinet I noticed a small pile of newspapers and on going straight to the sport pages I was delighted to find in all three their football result forecasts for the matches to be played that Saturday. Knowing I had the football pools I set about searching for my forecast draws for the 'Treble Chance'. That was after I had visited the washroom for a glass of water for my tablets and to freshen up it being too late to even snatch forty winks. All I did was take the draw fore-casts from all three papers and select the eleven or twelve required for my needs and then entered them onto the coupon. That was Something I had never done before. With everything completed I got dressed and took an early morning stroll towards the camp postbox and as I was about to post the coupon the Airman on duty in the Guardroom shouted similar words to "Not even you can be that lucky". I remember smiling and going over to have a chat and in doing so I was offered a cup of tea. If it wasn't for the strength and sweetness of the tea I wouldn't have remembered that incident.

I had noticed one of the 'Pools' syndicate wasn't joining in with the the rest of us that were on the camp and I also sensed an acute shortage of money was the reason behind it. During our conversation I offered him the chance of putting a little towards the already posted 'Coupon'. The reluctant investor came up with half his usual stake. Although his returns were not as great as mine that Airman was probably equally delighted as I, if not more so. You see John and his mother found life very difficult and the financial burden only eased a little with John joining the R.A.F. The syndicate broke up after that win with nobody expecting a winning coupon again. Even after my £60.00 win three weeks later couldn't convince anyone that the 'Pools' were a good investment.

Was 1958 going to be another glorious year for me?

Well apart from someone from above looking after my financial affairs of which I can't record any spectacular wind there was an earthly guardian looking after my material comforts. I mentioned a single earthly person when in fact there were three. Mr and Mrs Pickman of 19 Chaucer Crescent, in that charming village of Braintree looked after me as if I were their own son. At nights I would be invited to their beautiful home for a family evening; and at weekends and holidays I now and then played tennis on the courts at the rear of their house. Then there was the country girl with whom I dated quite often who always wanted to prove she wasn't slow off the mark when we were alone in different parts of that sun baked countryside.

Before the sun came out I was on my way on a 500cc motorbike with my friend Tony to visit my girlfriend in Blackpool when there was an interruption in our journey; because of the motorbike and I swiftly parting company during a speedy journey at the dark of the evening. Within seconds I was catapulted into the darkness and heaped only inches from a severe drop down a very deep and narrow ravine somewhere in Derbyshire. I can remember a small audience gathered and either a policeman or an ambulance man saying to me when I regained my senses that I must have had someone looking over me because he didn't know what prevented me from falling into that ravine; I was that close to certain death. Just like all young, fit and healthy young men who would have been in that position with a girlfriend eagerly waiting, I ignored the advice of the nurses and the doctors who attended me and I signed myself 'out' and hitch-hiked it to Blackpool. Thankfully I was wearing several layers of clothing and a crash helmet otherwise my cuts and bruises, etc., would have been more severe. The understanding and wonderful nursing staff I thanked for taking care of me and I also apologised for the inconvenience that I may have caused; and one of the nurses actually telephoned my girlfriends home to let her and her parents know what had happened and that I was on my way. On that visit to Blackpool my girlfriend and I agreed to call it a day and that we would remain friends. The motorbike was collected by the owner, Tony, the following weekend. There wasn't many boxing contests for me that year and what there was I had no difficulty in winning.

Now we are in the month of July and it is the camps Sports Day. On rising and looking out of the bedroom window I could see we were in for anther scorcher as we experienced the day before. By about three o'clock that afternoon we were getting ready for the 3000 meters when I was informed by a junior ranking commissioned officer that there was a fair bit of gambling on the winner of the race and that I was the hot favourite. That information so close to the 'off' unsettled me a little and tightened the stomach muscles but after a short while on my own I was feeling good again, though still surprised

123

at what the officer had told me. Twenty or so lined up for the off and on the gun I was away like a greyhound out if its trap only to limp off with that painful leg just as I passed the starting point for the first time.

From that moment my popularity ceased at the camp and that was due to devious talk about me doing some sort of a deal with the officer with whom I was seen talking with before the race started. My next five months excused me from taking part in all parades and camp duties together with my daily visits to the camp Physical Training Instructor, didn't go down at all well with several of the Airmen on the camp all of whom believed or wanted to believe I was skirting my duties. The camp Medical Officer also had something in his mind when he had me admitted to the R.A.F. Hospital at Ely just across the border and into Cambridgeshire. The staff at the hospital seemed gloomy and I didn't know if it was my being there or because they had just returned after their Christmas leave, was the cause of their miserable faces. After a couple of days of tests I was handed a form to which required my signature. "Sign here," said the orderly with his fountain pen at the ready and pointing to where my signature was to be. "Right, you are discharged. Get yourself dressed and go to the front entrance where transport will be provided to take you back to your camp." The driver of the transport didn't seem inclined to talk and all I can remember him saying was that I was to report to the Guardroom on arriving at the camp. That I did and was told by one of the military police not to report for work that morning and to be at the Station Commanders office at a certain time early that afternoon. The Group Captain started talking to me and within seconds I was watching a mouth opening and closing and no sound coming from it. At Ely Hospital I signed my R.A.F. discharge papers thinking it to be the hospital discharge papers.

20th February 1959 and now I am a reluctant civilian discharged unfit for the Air Force although fit for employment in civilian life. It was sad leaving behind the mystical environment of Saffron Walden and the beauty and warmth of its neighbouring villages and, everyone living in that beautiful county of Essex with its solidness which was in its village greens where, white clad figures scattered across the green cricket fields. It also was sad to leave behind a life of 'Glorious Years' while I was serving in Her Majesty's Royal Air Force.

RETURNING TO THE UNKNOWN

Being catapulted back into civilian life sent my mind into turmoil after glorious years of uninterrupted tranquillity and it also brought an inner discomfort of spiritual loneliness like I have never experienced before. Instead of looking forward to the future my long journey north and to really nowhere had me reminiscing and that wasn't doing me any good,

Kirkham railway station loomed in front of me as the train ground to a halt bringing my mind back to reality and the worry of what lay ahead of me. By the time the shorter version of the train arrived at the old Blackpool Central railway Station by having my faith restored in whoever was watching over me from above, A warm welcome awaited me when the taxi from the station pulled into the drive to stop at the front entrance of my ex girlfriends and parents bungalow on Preston New Road in the Marton area of Blackpool. After a good nights sleep I had to travel to Preston for a visit to the Forces Medical Centre for confirmation of some sort regarding being discharged from the Air Force for having 'Flat Feet'. On my return to Blackpool later that afternoon I called for an interview at a prearranged time for the vacancy of a toolmaker at the then well known household name of 'Nutbrowns' the kitchen gadget manufacturers, "You are too smartly dressed and too well presented to be working in a toolroom," were the words first spoken by one of the companies directors. "You will be a better asset to us selling our products to the general public," were the following words to reach my unbelieving ears. After minutes of standing face to face in one of the factory corridors with the Director trying desperately hard to convince me of a great financial future if I listened to him and with I dogmatically refusing to budge from the reason that brought me there the Director thinking that by showing me his demonstrated products in his exhibition room downstairs he would have a better chance of getting me to change my mind. I wasn't all that impressed although the novelty of it all took my imagination. "Look, sorry, what is your first name ?" "Andy," I replied. "Andy, with your healthy rugged looks, your smart appearance and that lovely Scottish accent that every woman loves to hear, makes you a natural for being a good salesman." I left saying I will think over what had been said and thanked the Director for the interest he has in me.

Unemployment was high in the sea resort forcing many of its citizens to seek work outside of the town so I had no choice but to return days later with the hope that the offer of employment was still in the offering. On a commission basis I began the following day in Nutbrowns arcade situated on 'The Promenade' just a few yards north of North Pier. A couple of weeks later I was on the road with a slightly better commission rate. My travels were to Departmental Stores and Exhibition Halls in towns and cities south of Blackpool. Although the freedom of travel and the opportunity of meeting people greatly appealed to me and of course the requests and attention received mostly from the females who were employed in the different stores, the 'man in a suitcase' style of living wasn't for me. So after only five months of demonstration, I thought, behind me I returned to the bungalow on Preston New Road in Blackpool to decide my next move. A couple of days later I was on the move again but on a daily basis.

With my part of my savings I purchased several German imported vacuum cleaners and all the attachments including a hair drier. Gathering together a team of demonstrators wasn't difficult, it never is in places such as Blackpool. Because of my inexperience of life in general, not to mention any business knowledge, I required a team leader and he also had to be my reliable advisor. With my gathered hopefuls selected by my advisor, arrangements were then made for all of us to meet at my advisors home which was off Preston New Road a little further down from the bungalow and on the opposite side. I arrived early and Bert introduced me to his wife who then went into another room so as Bert and I could start talking about what was ahead of us. Prior to the arrival of the first team member I agreed, because of my age, to give Bert full control of the demonstrators and that they would have to accept him as their boss. At the count of seven arrivals Bert decided to start discussions with all who were present.

I listened with keen ears and senses but my feelings were not that exciting. Nevertheless I agreed to how my new venture was to proceed and each member of the team left with a demonstrating only vacuum. Were the lonely women- of the potteries to blame for the bizarre excuses feeding back to me the reason for a quick ending to my first business venture or was it also my naivete, age and the silver Armstrong Sidley which I purchased for the job. Whatever the reasons I wasn't going to be 'ripped off' so after five weeks I was 'Signing on'.

It isn't often my brothers and sisters are far from my mind so I decided Aberdeen would be my first port of call. Mind you I had another reason for wanting to 'show off' my car to certain people in the Silver City and that was, when I was stopped by the police on one of my journeys to the Potteries I was without the required documents and they accepted my promise to produce them at the Central Police Station in Aberdeen. Early on the morning of my travel I called at the house of friends to enquire whether or not Nick (The Protagonist) would like to keep me company. Nick as expected, jumped at the opportunity and within five minutes I was 'filling up' and having the water, etc. checked before we headed north. When Nick stopped talking which wasn't for at least one hundred miles, I had the opportunity to feel sad that I had let down all my brothers and sisters by not

126

being successful at my 'door to door' adventure. Nick and I had an experience we will never forget when we were given an officers salute by a 'Bobby' when the silver Armstrong Sidley cruised towards the arched entrance to the Aberdeen Police Station. How on earth I managed to keep a bland expression on my face when at the police window with my driving licence and car insurance I will never know. Nick was in hysterical laughter and had the members of the police force in smiles when they passed the car when stationary in the police yard; and not only was it there that Nick was cracking his ribs, it was almost everywhere we were when the occasion entered his mind. I am certain that to this day Nick tickles his ribs over those few seconds.

On my way to Nazareth House where I hoped to see my youngest sister, I dropped Nick off at the bottom of a street of which a friend had a spare bedroom in a flat he was renting, later I was to spend the night there before returning south. I couldn't see my sister, she was living with a very 'good' catholic family somewhere in England and it was better for her I didn't know of her whereabouts. The laughter I had within from that earlier experience was immediately replaced with the inhuman ashes of Catholicism. And with the words of the nun whirling around the inside of my head like a darken storm cloud I left Nazareth House behind forever.

It was only a single bed, so Nick and I, after talking for most of the night, fell asleep sitting up with our backs to the emulsioned wall. Although the flat was rented by a friend of Nicks he wasn't that delighted to see me, we both being rejects from the 'House of God!' This, Nick was sharp to sense and out of fairness to me, he rejected all other hospitalities offered including the chance to wash and brush up before we left on our return journey. Being unwashed, unshaven and unfed didn't appear to have any affect on Nick as we travelled, he being as chirpy as always, that was good for me as not only did it keep me awake it also prevented me from thinking too deeply and too long on my disappointment of the previous day. Preston is where Nick and I parted company late that night, then I wearily made my way to Blackpool where I was to hear something really amazing the following morning.

Sitting at the breakfast table with myself were my ex girlfriend and her mother, when I was stunned to hear my ex girlfriends mother say to me, "You have won the 'Pools'." I was amazed! With obvious disbelief written across my face, my ex girlfriends mother went on to say that she had known for months and it was due to dire financial problems that she belittled herself and her daughter in requesting a loan of. a few hundred pounds to further invest in what at that time was 'BIG' business and that was Miniature Poodle breeding. Brushing aside any legal connections I parted with a

127

cheque to the amount requested. Although the Poodle business wasn't profitable, I had no problems getting back my money when I needed it, when I married. I was never told who informed that lovely, warm, kind hearted, amazing lady of my winnings but now I do know it wasn't a person on this earth but someone in the Spirit World.

I hadn't the slightest idea what to expect when I arrived at Wheeleys Road when I took a flying visit to see my sisters and to show off my glittering silver Armstrong motor. My return journey was first of all of delight to find out my sisters were married and each with a child; and of horror, disgust, shame and sorrow all being quickly followed by anger at the appalling living conditions in which my sisters and their families were living and that they were paying rent to the 'Old Man' for those squalid conditions. It took a knock on the bedroom door by one of my sisters to get the Landlord out of his bed and it was well past two o'clock in the afternoon. Not surprised in the least when the 'Old Man' asked for the keys to the Armstrong even before he washed and shaved. Surprisingly though, he didn't make any enquiries as to my sudden and unexpected departure years earlier when I was one of his tenants at Islington Row. I was left with one vacuum cleaner and that was bought by one of my sisters before I said my farewells with a promise to keep in touch with them both. Another disappointment was when I knocked at the door of my old friend Bill from the factory, to find that Bill wasn't there anymore and that he passed away a year earlier.

One of the engineering companies I applied to for employment after being turned down as a toolmaker by Nutbrowns was British Aerospace at Preston, so I made enquiries soon after nine o'clock the following morning. "We have you on file sir, and as soon as we have a suitable vacancy you will be called for an interview. Good morning." And that was my last ever contact with the company who are supposed to give preference to ex-serving Airmen with engineering skills. The car had problems which I could ill afford to get put right so we parted company as did I and my friends at the bungalow on Preston New Road.

INTO FASHION

In a strange sort of way I strongly felt my life was being taken out of my own hands and that I was being guided, or was I drifting? I put my sales ability to good use immediately on joining a Mens Wear retail company on the sea front in Blackpool. First of all the boss had me 'Market' selling shirts in his Clifton Arcade walk round, with an entrance on the sea front. Soon I was to be selling a full range of mens clothes with the Diana Warren Company.

I would have been in my attic flat in Charles Street about a week when I met my flat neighbour. This attractive, honey blonde, months later became my wife and that meant moving to another flat, but only a short distance from the attic flat close to the towns bus station. After another few months we had a lovely little baby boy, who was to be a great part of my life, and still is. What little money I had before getting married had gone and if it wasn't for having a loan from the British Legion to put down the deposit on our first house, I don't know where I would be today. Well it was farewell to our flat in Clinton Avenue and welcome to our home in Blenhiem Avenue only a stones throw away, but in beautiful surrounds. Although the front and rear gardens were in good condition and not showing any signs of hard upkeep, the house interior required a little attention and furnishing. The pain in my leg was now causing me some anxiety, only to be relieved by tablets of which I was taking too many. My sons half brother was living in Nelson with his grandparents and at about that time of staying in Clinton Avenue it was decided it was right for him to be with his mum, new dad and his brother. We had an unexpected and uninvited guest in our house during the night which unnerved my wife. Although I had floored the big Irish intruder, it only made my wife more hysterical she thinking that I would be in trouble with the police when they arrived and they finding out of my boxing experience. With a few shakes from the police the big Irishman was on his feet and on his way out of the living room to be pushed into the waiting police car on our doorstep. It was the police who suggested I called a doctor to give a mild sedative to my wife, otherwise I would be in for a difficult night of what was left of it. On strong advice from the doctor a 'House for Sale' board was erected outside in the front garden. The house was soon sold and it was to be just another of several moves in our marriage. We both liked the area in which we lived so it was another short transfer to around the corner to Keswick Road to the bottom of which were Guest Houses and a few Holiday Flats.

I was working with a great bunch of fellows but the higher wage offer from a competitive company couldn't be refused. Although based in

Blackpool, Carleys Outfitters had shops in Southport, Wigan, Leigh and Preston and it was to those shops I owe my living, especially at managerial level. Feeding four mouths on one income isn't easy and never will be, it is with that in mind that I take you back to my days of employment with that world famous name 'Diana Warren'.

It was during the early days of working with that company that my midas touch returned. Again I didn't lay out silly money to get rich quickly, no I controlled my betting and I can tell you it wasn't easy. Soon the words 'Golden Bullocks' were being used and with other descriptives such as, "If you fell in a barrel of dog - - - you would come out covered in chocolate". No one in my circle of friends or associates could find room to complain about my 'Magical Finger' for I always shared my 'findings' with them and I know of only one who didn't take advantage of the information given. In saying that I, also know or heard of several who had a few quid and who did very well out of my Gift and not one of them ever said "Thank You" financially.

My constant winnings were soon to become a bit of a headache to the Bookmaker around the corner in Hull Road so he sent a message to me not to bother placing anymore bets with him. Of course I got round that by using a different Nom-De-Plume and by asking whoever was available in the shop to place my bet for me. It was during my third and final year at the shop and we were well into the Illuminations, the last week if my memory serves me correctly, when one of Blackpools flamboyant playboys was walking towards me and as we met we exchanged greetings then on receiving from me the names of three horses we parted company but not before that character had said to me, "These are all outsiders, are you sure they are on the job?" 100/6 ... 100/8 ... 11/2 ... were about the prices, if not the prices of the three winners and I was unable to place a bet, I being flat broke.

It was about six years later when we next met and I had the gut feeling he was as penniless as I those many years ago. Thirteen hours, seven days per week, June to end of October trying to keep body and soul together and at the end of the day you find your pockets empty. That is hard and not only hard on myself and my family but on hundreds of other families in the service industry in Blackpool who only had one breadwinner. I was lucky ... I had that magical finger.

By now retailing in mens clothing had well and truly got into my bloodstream and it wasn't far off becoming a hobby. I aimed for the best in every shop and achieved the best in every shop and that included stock turnover and highest takings. I hated the thought of being a loser and a loser I was not. I desired a reputation of being a good manager and I ended up being the best when with Carleys.

Leaving Diana Warren in November 1963 to take up a managerial position with Carleys still left me with little time with my family but at least it was steady all year round employment with the Sunday off. Usually it was by train that I travelled to the out of town shops but there was this particular week when I couldn't settle myself. "Was this unsettledness due to a change of transport from rail to road with the use of the companies 15cwt van for that week?" It was late one Autumn evening with frost in the air and that killer fog was hovering about waiting for its selected victims of which I didn't wish to be one. Head Office in Blackpool requested the return of about four full length display models, red, blue and black poster paint along with other materials used for home made advertising benefits. Several items of clothing and footwear were also put into the van before I set off for my home town.

The accident happened on a winding country lane outside the town of St. Helens and close to its rugby rival town of Wigan. Without giving it much thought I was probably going faster than the underground conditions permitted. There was this two seater sports car closing on me with full headlights and horn at full blast. Refusing to allow any room for the driver of the sports car to pass me sent that driver into a dangerous one, so I put my foot down a little more on the knowing there was an opportunity to let him pass just a couple of hundred of yards further along the winding descending road. It was at that opening and on impact with a lamp-post nestling close to a quasi of cottages that I had my first experience of my spirit leaving my body. That experience only lasted a couple of seconds but it seemed much longer. Voices were echoing in the distance and were gradually getting closer until I recognised they were human, some of which belonged to the ambulance men, some from the police and there was the soothing voice of a woman. At first nothing made sense to me the voices were just a blur of mixed tones. There were no witness's to the accident so everyone in the room had to rely on me for information. I wasn't very helpful and didn't know I was charged with a motoring offence until being reminded the following day. And it was only then that I fully understood what had happened and how lucky I was to be living.

It isn't often the police and ambulance men get a laugh out of an accident on the road, but this one had a few of them in stitches. On impact with the lamp-post the van windscreen simply shattered and dropped mainly to the floor of the van allowing me to go flying through the empty space provided and to have me lying on the ground unconscious and with cuts and bruises mainly to the face area and arms and hands. When the van bounced off the lamp-post the rear end hit something else, what, I can't remember, but I do remember being told that on seeing the spilled red poster paint trickling from the rear of the van and onto the street the police and ambulance men all thought they had another fatality on their hands. I vaguely remember being asked if I was carrying a passenger while others were trying to open the badly dented rear doors of the van. When they did manage to prize open the doors, one of the model heads, hair and all covered in red poster paint, dropped out of the van and immediately they were thinking they had a murder investigation on their hands. Although it was late into the evening, the police were able to contact my boss who was waiting for me in his office. Arrangements were then made for the Manager of the Blackpool shop to come and pick me up and take me directly home.

It was late Friday night and again I was in the land of an uncertain future. They were troublesome hours for myself and my wife, neither of us knowing if I was to be 'signing on' or not. Well that fear was put to rest the following evening when we were visited by John Higgs the Blackpool Branch Manager and the person who was sent to pick me up at the cottage the evening before. It was from John that I learnt that I was attended by a local 'doctor and surgeon who lived close to the scene of the accident and it was he who decided it was o.k. for me to travel home after treatment and a little rest on the promise I was to attend my local doctors on the Monday. Most of my information came from John including the address of the lady occupier of the cottage in which I was treated. After a weeks rest and with a bunch of flowers in my hand and in a taxi I left home for St. Helens, but calling to say 'Thank You' to the kind and gentle elderly lady who accepted me into her home and in which apart from everything else mentioned I enjoyed a good cup of tea.

Being hungry for success and everything that went with it always had me on the lookout for better career opportunities. In July the following year an advertisement in an evening paper had me putting pen to paper in great expectations. The Coop Retail Services were for the first time to my knowledge and to others to whom I inquired, advertising for a manager outside of their own movement. A couple of weeks later and into the month of August, I received an interview and days later followed an acceptance of the job offered. I and my wife were over the moon, but the boys didn't like the idea of leaving behind their friends and the generosity of which Blackpool is famous.

On arriving at the new Departmental Store I suddenly felt an inner calm and an outer warmth, I felt with great faith this was where I was to be going places. The fittings and fixtures were already in place in the Mens Wear Department, it was obvious the layout was well planned long in advance of our being there, that being the case Mr Gill, my immediate boss, and I only had the merchandise to display. After the traditional opening ceremony was over it was down to business. Having been given a free hand was pleasing to me unfortunately my 'out with the old, in with the new' policy didn't go down well, both staff and customer were quick to make their dislike of what I was doing known to me. The store had an excellent school uniform trade and nothing else to offer the young fashion demanding younger generation. Fashion shirts, jeans and trousers were quickly replacing the old and terribly slow selling old fashioned tunic shirts and their separate collars and the back to front studs that went with them, 'Flair' styled school trousers and jeans were quicker off the mark than the shirts and they were selling fast. Within weeks two thirds of the Mens Wear Department was geared to male fashion. That quick turnover of fashion didn't make life easy for Mr Gill, for unknown to me at that time he only had a budget to work with and when the Area General Manager was informed that the Mens Wear budget had reached its limit only half way through its allotted time, Mr Gill had questions to answer. We had a problem on our hands because the older mens wear was not paying for the space it was taking, as a matter of fact it just was not selling and I inherited a lot of it. Much to the dislike of the Branch Managers at Accrington and Haslington they were used as a dumping ground for my unwanted, heavy all wool, long Johns and their buttoned matching vests and nearly all that was associated with that sales market.

I remember Mr Gill telling me about the changing textile world and we had lost our wool and cotton industry to the Far Eastern countries and that they were now cutting our throats and importing at a much lower price than what we could ever achieve. There I was satisfying the needs of the younger generation and bringing in desperately wanted money to the Co-op shareholders and boosting the areas bank account and I was being blamed for angering five per cent of the customers by displaying imported goods in a historical mill town. It was sad hearing about the slave labour in the closed cotton mills and the long and awkward shifts those people endured and for them to be sold down stream, my those who invited the Far Eastern countries to come in like a thief in the night and take away 'a way of life' from the mill workers and families. After a dip in morale and sales things began to look brighter again in the Mens Wear Department, and with the departure of two lady Departmental Managers in my time with the mens side I was to be given the opportunity I never thought about.

Before the interview Mr Brookside the Area General Manager

and father of two of the Staff employed in the departments of which I was expected to take over as Manager. The Area Manager and relative of two of the women involved in the departments of which I was expected to take charge called me into his office for a quiet piece of advice and that included he answering most of the questions that would probably be put to me during my interview with the Committee members, himself and the big boss of the Co-op Retail Services, Mr Murrayfield.

Monday morning 10 o'clock and I was nervously excited and knocking on the Committee room door. Mr Murrayfield said, "Well Mr Gorman, you have made quite an impression in the short time you have been with us. We are most pleased to have such talent working with us. To show our appreciation we are offering you a unique opportunity in career advancement." One man at the table said, "You certainly have made an impression as a young man with prospects. Do you believe you have prospects ?" I gave him the answer that seemed to satisfy the man who asked the question. At the far end of the large solid oak and oblong table were seated Mr Brookside and next, to the left of him, Mr Murrayfield, the Committee members which included the U.S.D.A.W. Area Representative were seated at either side of the table at which I was the lone figure at the bottom end. A woman to the left of me put this question to me, "If you are accepted as our Ladies Departmental Manager and Buyer, what will you be offering me and other ladies of my age that we don't already get in the Ladies Department?" "Looking over the garden fence I can see your age group is more than adequately catered for." "Are you telling me it is your intention to either do away with or severely cut back on present stock levels in the department and in the two shops; and if so what do you intend using to replace what we have been successfully offering our lady members over the past years ?" Before I could open my mouth, Mr Brookside answered that question for me by saying something like, "Before any changes, if any are made, Mr Gorman obviously will be talking with the ladies on the department and the Manageress's in the shops, then we will further discuss what they have talked about." Inside of me was nervously boiling. I wanted to voice my opinion but couldn't. Anyway Mr Brookside's words didn't receive the backing he obviously wanted. Mr Murrayfield thanked the Area Manager for his words of comfort saying, "I am sure Mr Gorman found your advice most acceptable and pleasing." I gathered there and then there was no love lost between them, of which I had previously learnt from the Trade Union Representative. The voice from another of the ladies on the Committee asked me what is it she is hearing about High Fashion and would I explain it to her and to the other members present. "After all it is a fashion department that we have within the ladies wear in the store." No sooner had I given my explanation another voice from a male member at the table put this question to me, "High fashion as you describe it is unknown territory as far as our Co-Operative is concerned. What makes you think you will be successful and what makes you different from our previous managers who all in the past gave us hope of better days ahead, but failed to reach their promises ?" Then removing his eyes from my right shoulder the speaker then returned them to the papers on the table immediately in front of him. I, without looking in his direction could feel Mr Brookside enviously glaring at me as I was about to answer the questions put to me. The Union Representative and Mr Murrayfield both had what I can only describe as a confident go ahead smile on their faces; both nodding their head in my direction. I couldn't answer for the past managers so I just said to all around the table, "Guess right and often you win. Guess wrong too many times and you go under." "Are you prepared to take risks with our money if you are offered the position that is currently vacant ?" asked the man sitting at the righthand side of the table and in between two younger men, younger only by about five years. The man was clearly in his sixties, small in build and height, his handlebar moustache under a thin pointed nose covered most of his serious looking face. "Calculated risks but not stupid risks," was my reply as I glanced at Mr Brookside, who at this stage was fidgety. "Do you find Mr Gormans answer to your satisfaction," Mr Murrayfield asked Mr Walker. "Most satisfactory," was the reply. I sensed anger from Mr Brookside and I wasn't wrong, he immediately saying, "I am informed of your reliability to your animal instinct for your success. Is that the case Mr Gorman?" "During my life I have developed an instinct for certain things in life just as an animal has the built-in instinct for danger," was my unacceptable reply for Mr Brookside as he slapped the palm of his right hand on top of the papers on the table. "Mr Gorman, you cannot expect us to offer you the responsibilities of our Ladies Departments and Shops because of your 'animal instincts'. We need more ground than that!" His face flushed, he withdrew his hand from the papers and placed it on top of his other hand which was gripping his left knee. I stood there, my heart pounding. For a moment I had the overwhelming desire to tell Brookside he had got it all wrong, but my instinct told me otherwise. Mr Murrayfield leaned towards the Area Manager resulting in the Manager reaching for the telephone. It was standing on a pile of books, on an open bookshelf immediately behind where he was sitting, just an arms length away from him and just about level with his head. What seemed a couple of minutes after the Area Manager replaced the receiver, the tea arrived; being brought in on a wooden tray carried by a teenage girl. I didn't take much notice of her, I being too absorbent in thought about the position I was in. At that time everyone in the room, myself included, began talking about anything except what the meeting was about. The tea, hot, wet and sweet, brought instant relief to my nervous and excited body and it was then that I noticed the Tea-Set to be of Bone China and of blue floral design, the teaspoons used were white plastic. Having finished whatever we were talking about we replaced our cups and saucers on the wooden tray which rested on the highly polished table of which we were sitting.

Mr Murrayfield, looking at me said, "Mr Gorman, you have impressed all of us enormously. Now before we end this most interesting and enjoyable interview I would just like to ask you if you have anything else to say to us regarding the position on offer?" "All I wish to say is, you can't linger in the past and you can't maintain business attitudes that are years out of date in a changing world. One has to adapt." "Here! Here!" said the Trade Union Representative. "I think that is all Mr Gorman." Turning in the direction of Mr Brookside, Mr Murrayfield asked him if he had anything further to say to me. Blowing from his nose the Area Managers answer was, "No!" Then I was asked to return to my Mens Wear Department by Mr Murrayfield. I immediately got up from my sitting position, thanked everyone in the room for their time and left with my stomach tense with anxiety.

We were into the month of June and there was a lot of work to be done before it was too late for that summer trade. Prior to my taking over, Mr Brookside and the Departmental Manageress had carried out the 'stock-take' of all departments. That was to my dislike but at least if anything didn't add up at the next 'stock-take' they couldn't blame me.

Before leaving the store for the two shops I telephoned three ladies warehouses that I had known to be 'on the ball', arrangements made, I then set off. Haslingden was more fashion conscious than its blood-line shop in Accrington where corsitory, overalls and school clothing were the main trade. The Haslingden staff were very keen to see their well kept but old fashioned shop change with the introduction of more interesting lines to display and sell. It was when on my first visit to Haslingden that I received further warning signals about Mr Brookside. The departmental store had virtually nothing to offer the sixteen to twenty-five year old female so it was with that in mind I set up a High Fashion Department within the fashion department and it had the prime position.

It is September and the very latest in fashion was delivered on the doorstep and my selection of dresses and fun fabrics were immediately on display after being priced. There was thick animosity hanging about

136

mingled with delight, sharpness of the eye and a great uplift in spirit from the younger members of the staff in the store, most of whom now wanted to be on the ladies High Fashion Section. Word spread that I was only going to employ 'Dolly Birds' throughout the entire ladies and childrens sections. Although that would be good for me it wouldn't be for business. I couldn't get my own way as regarding the staff I needed but the dowdy Manageress of the fashion department did make an effort in changing her hairstyle and presentation as a whole. Having to be satisfied with the staff available on that one section I then turned my attention and interests to the other side of the ladies department. Corsitory is a specialist section and I was very grateful that I had what was described to me by several people as, best in the trade. Mrs Trimmir was also responsible for the Haberdashery and Soft Furnishing Sections of which also were under my control as was the Childrens Wear Section of which Mr Brookside seemed to take an unusual interest.

The High Fashion sales were beyond all expectations in the store and when the two shops heard of the success they too wanted a slice of the cake. This great success was also to be a great problem, firstly because I again was up against a strictly controlled cash budget, secondly I wasn't giving the other sections in the department the attention required and the third reason was the dislike of me by Mr Brookside. The new section was for reasons known only to himself an embarrassment but there was little he could do about it but he could have the final say in all aspects of my adverts in the local newspaper. Now, I am not a mathematician but I do know about pluses and minuses when it comes to stock control, but Mr Brookside didn't agree with me, nor did he agree with the previous managers. This brick wall was to be a major problem to me. He obviously didn't like the attention I was receiving from Head Office, neither did he like the way in which I was ignoring our merchandise at our warehouse in Manchester.

I arrived with my family and I arrived with a good reputation. Len Dole who during this time was a pillar of strength within the Labour Party, Len being the Divisional Labour Party agent for Nelson and Colne. Len and I became good friends starting from our first meeting during my early days in the Mens Wear Department and it was in those days that Len introduced me to Socialism, soon I became involved and the interest grew stronger with every opportune meeting in and outside the Local Party meeting rooms. Although I helped people in the past and felt sadness for most of them it was through meeting Len and his lovely wife Betty that I really felt the need to make helping others a part of my every day life and as time went marching on that need went marching along with it.

137

Nelson and Colne Constituency Labour Party held its first Annual Dinner and Social Evening at the Silverman Hall in Nelson at 7.30 p.m. on Tuesday 10th March 1970 and my invite was of great surprise and delight.

MENU

Soup or Fruit juice

+

Roast Spring Chicken and Sausage

+

Sage and Onion Stuffing

+

Green Peas cooked with Ham

+

Buttered Carrots

+

Game Chips Cream Potatoes

+

Swan Lake

+

Cheese Tray

+

Coffee

Presentations were made to two Aldermen by Mrs Mary Wilson the wife of the famous 'Pipe and Mack' man.

Owing to the demanding needs for the envious older women the High Fashion section was blended in with a more update Fashion Department displaying up to the minute trendy clothes to suit the needs of the over twenty-five female. And that need led to the first of our Fashion Shows for our very own customers. To make the night more exciting we used ladies from the Lucy Fields Fashion Model Agency to advertise our new seasonal ranges and on the spot orders were in abundance on the night.

Mr Brookside just did not want me for his Fashion Buyer or for anything else for that matter so we parted company. My forced resignation had me in uncontrollable tears for a couple of minutes after stepping outside the Store and on my way home with the news to my family. But it wasn't all gloom that I brought with me through the front door. Mr Murrayfield had heard Brooksides dislike of me and of his poor opinion of me as a Departmental Manager and Buyer, so with an emergency vacancy for a Mens Wear Manager and Buyer waiting to be filled the opportunity of offer was accepted and soon my family and I were in the over crowded and historical town of Maidstone in Kent.

Even before I arrived they were betting 7/1 I wouldn't fit the shoes of their blue eyed boy of the southern area of the Cooperative Retail Services. But the man from the north as I was known had them all in the south wishing they weren't so biassed. Seeing the weekly sales for the Mens Wear Department increased on the corresponding period for the previous three years was of immense delight to me and of course to my southern bosses and as I found out to Mr Murrayfield as well.

The boys really loved and enjoyed that part of the country and we made the best of it with visiting all the historical places in and around Maidstone and by being in places such as Deal, Dover, Hastings and Rye. "Oh God, what a beautiful place Rye is". My income more than covered the rent of the lovely flat we rented in that beautiful quaint southern town on the River Medway, but unfortunately our house in Nelson didn't sell and the mortgage repayments became a burden. Both boys were very disappointed at having to leave their new friends and a different and better way of living, that brought sadness to my heart but I had no alternative but to move.

After a couple of weeks back in the old mill town I was travelling south again, this time on my own with a paid return train ticket to Bristol where I was to 'be chauffeured in a limousine to the 'as God' created, village of Street in that God made county of Somerset. What was I doing there, you might well ask! Training to become a qualified shoe fitter can be the only answer. What a wonderful, fantastic fortnight that was. Training apart it was like being on a five star holiday. All on the training course were treated like Royalty. The food, the wine, the cream, the attention, the weather, the hospitality, everything made me feel as if I were being punished the day I left it all behind. Well it was back to the real world and to further clashes with that Area Manager, Mr Brookside.

Although not the Footwear Buyer, Mr Bootie the Buyer allowed me the privilege of buying for the shop I managed and also to be responsible for the advertising of the shoes. Listening to the experienced shoe senior sales woman, my first bulk purchase was one of mens shoes and they required an attractive advert in the local paper to have any chance of selling them in quantity. It was that advert when it appeared in the local paper that was the cause of the blocked lines to Mr Brooksides office, and the irate callers that were fortunate to get through to Mr Brookside had him hopping mad.

MEN, THE HUNT IS OVER.
SHOP AT THE 'IN' SHOP
OF THE MOMENT.

That caption along with a picture of woman holding a shot-gun and the top half of her Safari Suit unbuttoned showing what nearly all men like to, look at was the reason for the concern. The advert may not have gone down well with the Victorian minded of the mill town but it certainly had the local school kids buzzing and my two boys loved every minute of their new found popularity. Of course the advert sold shoes, lots of them. In fact that many shoes were sold at the end of that Saturday the staff were absolutely shattered and glad to get home to put their feet up.

It was several weeks before the shoe shop required another advert because we had lost customers return, and new ones gained from elsewhere. A disturbance was blowing in the wind and it had me again clasping my hands, looking up at the sky praying to my God for spiritual help and guidance. "Whoever else is looking after me, I also need your help and guidance," I can remember that day well as it was mostly spent in prayer.

It was yet again another return to Blackpool for me this time to open my own fashion Shop.

A PERIOD OF TREPIDATION

For several years it had been a Toy and Fancy Goods Shop but the landlord to be, allowed the shop to be used as a Fashion Outlet. That was tremendously good news, there not being a shop anywhere near, selling Male fashion.

Trading on the bustling Central Drive in a corner position close to The Mecca, Blackpool Rugby and Greyhound Grounds, and with two of the resorts busiest Working Mens Clubs just around the corner, just had to be good for business and it was close enough to the Guest House to have a direct link with the telephone. With the Guest House catering only for Bed and Breakfast I found it convenient to also earn an extra living working late shifts on Blackpools Corporation Trams and Buses that brought in extra money for rapid business growth. At least that was the plan. Then after three hard but rewarding years, for domestic reasons the shop had to be sold. There was no problem selling, the first response to the advert was in no doubt it was exactly what he was looking for. Within two weeks everything was signed, sealed and delivered.

Again my mind was clogged with briars and weeds, I not knowing or understanding what was going on in my life. This agonising and disruptive period brought the thoughts of my brothers and sisters into the entanglement with what I was now experiencing, also the darker days we spent in Nazareth House in Aberdeen. Mangled with the thoughts of my kin were memories of the past ten years or so and with the unthinkable thoughts of that time. Selling the Guest House was a relief, it ought not to have been purchased in the first place. Tension never left me after the two sales so I decided to have more freedom by working longer than usual hours on the trams and buses. I don't think a day passed without me taking some form of pain killers. I knew they weren't the answer to my problem but at least they kept me sane, but somehow they dulled the brain and I was becoming forgetful. The telephone bill was overdue so I put it in a prominent place on the mantle-piece before retiring to bed the night before.

I was the Guard on the Blackpool South to Cleveleys Bus Station when a woman traveller on the bus handed me a handbag that another woman passenger left behind. I went through the procedure of checking the handbag in the presence of a man on the bus then placed the handbag in the small compartment used by all bus guards for their ticket machine and its metal box plus other things such as flasks and sandwiches. This happened on our final trip to Cleveleys and it was when nearing the town the incident took place. Then as we approached Cleveleys Bus Station with an empty bus I decided to check the handbag for a name and address and in doing so I came across a compartment with paper money, on counting there was

141

£25.00. The driver of the bus had already got out of his cab and was in the staff waiting room ready to pour out the can of tea he had brewed. With me feeling numb with the cold of the night and with the effects of my headaches I returned the handbag and money to the compartment and put the hook on. Not knowing what response I would receive from the driver I only mentioned the handing over of the handbag thinking it was safer that way, after all I didn't know him that well.

The further we travelled through Cleveleys and into Bispham the more travellers boarded the bus and it had to be on a night when my head was spinning and I feeling bitterly cold and in no mood for jokes, although I tried to be as civil as possible. It was at a bus stop well into Bispham that a solitary woman signalled for the bus driver to stop and as he did the woman asked if a handbag was found and after I received a good description of the handbag and one or two of its contents I handed it over to the claimant. As far as I was concerned that was the last of the matter and then whilst just about to leave the south shore terminal to return to the bus depot to complete our shift a man jumped onto the bus saying, "Oh no you don't. You have some explaining to do. Where is the money?" In total puzzlement I looked at him and said, "I don't know what you are on about!" "Oh yes you do. I am talking about the £100.00 that was in the handbag." My mind couldn't function properly so I called the driver of the bus for his assistance. Having noticed I hadn't changed the rear bus number he did it whilst I was sitting on the seat nearest to the platform. From there I shouted to the driver that the man standing outside is saying there was £100.00 in the handbag handed to me. The irate male wasn't believing anything that was said and he decided to follow the bus in his car and that he would be watching every move that I would make.

Once in the depot the bus driver dropped me off at the offices then he drove the double decker to the garage just a few yards away. Having checked my ticket machine, log card and money that all was correct the supervisor that was sent to watch me then took all three to the checking office. There was a heated argument going on outside the checking room close to the control room. The chap who was accusing me of not telling the truth turned out to be a son of the owner of the handbag. He was of stocky build, raucous type of a man who used four letter words frequently. This disturbance brought together several of my work mates and a handful of different ranking inspectors nearly all of whom were either trying to calm the raging man and/or trying to convince me it will be sorted out without the need for the police to be called. The man wasn't having any of it and several minutes later his mother arrived with two C.I.D. men.

In the presence of the Chief Inspector and in his office I was ques-

142

tioned by two from the police force and before agreeing to being searched I voluntary removed every thing from all of my pockets. With other bits and pieces there was £75.00 in cash on the table that being all of my pocket contents. "Where is the other £25.00, one of the C.I.D. asked. Puzzled, I answered, "That is my money." "Where is the other £25.00," that same voice said, this time there was a threatening tone to his voice. Several other questions were put to me by that same person then the Chief Inspector began to ask the C.I.D. men questions. Then turning to me I was asked if I could prove the £75.00 was mine. I explained to the Inspector as I did to the C.I.D. that the £75.00 was my telephone money that I intended to pay that day but couldn't because I had left the telephone bill at home. Because of a final demand I placed the telephone bill in a prominent position on the mantle-piece the night before.

The C.I.D. wanted the proof of the bill and I was allowed to go home and bring it back for all to see. Having done that, still they were not convinced and they asked the Chief Inspector permission to take me to the police station for further questioning. That request didn't suit the Chief or myself but with reluctance the Chief allowed the two men to take me with them to the police station where all promises made to the Chief were broken. By this time my brain was numb. Sitting in the plain C.I.D. car on the way to the police station I was trying to fathom out why no one in the Chief Inspectors room questioned my £49.00 plus telephone bill when I had told them that the £75.00 was my telephone money. Then I said to myself, "Stop thinking! Stop thinking!"

Once inside the station I was put in an empty room, bar a large and old wooden table with a telephone resting on it at the other end to where I was told to sit. Having seated comfortably for the first time in hours and with the aid of the dimly lit room I began trying to put my thoughts together. I was just thinking that the extra £25.00 in my pocket was the money from that handbag, but they are saying there was £100.00 in the handbag and they wanted to know what has happened to it. I still had no answers when I was joined by the two C.I.D. men for what they said would be straight forward and simple questions that would require similar answers. At first I wasn't afraid, just totally confused at the questions put to me and in the manner in which they were being asked. "You are entitled to one phone call and that is up to you whether it is your wife or your solicitor you call." And when the senior of the two men put his finger on the telephone receiver as I was about to call my solicitors home number, I was afraid. Scared to death is a better description of that moment.

After a lengthy and mentally brutal interrogation I was forced to hand over the £75.00 and told if I didn't sign a guilty confession, police pre-hand written statement I would be locked up for the night. On fearing what I heard and with the words, "We will plant drugs on your older boy and at home," still tormenting my mind I signed what was demanded of me. Then I was in Hell ! ! ! The following morning I was at the newly built police station in Chapel Street for photographs and fingerprinting both of which stirred the flames within me. I left the station not hearing that the charge against me had been changed to stealing £75.00 and not the £100.00 because after the C.I.D. informed the owner of the handbag that that was the amount of money found in my possession she suddenly remembered she had paid £25.00 earlier that morning for an electric fire.

At my solicitors the following morning Hell was still within and around me and I wanted to commit suicide there and then. Getting across to the doctors was like battling my way through the fires of Hell. Not for weeks but for months I went about in body only my mind had left me, that is the way I felt and to me that could only be in the fires of Hell. Later in life I learnt that Hell isn't what was put into my mind by the Catholic Nuns but Hell is here on earth and once in it, it takes some getting out of.

Yes, part of that Hell was the suffering I was carrying for the misery I brought on my family, but not being guilty as charged I had no reason to put the house up for sale and move out of town. My plea of Not Guilty at the local Magistrates Court had me waiting to be heard at the Crown Court where the hearing was to be at Preston. In the meantime I continued with my weekly visits to the Bus Depot to pay my full Union Fees even though I was suspended from work without pay. As I did, so did almost everyone at the Depot know I was innocent of the offence brought against me, most of them convinced it was a 'set up'. After several months of agonising, suffering and painful hell my case was held in Blackpool, it being switched from Preston only weeks earlier. Standing in the 'Dock' I still was of the feeling I was being charged with the theft of £100.00. My paralysed brain just wouldn't work for me. What questions I did answer in my defence were said with the fear of what the two C.I.D. men sitting close to me had said about planting drugs if I was round not guilty. Before the jury went out to reach their verdict I was given permission to leave the court buildings for a break if I so wished. My wife and I made the best of allotted time by having a stroll and then visiting a friends care where all three of us talked about what was said during the trial. And with our friend saying being allowed out of the court building was in itself a pointer of not guilty. With those comforting words nestling around me, we returned for the conclusion of my trial.

It was a long and nail biting experience waiting with my court escorts in the cells, waiting for the jury to present themselves to the court chambers. According to my escorts the jury were out a long time for such a minor offence and that I should consider myself 'Not Guilty'. Their words did penetrate my healing mind and it was with those words that I gave the 'Thumbs up' sign to my wife as I passed her on my way to the hearing box.

'Guilty!' was the verdict.

And these were I believe the summing up words of the trial Judge, "How in earth you have arrived at such a decision I will never know. But it is a verdict I have to accept." With the majority verdict from the jury and my few months probation period erasing my earlier hopes I must have dragged my unbelieving self back home because I could never remember getting there and out of the court building. The three months that followed were of a wondering aimless existence when restrictions, adversities, sorrows, echoes of past unhappiness kept penetrating my mind and my emotions were subject to muddle and confusion. What followed was a period of sifting the ashes of despair, the fires of hell having gradually burnt out. It was through those ashes I tread an uncertain path to Blackpools Town Hall for an application form to drive a taxi for one of the towns leading taxi companies. It was painful having to put pen to the question, "Have you been guilty of an offence and were you given a legal conviction for that offence ?" The special panel made up of councillors from the local area heard each culprit separately and fortunately for me my case was remembered and there were no hesitations in allowing me to go for the required medical and to take the knowledge of the town examination. With a letter from the taxi company my licence fee was accepted then I was sent for a badge photograph.

It was now March 1975 and my freedom and the right to earn a living were of enormous importance to my morale. At first the money was poor but at least I was in a friendly environment where I was getting the hang of things, meaning good communications with the radio operators and the crafty moves that certain drivers were using to gain from others. Well it was a busy and hectic season and the seven days a week, twelve hours a day took its toll in as much as it was painful going to bed and more painful getting out of it. With that in mind and of the quiet months ahead when the residents only speak to seagulls, I scanned the local paper for another source of income but still hoping to taxi on a part time basis. Three weeks before an advert caught my eye for a Managerial position with a famous mens tailoring company I was subjected to another frightening ordeal.

A larger than large bloodhound faced, long dark baited monster of a man with a dark thick drooping moustache and with a tray of chips in his large fat hands squeezed into my taxi on the taxi rank in Cedar Square at the back of the well known indoor market close to the Winter Gardens. "South shore," he growled as he made himself comfortable on the back seat and immediately behind me. "Where in south shore," politely I asked. "Just drive and I will tell you where to go," he snapped. After several demands of 'turn left here, turn right there' I began to get a little nervous and without turning around but by looking at his grizzly appearance in the interior mirror I asked, "What on earth are you playing at?" The reply to that question was the introduction of a sharp and shiny looking object which was prickling the back of my neck. I then slowed to a few miles per hour and began fidgeting with the taxi microphone not really knowing what to say or when to say it. "Try and get in touch with the police and you will be sorry." Then I was a frightened rabbit with thoughts mangled with thoughts. Silently and eagerly I started putting a plan of rescue together which was made all the easier when the passenger ordered me to turn the taxi and head north of the town, at that point I was nearing Blackpool Airport and approximately three miles from the said destination. The number of the road given didn't exist, this I knew by experience of that area. Within half a minute of my demanded 'U-Turn' I had the opportunity of putting the first part of my plan into action. Control Office were giving out and receiving messages and I started pretending the messages were for me, this I did by fiddling about with the microphone button so as the passenger couldn't understand what was being given over the radio. And to make it sound genuine I gave my taxi name out on a couple of occasions but was soon interrupted and told to switch off. Only by telling the passenger that by switching off it would draw attention to the office and that would lead to a message for all other drivers to be on the look out for me.

The second part of my plan was soon put into operation as we neared the taxi rank at Talbot Square opposite the North Pier. With my empty flask nestling on the passenger seat beside me I nervously told the passenger that the flask had to be handed over to the driver of one our other taxi drivers at more or less a given time and that this was done on a regular basis, failing to carry out the procedure would again lead to suspicion as to why I was a long time before accepting a call from the office. He fell for the tale and wasn't I relieved. Now all I could ask for was for one of our taxi's to be on that taxi rank. I was in luck, I took a long intake of breath and immediately let it out again as I almost lost control of the wheel on turning off the promenade and into Talbot Square. The taxi driver was quick to get the point when I pulled alongside of his taxi and with the empty flask being handed over to him and I saying quietly but well pronounced "Police".

Pulling away from my colleague I was less nervous but still concerned about the position in which I found myself. Having arrived at the end of Carshalton Road in the north end of the town and without moving my head I said to the driver, "This is the road you asked for and it doesn't go near the number you mentioned," I had forgotten it anyway. There was deadly silence and when I glanced up at the mirror in front of me I could see a clearer description of the huge, surly, morose, heavy jowled, long greasy black haired, close to the nose dark narrow eyed monster of a man. As he sat staring into space with those piercing and evil looking eyes he ordered me back to south shore. Without another word spoken I started the taxi and started to move off and then my heart jumped into my mouth when that huge lump leaned over the seat and switched off the radio. Fearing a return to the back of the neck of that sharp and shiny object or even worse, I didn't do or say anything about the incident until a good way into the return journey. Again luck was with me when, at the traffic lights and positioned to go in the direction of Lytham Road and the Airport, a fellow taxi driver from the same company as I pulled alongside of me and just managed to shout to me before the traffic lights turned to green, "The office have been trying for ages to contact you." Permission granted to switch on the radio and within moments of doing so a very welcome female voice called me and inquired as to my whereabouts. "Tell them you are heading in the direction of the airport," were the words whispered into my ear as I inhaled the outlet of his foul smelling breath. Later and within two minutes of conveying my instructions I was approached by a police patrol car and told to pull up just past the traffic lights and the last ones before reaching the airport. Nervously but willingly I did as I was asked and after getting out of the taxi to talk over my ordeal with the police the fat man was ordered to join us. It was my first look at the full frame of my tormentor and my 5'7", nine stone seven frame was certainly no competition for a huge over sixteen stone 6ft plus meaty frame, whose dark jacket would have made a good fitting overcoat for Harry Seacombe. Asked by the police if I wanted to bring charges against the man and with me gratefully refusing, the police then turned to the giant and asked him to pay the fare registered on the meter. He did, then had the nerve to request I take him back to Carshalton Road to which I instantly refused. With the clearance from the police I threw myself into the taxi and drove off to carry on with my way of earning a living.

The 'Lights' were out and the long, tiring and weary season had left its mark, I was totally dejected and in need of a holiday but not even affording one day off from earning the bread money, I went straight into my new job hoping it would be a happy and long lasting one.

UNDER THE WRONG STAR

With my metal ended tape measure snugly resting in the inside ticket pocket of one of my long time unused two piece suits, I entered the staff entrance of R.H.O. HILLS Departmental Store in plenty of time before the opening time of nine o'clock. The date? 25th November 1975. My position? Tailoring Manager for a well known high class clothing company. As in all Departmental Stores the arrival of arrival 'shop within shop' inevitably caused hiccups but they are soon soothed by better understandings of ones positions and loyalties.

At work all was going well and after twelve months of being with the company I was allowed to go along to our clothing factory in Leeds to select the clothes and styles I thought would sell well in Blackpool. Not only did my regular visits to the factory work wonders for that instinct of mine it also gave me the opportunity to meet other managers from other branches. Not only were the meetings friendly they also were essential to all concerned with the company as a way of finding out what clothes, styles, prices, etc. sold better in some areas than others. This information was most useful in cost control by branches exchanging quantities of stock thus cutting production costs. By Spring 1977 R.H.O. Hills was just a memory for most of the staff employed in the store and for most of the general public in the area, it being another victim of the giant conglomerates, House of Fraser. By the end of 1977 I was unwell and found it painful to get about resulting in me having to be admitted to the Manchester Royal Hospital in Manchester for a major operation. It was April 7th the day before my 44th birthday when the operation to remove part of my Aortic artery and other arteries from both sides of my stomach into my groin and replace those defunct arteries with synthetic tubes. My fortnights stay in hospital was soon followed by a return visit only days after being released, this was due to me having a haematoma as a result of negligence of the Sister in Charge of the ward on duty at the time of my release. Three months after my re-release and I was back at work but only on light duties during which time my company allowed me to use taxis to take me to work at their expense. The kindness and hospitality given to me and my family during that period of ill health can never be forgotten especially when I was assured before entering hospital my employment with the company was assured no matter how long I was away from work.

In the July of that year, all roads led to Southport as the Worlds Best Golfers bid for the greatest title of them all. Under canvass at the Royal Birkdale Golf Course, pleased to be representing the great Californian Johnny Miller. The famous Californian would have done well to bring with him gallons of his own quality orange juice; chilled, his product would have sold well in the almost unbearable heat wave in our country at that time. In hot, scorching heat and under canvass I managed the Johnny Miller Golf Shop and trade was just steady with the Johnny Miller Trousers selling better than his Blazers and other items. All were immaculately tailored by the famous Leeds Tailors Benjamin Simon with whom my company was part of. The only name that was causing excitement was the up in coming 19 year old Spaniard called Severiano Ballesteros. In the heat wave the handsome Spaniard led by 2 at the half way stage and maintained that lead over the 3rd round. That being so my Boss suggested I started packing the stock; minutes later I sensed a change of excitement in the air, the young Spaniard couldn't make a dream come true, the man to deny him was Johnny Miller playing one of the greatest rounds in Open history - a 66 that gave the orange juice giant a 6 stroke wining margin. And trying but failing to keep his composure, my Boss returned to the shop quietly and nervously shouting at me to unpack the stock. All hell let loose, everyone wanted to buy Johnny Miller Trousers, Blazers, etc. etc. I slept well that night and well into the following morning. What a once in a lifetime experience I had, never having a golf club in my hand.

I waited until late November that year before resuming my part time job as a taxi driver; and on a cold, wet and windy night in December fate yet again struck me another nasty blow. I had a call from the taxi office to pick up a man from a working mens club about two miles from the centre of Blackpool. The 'Fare' as we call them in the taxi business, seemed to be like any other until half a mile into the journey when he didn't like the amount shown on the meter and ordered me in a broad Scottish accent to turn off the meter and that he wasn't going to pay his fare. With about half a mile to go before getting into town I stopped the taxi and asked the passenger why he continues to say he is being ripped off and that he has no intention of paying the fare registered on the meter. Not getting any satisfactory response to my questions I then contacted the office and reported the matter to them and the reply I received was to advise the passenger to pay the full fare at the end of his journey if not agreeable to this then to take him to the police station. On hearing what was being said the irate Scotsman warned me that if I took him to the police station I would be a dead man. Afraid by what I had heard and not wishing to be involved with the police on my own I drove to the taxi office at the corner of Grasmere Road and Central Drive just a minutes drive from the Central Police Station. Having again been told to take the non payer to the Police Station I left the office feeling uncomfortable and in need of encouragement but there were no male drivers in the immediate area at that precise moment. So alone I approached the man in the taxi and told him what I was told to do, then I walked around the front

149

of the car and was about to open the door for myself to get in when the toothless idiot walked past me stopping inches in front of me, and with his back to me bent down as if to tie his shoe laces then, with one almighty swoop from ground level he landed a crushing blow to my chin which had me unconscious lying on the street on the blind side of the taxi to the office. I was in pain, dirty, soaking wet and down in the mouth so I decided to call it a day even though it was only about ten o'clock in the night. After filling up with petrol and checking what was routine at the close by filling station I drove home and at the end of the third of a mile journey I remained seated in the taxi for a few minutes chewing things over and pondering on what sort of a reception was waiting for me inside the house. Although I arrived at work on time the following morning I was, I believe for the first time in my life not interested in what I have always regarded as an essential part of my living.

For a few, Christmas has no meaning and for me it never had except, to see the happiness and feel the joy that it gave to the two boys. That isn't to say, I never joined the parties at that time of year. Below the colourful Christmas tinsel I sat alone in the stores comfortable Coffee House. Then I was joined by two lovely and interesting ladies. They were much older than I and one of them had what some people called a gift and others, myself included, a load of cods wallop. But unknown to me at that time and for sometime later I was to be still one of the Ha, Ha, group.

The Manageress of the Coffee House was having matrimonial problems as well as myself but I did not know of her situation. Having poured herself a cup of tea the Manageress then joined myself, the two other ladies that I have mentioned and another female much younger in years than any of us at the table. Flo, the gifted lady turned to the Coffee House Manageress and said, when you have finished drinking your tea I would like to read your cup." Silently I chuckled. It was over my time allowed for my morning break but I wasn't concerned. What the gifted lady had told the Coffee House Manageress amazed me and I fully expected an angry remark from the lady who had her cup reading. She was told by Flo the gifted lady, that within a couple of weeks something drastic was going to happen but out of it she would find happiness greater than she could ever imagine. Turning to me the gifted lady told me that a huge dark cloud would darken my days for a very long time and that I would have no control over it. I was also given the date of 25th November. At that the younger woman laughed aloud only to hear from the gifted woman that she was pregnant. "Oh no I'm not," was the adamant reply. Well she was pregnant and she was shocked on being told on her visit to the doctors only a couple of days later. After a couple of weeks of being told that something drastic

150

was going to happen the husband of the Coffee House Manageress was killed in an accident. Months later the bereaved woman went to Australia on a holiday where she met and later married a wealthy business man.

Although there was trouble within my marriage no one in the store knew about it at that time and as I was leaving the Coffee House after my extended morning break I was thinking to myself, "It would me interesting if Flo, the gifted lady was seeing something that was to the foremost in my mind and of which day by day was getting me down." Three months after that warning my wife demanded a divorce and this time it was mentioned once too often and she began divorce proceedings towards the month of May 1980. Just days before the divorce absolute on the 19th November of the same year, I again found myself in deep waters. I was summoned to the office of the Accounts Manager where in presence of another senior member of the company I was questioned about an incident that had taken place on their Mens Wear Department regarding the mishandling of money tendered by a certain person. It would have been two to three weeks prior to being called to the office and when I was given the added responsibility of looking after the other Mens Wear Department owing to their new manager being allowed to take his prearranged holiday, booked before accepting his position. That responsibility was the last thing I could have done with under those present circumstances.

The day of the incident I was in the worst mood I have ever been in in my entire life and the anti-depressants weren't helped with the pain killers that were taken with them. For some unknown reason the shared department telephone was constantly ringing and several times I had the urge to remove the receiver. There was activity close to the shared cash terminal and at first I ignored what was going on, then on noticing there was a queue of about five or more people at the terminal and nobody around to serve them I had no alternative but to go and accept their payments and wrap their purchases. At the time I was with the fourth customer I was thinking it unusual for so many people to have the correct money readily available, this I mentioned to the fifth or sixth person, I think it was the fifth and it was a lady, her remark of, "Is that so," made me see black. For how long I was in that darkness I will never know, but it couldn't have been for long as the same people were at the terminal when I glanced at them from the seat in my-own department. Opening my hand there was money in it though at that time that didn't register with me, anyhow the telephone was ringing and it probably was the result of me coming out of the darkness I was in. Having answered the telephone and on turning to the other department and seeing nobody that was the last I remember of that day, and the days that followed prior to being summoned to the office were days really

151

no different from most others. It was after being asked about staff customer service and having given correct answers to probably all the questions that I noticed the office table was cleared of everything including the telephone which I later saw on the floor under the cleared table. It was immediately after the what I thought to be normal procedure within the House of Fraser Group that I was accused of mishandling money belonging to the company. On hearing the words I momentarily stunned as I sat at the table. I closed my eyes and tried to shut out the words that were being spoken. The only other memory I have of that day is walking through an empty store and getting home to a barrage of hell fire remarks then going to bed where I stared at the window for a while before going into a restless sleep in what was a nightmare web of plots and counter plots.

The following day I returned for work as usual, not being told not to do so. It was obvious by the expression of my face and of the colour of it that there was something terribly wrong with me but nobody was sensing that my life was in shatters, ripped apart by fate and I wondering how much more I could take before a vein popped in my head. The date: 25th November 1980. Late into that morning I was again summoned upstairs this time in front of the enigmatic Store Manager who added me to his list of unwanted managers under his roof. Again and later into that day I was being questioned, this time it was by my own Area Manager and it was from him that I heard the devastating news that I could no longer be employed by the House of Fraser Group and that our company couldn't employ me anywhere else owing to unclosed circumstances.

In a state of shock I arrived at my solicitors which was a few hundred yards from the store. Once in the reception room my solicitor was informed of my presence and of my stressful condition. Having told what had happened and before advising me to go across to the doctors I left the office with the words something like, "Leave it to me Andy, I will see what I can sort out." With another prescription of anti-depressants in my hand I found my way to the house and more trouble. In the past I could cope with my problems but not now. Everything seemed to be out of my control. Mentally I was sealed into the emptiness and darkness of a large oil drum that was being pounded along the promenade in a gale force wind. It was the following day I called the solicitors receptionist hoping to hear if my solicitor had been in contact with my Head Office but it wasn't until a few days later that I was informed that I wasn't sacked for mishandling company money but of a lesser offence of failing to carry out technical procedures.

After another few months living on state benefit I was back in retail management in the shopping precinct and only yards away from where I was previously employed. Six months later and for no valid reason I was handed a letter from one of that companies senior managers and its contents were of startling reading ... Fate got at me yet again causing me further mental agony as I returned to state handouts. Only weeks after my dismissal the company changed hands only to be closed down along with all its other off shoots. Then as before I sought help from my solicitor who unfortunately was refused any link with the people responsible for ending my six months stay with that company. At the time of my dismissal I believed it was the result of me knowing more about retail managing than my immediate bosses but with the company changing hands only a couple of months later I dismissed the thought from my mind.

By that time there was only my son Glen and I at home, his mother having left weeks earlier to live elsewhere and out of Blackpool. Painful as it was the divorce was of great relief to me and for the first time in years my mind and body began to relax. But I was still in need of love, care and attention to give me the spiritual strength I needed to survive. All my needs were from Glen and whoever was looking after me for at that time my faith in God had somewhat diminished. Of course I couldn't expect too much from Glen and it would have been cruelly unfair for me to burden him with all my problems. So for that extra help I turned to my R.A.F. Association Branch and my colleagues for the extra inner strength I so badly needed. Soon I was involved, not only in being friendly with all our members but also getting involved in fund raising for those of our friends who found life in many and many different ways unfair to them. In February 1982 I was serving on the branch committee as Press Officer of which I was responsible for gaining as much free publicity as possible and where possible to boost our membership and to raise funds for the R.A.F. Association Welfare Funds. This was good for me as it took my mind away from my own problems and I was soon to learn that my future happiness was to be with helping others. The Falkland Crisis got me off to a good start in my new role as Press Officer because at that time the R.A.F. Association were holding their Annual Conference and delegates from all over the world were expected to attend the conference at the Winter Gardens from May 7th to 9th that year. With a delegation expected from Argentina the local press were greatly interested, unfortunately no member of the association left that country to attend the conference, never the less we received front page-coverage in the local paper the Blackpool Gazette.

In February the following year I was appointed Honorary Secretary of our Branch further involving me with the fund raising and increasing my need to see people happy and enjoying themselves at different social events and with increased branch membership. Foremost in my

153

mind are the Miss R.A.F. Competitions, the Mini Cruise and coach tour to the Dutch Bulbfields and the two occasions when we achieved by hard work and companionship two Branch Wings Appeal Collections. And I surely must mention those magnificent people from that devastated country of Poland who came to live in Blackpool and to build that wonderful and friendly club of theirs, The White Eagle Club on Hornby Road, Blackpool. Without them and their generosity in allowing the R.A.F. members of Blackpool the honour of using their club for our meeting place and for a base from which we organised everything associated with the branch; a final word to those magnificent people, "Thank you for your warmth and kindness and generosity in allowing us to be your guests and for allowing us the use of your wonderful premises for all those lovely and unforgettable joint social evenings when we danced, sang and drank the night away."

My brothers and sisters are rarely out of my mind and I dearly wanted us brought together. We all had been sent on separate ways on leaving the-orphanage in Aberdeen and never have been together as a family. In the early days of October 1982 I contacted the Salvation Army in London and for a nominal fee of £3.00 within three months they had traced my two brothers and two sisters. My sisters Yvonne and Anne were still living in the Birmingham area, my brother Bill was living in the 'Sticks' down in the county of Sussex and my youngest brother Anthony, the only one of us not to wed was traced under the care of the Warwickshire Health Authorities during his twelve years as a mental patient at their hospital in Warwick. Betsy, the youngest of the family and who was only a few months old when entering the orphanage was traced to South Africa. Although we have not been able to be brought together even for a short while at least we know we are all living. Yvonne, Anne, Bill, myself and my son Glen have met as individual families from time to time. Anthony we have met on a couple of occasions but since he was allowed out of the mental institution he had gone his own way. I have been in correspondence with my sister in South Africa and hope and pray that one day we will meet and if it isn't asking too much it would be a dream if all our families could be together if only for a brief period.

Life for the first time in many years was good to me so I returned to earning a living by returning to the taxi way of life. It was March 1983 when I turned on the taxi meter again and it was on the eve of my birthday a couple of weeks later when my taxi exploded, or so I thought at that time. Having been given the order to go mobile to pick up a fare from the George Hotel on Central Drive and to wait until that person came out of the pub I parked the taxi almost outside of the front entrance. Anticipating a wait of several minutes as nearly always is the case on closing time at night, I settled with a book in my hand. Then ... what I described as an explosion happened. Colourful lights mixed with darkness were all around me and the shattering of glass and metal was deafening, I thought I and the taxi had been blown to pieces. The young male driver of a stolen car lost control of the car when travelling at a high speed. Out of all the other cars to the front and rear of me and all empty, I was the unfortunate victim. According to eye witnesses, the police and later the Ambulance men it was a miracle no one was seriously injured or killed. Being lifted out of the taxi and carried into the ambulance was painful, I was aching all over. It wasn't all bad luck as something I did before the accident was fasten around me, my seat belt. That is something I can never remember doing previously with it not being compulsory for taxi drivers to wear seat belts. At hospital my whiplash and other injuries were passed as painful but not all that serious so I was allowed home.

The following day I learnt that both the hired taxi and the other car were 'write offs' and that a large part of the other car was still embedded in the taxi when it was taken away. A week later the young culprit was given a six months prison sentence for unauthorised taking of the car, and further twelve months for driving while disqualified and for having blood alcohol count above the prescribed limit. Separate fines of £60.00 were also imposed on the driver for using the car with no insurance cover and for driving without due care and attention.

Days after that court hearing and with my solicitor I applied for Legal Aid for loss of income and personal damages. It was towards the end of our talk that the solicitor looked up at me and with me sensing the unbelievable look on his face I got to my feet and said,

"Yes, I must have been born under the wrong star."

It wasn't all doom and gloom for as I entered the Polish Club on our weekly Thursday night out I was met with the expected outburst of laughter from my R.A.F. friends on seeing me wearing the large white polystyrene covered neck support; and it was just coincidental that that night one of my friends had a red plastic 'nose' in his pocket and another with his camera and flashbulb. The photograph I will keep forever. It is another memorable night with those LADS and I am grateful for all the free drinks. "Thanks Lads!"

SEARCHING

For what I was forever searching could possibly be in the stars, or so I thought, but I wasn't to be far wrong, speaking in an earthly manner that is. To all of you who are interested in Astrology you might be interested in the birth dates of myself, my sister Anne and my brother Bill of which I have noted at the beginning of the book. You may also find to your interest that I an Arian born in 1934 married a Scorpion from the same year.

John, a good friend of mine owned a watch repair business in the town centre and it was on one of my regular visits to him when a lady customer and friend of John was with him when I arrived. It was a chance meeting, the lady gave me the name and telephone number of a qualified teacher on Astrology. "I haven't a class going at the moment, but if you care to let me have details of your date and time and place of your birth I will do your life chart for you." Without hesitation I sent off by post the information the Astrologer required. As I also was interested in knowing about the science of Astrology an appointment was made for a meeting. About a week later the appointment was met.

After being welcomed and on returning from the kitchen with the offered and gratefully accepted cup of coffee, the Astrologer startled me after placing the cup and saucer on the coffee table beside where I was sitting. "You are going to join the Samaritans." After a few moments of silent disbelief at what was said to me I replied by saying in an uncertain tone of voice, "The Samaritans!" "Yes, no other organisation but the Samaritans." "I am at present involved in helping with the welfare of the members of the R.A.F.A. and their families," I hesitantly replied. "Just remember what I have just mentioned and there is going to be a very good reason for you wanting to be with that organisation." Those were I believe the concluding words on that matter. What was said about my birth chart didn't sink into my mind and what I did hear before had had me walking away with my mind as nebulous as the day itself.

I was desperately in need of a hobby, something, anything that required a great deal of concentration and for the reasons mentioned earlier it had to be Astrology and I don't mean the Fun Stars one reads in some newspapers, magazines and periodicals. I began purchasing a handful of books written by different Astrologers then with the information from my Birth Chart I got to work on trying to discover the Astrological me. My findings spread over a period of about ten or so months were both interesting and of great use for the years ahead. In saying that I don't mean I could forecast what was in store for me in the years ahead, I am not that clever to be able to work that out! What I believe I did find out from studying Astrology was, that in a way life is planned therefore we are all subjects of fate. There was something else I discovered from my studies that was to a certain extent responsible for a different way of life for myself, more about that in a minute.

I was into the fourth of my five years of following the 'Stars', when on a social night at the Polish Club and not on one of our regular R.A.F.A. nights my friend Brian got into one of his usual conversations with a group of women friends of ours and out of that conversation came my first chance to do a yearly forecast. With the date of birth and nothing else I set out to try my hand at pleasing three of the four women who were willing to place their future in my hands. Putting health aside I got down to work and that strange GIFT was with me again. With the information from my books and knowing the aspects of the Sun and the Moon, I worked on each birth date separately. The first forecast I attempted was a dismal failure, I just couldn't get into doing it so I put it to one side and began on the second. It was during the second birth reading that that feeling from the past was with me again and as I continued the feeling grew stronger. It was as if some unseen force was around or within me. With what little information available to me and from that wonderful feeling I managed to present my year forecast to the three women. During the following months the three women and myself were amazed at the accuracy of my attempted forecasts and at the end of the year I had other women giving me their dates of birth.

We all know we all posses psychic abilities and most of us know that to make good use of it it requires developing. Up to and during my studies on Astrology I had no idea what that Gift was that I had. But at that time I had a powerful feeling that all Astrologers were in possession of a developed psychic gift and that that gift was used to forecast events, but where that power came from I was not to know until several months later.

My son Glen had told his girlfriend of my unusual gift and at Christmas of 1984 she tested me when on arriving at our home with my present she said something like, "So you can guess what is inside parcels?" and on throwing my wrapped parcel to me I had said, "It is a pair of slippers." And on getting hold of the wrapped box I knew I was right in what I had said. Glen was in stitches laughing at the disbelief written all over the face of Tracy and at being slapped across the head and shoulders with the words, "I don't believe it. You have told him," being bellowed into his ears. Turning to me Tracy then said, "Alright then, what kind of slippers are they?" "Sheepskin!" I replied. Sheepskin they were. But Tracy was not convinced so she had Glen empty a large whiskey bottle that was about half full of coins. My said total was wrong ... I was five pence short of whatever sum of money was in the bottle. Although happenings such as that were a source of laughter for myself and others it also had a strange feeling of awareness about it, it was a feeling of being aware of something or someone unknown around or within me.

Using government time to dish out free forecasts and to load myself with paper work for the Blackpool Branch of the R.A.F.A. was all good for my morale but it didn't come anywhere near fulfilling that in which I was in need. I have jumped the gun a little by taking you into Christmas 1984 and now I have to take you back to the last week of October the year before.

It was on a night I had my brother Anthony staying with me, a night in which he wondered off and lost his bearings. Someone directed Anthony to the Salvation Army Citadel situated about a mile from my house. It was from the Citadel that I learned of Anthony's fate and that they had directed him to the house and to expect him at any moment. Anthony had with him a Samaritan leaflet when he arrived home. On seeing the telephone number on the back of the leaflet I rang the Blackpool Branch of the Samaritans saying I would like to be one of them. My name, address, age and telephone number were taken by the voice on the other side of the line and it said someone would be in touch with me in a couple of days. After several months training and on the 6th September 1984 I was accepted as a Samaritan with the Branch in Blackpool. That was fantastic news and it had me thinking; 'If the doorway to happiness is found by helping other people then surely by giving a few hours a week with the Samaritans was the finding of my years of searching for whatever I didn't have.' However I was still unemployed and for health and age reasons employment was not available for me. Everyday I called at the Job Office and when a vacancy did arise that I felt capable of I was told by who interviewed me that I was either too old, over experienced, not educationally qualified and on the odd occasion I was informed that a medical was required; and with my G.P.'s words, "If I were an employer I wouldn't take the risk and employ you," ringing in my ears, I still didn't give up hope. Buying extra newspapers to seek employment was a financial burden and after months of failing to obtain a job I had to concentrate on my local area to hopefully fulfil that wish. Although I must say that out of thirty applications only one company didn't reply, that in a way was heartening, especially when one hears of so many people saying they never receive a reply to their applications.

January 1984 was nail in coffin month for the matrimonial home when the mortgage transfer took place and lumbered me with repayments almost treble that of which I struggled to pay during the past few months. That being the case I urgently required employment so I hastily returned to driving a taxi, unfortunately after three days and very little reward I resigned for health reasons. But before I leave you with my last ever day of

158

taxi driving I want to bring into your lives a sniff of mystery and intrigue and perhaps a little laughter to the unbelievers.

During the first of those three nights on my return as a taxi driver I was surprised to be given an out of town job. The fare was from a house somewhere in Blackpool and I was told over the taxi radio that the gentleman was a regular to the inland town of Darwin and that a fixed fee was in operation. It would have been about one o'clock in the morning when we set off on our journey and after giving me instructions as how best to arrive at the gentlemans destination the passenger fell asleep. Well I was in Darwin after about a drive of about fifty minutes and on acting on instructions I awoke the passenger from his deep sleep. "Ah, your fortunate, other drivers go miles past," and then saying, "See that pub halfway up that brow, that's where I want to be. I am the Landlord." Having handed over his agreed fare and a generous tip, the passenger then opened his near rear door and slipped into the darkness of the night. On my arrival at that pub I noticed there were no houses next to or near the pub building and if there were any at all nearby they all were without light, that's not surprising at about two o'clock in the morning. I had just put away the money tendered and then gave myself a good stretch to relieve the discomfort of sitting in one position for a long period of time. Then as I was about to restart the engine something strange took place. I was watching a group of soldiers in steel armour and on horse back immediately past the pub and I was one of them and it was I that was leaning over to my right demanding from a peasant the way to somewhere. I sat in great disbelief at what I was watching, it was like looking at a wide cinema screen. For minutes after I was rubbing my eyes, slapping my cheeks, flexing my fingers, stamping my feet, thumping my hands against my chest, you think of it and I probably did it. I thought to myself, "God keep this to yourself otherwise you will be sent to the loony bin." Then I switched on the engine, hand brake off, foot gently and nervously on the pedal and I was off only moments later to be watching another large cinema screen of military epic. It was really and truly unbelievable.

The all night petrol filling station ahead and to the left of me appeared to disappear and was replaced by an old and small thatched top wooden hut and outside of which were the same group of soldiers I had seen earlier, this time I was leaning over the left hand side of my horse again seemingly asking directions. I was about to stop the taxi when the filling station loomed up in front of me and on entering I inquired the best way out of town.

I wasn't getting any younger and edging towards the age of 56 years in April and knowing I just had to find employment of some nature I began walking around the town looking at empty shops with living accommodation above the premises. With nothing to suit my requirements I then searched suitable areas bordering the town but again to no avail. Then I received a letter from my solicitors stating I was going to receive compensation from the Criminal Injuries Department arriving out of the accident on 4th April 1983. That meant I didn't have to sell my house and I concentrated my search towards seasonal or permanent indoor markets. I was in luck and in the month of May I was making plans for a stall different from any other to be built for the retail of gold and silver jewellery in Abingdon Street Market in the centre of Blackpool and close to the Winter Gardens.

With money borrowed from the bank I set about buying stock ready for the opening day nearing the end of the month of June. I had a feeling 1985 was going to be good for me and I was confident that I would be in a position of helping Glen and Tracy with their wedding four months later and on the 21st September. With not even knowing the difference between carat gold and gold plated, my first week was very pleasing and by the time of the wedding I was able to be of financial help to the great relief to both Glen and myself. The day Glen was born and his beautiful wedding, stand as the happiest days of my life, there is so much I owe Glen and he doesn't know how much. I know every parent is proud and happy on their son or daughters wedding day but I believe no one has or ever will be as happy or proud as I was that Septembers day.

Business continued to be satisfactory and I was learning more each day about jewellery from my customers and long before Christmas I knew the difference between a dangler and a sleeper. Not only were the women customers of use to me for my search for knowledge of the jewellery trade, my suppliers were of great assistance and most eager in helping what was to them a good customer. Christmas and New Year trading were good and for many a long year I had coppers in my pocket to spend on brightening up the house. On a bitterly cold winters morning I suffered a heart attack as I was about to open the stall for the days business. Fortunately my doctors surgery was only a few yards away and within minutes of calling for an ambulance I was on my way to Ward 11 for a fortnights free board and lodgings.

Well recovered from my treatment during the previous seven days and with a Wilbur Smith book I settled myself on top of my bed for a good nights read. Then it happened From the ward annex came noises. The Ward Sister passed me on her way to attend to another patient. On her return I beckoned the Sister to come over to me so as I could quietly tell her of what I had just been hearing. "Sister, are there women in the annex?" "You will be so lucky. Why?" "I have been hearing the voices of new born babies," I told her. "Oh no! Not you as well," the Ward Sister said in a low tone of

160

voice. Then after a deep intake of a commanding breath of the stifling hospital central heated air I was told to keep quiet about as she didn't want the Ward Nurses upset. Apparently those same voice were heard by another male patient just two years prior to my hearing. I was glad to learn what I had been told by the Sister if only because it was a good book I was reading and I wanted to finish reading it before slipping between the sheets for the nights sleep. I also learned from my quick exchange of words with the Ward Sister that the annex was at one time in the past a part of the hospitals maternity ward.

Apart from that slight setback life was going well for me except for that of which I was searching. It was several weeks before I was in a healthy position to return to work and those days of illness were made much easier knowing I had good people working on the stall for me. Later in the year I was readmitted to Victoria Hospital where in Ward 19 the doctors and staff carried out tests to see exactly which arteries were responsible for my condition. Although my stay was to be of a few days, an infection had me there a few days longer; and again on knowing my stall was in good hands I could relax and enjoy the company of the other patients and that band of beauty and love, dedication and care, the ward nursing staff.

By November I was advertising my stall for sale as I was in possession of information stating I would soon be called into hospital for three coronary by-passes and a possible clear out of two smaller arteries. No one in the market had much faith in my ability or luck in selling my business least of all as a going concern. Well they were proved wrong, everything went surprisingly smoothly with the seal firmly fixed on 6th December 1986. Disappointing as that was, 1986 was another good year for me and I would like to say for Glen and Tracy also.

17th February 1987 I was admitted to Ward 10 for my operation on the morning of the 20th. On the night before my operation I was lying awake waiting for my sleeping tablet, when standing to the right and close to the foot of my bed appeared a young girl of about ten or eleven years of age. The beautiful young girl was wearing a Victorian dull off white laced full length dress with either a blue or green ribbon around her waist and her neatly plaited brown hair also was tied in ribbons. After giving me a warm loving smile she then said, "Hello," then vanished. It was then I knew the operation was to be a success. Despite unfortunately having the hiccups for most of four days after my operation and not being able to eat during that time I still met the all clear predicted date for being discharged with those who also had their operation about the same time as I. But on the morning before my release I was taken ill and only a couple of minutes of being given the all clear by one of the nurses. I felt fine during the check then suddenly a wave of what I described as a wave of depression or sickness swept through my body. It was a Sunday morning with not many staff on the ward, so I was fortunate there was the nurse who gave me the check close at hand to give me another. Puzzled the nurse ran along the ward shouting I had a temperature. Soon I was answering questions to two doctors and having quickly grasped the dangerous situation I was in, me and my bed were whisked up to the top of the ward and even before the bed was in its position I was surrounded by white coats behind closed curtains. It was at a time during the early minutes that I was suspended outside my body and 'looking in'. It was a strange and wonderful experience told only to a very dear and close Samaritan friend the Branch Sick Auntie, a lady of great essence in all that is nice and the sincerity in supporting others goes a very long way to be equalled.

I was well connected to the heart monitoring unit and it was when being injected by morphine into the stomach the doctor said to me, "If we don't take these emergency precautionary procedures, to put it in lay-mans terms, the situation could be very grave indeed." The doctor then looked at me unbelieving what he had heard, when I replied, "Don't worry too much doctor," and looking upwards I continued by saying, "He isn't ready for me." In tacit silence the doctor left with his other white coats only for the doctor to return about half an hour later to insert more morphine into me.

For some reason mentioned to me at the time and now forgotten the lung equipment used to detect clots in the lung was not available for me, it being Sunday. First thing Monday morning I was wheeled to that department for rigid and at times painful tests. After being extensively scanned I was given a clean bill of health by the doctor when calling to see me later that morning when saying, "I am very pleased to say that the examinations have come up with nothing and whatever was on your lung, and there certainly was something, is no longer there. Nevertheless we will want to keep you in for a few days longer. Those three extra days were stepping stones in my life. Needing very little, if any medical attention I found time to search and think my life. One of the first and probably one of the most important things that could have been said to me was by a close friend in the R.A.F.A. "Andy, do you know what is your biggest enemy?" and before I could reply he continued by saying, "It's your pride." Those were very true spoken words and in hospital I searched my memory for the times my pride was my downfall. It is true that I required perfection or near perfection in my business and work relations, whether it be as a tram or bus conductor or the Fashion Buyer for an area of a big multiple company. During that time thinking I came to the conclusion my pride was also my weakness, because if I had spiritual strength to prevent me from getting into the difficulties of the past and the spiritual strength to prevent me hating myself for being in those situations I would never had experienced life in Hell. Then there was that burning hatred of the Nuns who mentally and physically ill treated myself and my brothers and sisters, I had that to get out of my system. That problem I still had with me on leaving the hospital.

Then there was the invisible that bugged me for years, that missing something I was badly in need of to build that inner weakness into a strong, stable and rewarding life. And I couldn't pass that golden opportunity without giving thought to those fantastic, encouraging and dedicated nurses and all the doctors from all the wards that saved my life from the time of my heart attack to the end of my stay in Ward 10. Then there was the loving care and attention also from my family and friends inside and outside the R.A.F.A. and the Samaritans. And whoever else was watching over me I thank you as well. Was it the Roman Catholic Nun who visited me one Sunday when I was in church?

Only days after leaving the hospital I tendered my resignation with the Blackpool Branch of the R.A.F.A. and then became a member of the Branch in St. Annes On Sea. It wasn't any easy decision to make but because of internal squabbles it had to be done. Unfortunately I have not been able to take an active role in that Branch due to health and other restrictive reasons.

I, then in need of a good tonic, what better than being told that you are the Grandad of a beautiful baby girl. Katie was born to Glen and Tracy on Wednesday 17th June just two weeks before I entered the Richard Peck Convalescent Home for the members of the R.A.F.A. and situated in the beautiful St. Annes On Sea just on my doorstep. A wonderful fortnight was had and I left with lasting good memories, much improved physical and mental health and not without adding more friends to my growing number over the past years.

Keeping body and soul together was a struggle so in March the following year I cash surrendered my small and only life insurance policy to open a Costume and Fashion Jewellery stall in the seasonal south shore area of Blackpool. Within a couple of days of opening in the month of May of that year I had to admit to other stall holders of knowing nothing at all about the growing number of requests for Hair Accessories. Pony-Tail Holders, Bulldog Clips, Banana Clips? "They must be having me on!" I kept repeating to myself until the demand was so great I had to turn to my daughter-in-law for the answers. Instead of shaking my head and saying sorry I don't stock them, I returned to my stall proudly saying, "They will be arriving soon," how soon I had no idea. Sooner than expected they arrived and only because on that morning following my phone call to my daughter-in-law a Representative carrying all the Hair Accessories I could afford to buy on the day arrived at the stall having been advised to do so by a friend who ran a Perfume and Cosmetic stall at the far end of the market. From that Representative I required all the knowledge I needed to build a lucrative Hair Accessory business alongside the jewellery. By the end of September I was up to date with my house mortgage, being almost three months in arrears when opening the stall, and other outstanding domestic bills were also met at that time. Altogether I was feeling good and pleased that someone is looking after me.

Four weeks later I was in agony, the long seasonal hours and the relentless flow of customers had me agonisingly exhausted to the point that one night I had to be helped off my seat and escorted to a waiting car outside the market for a stall holder to drive me home. On wakening the following morning I was shocked to find my body would not move. I couldn't and dare not try to move fearing a seizure of the heart. Frightened and in great pain, I lay trying to get my wits together. Instinct told me to slowly and gently relax and control regulated breathing then to attempt moving fingers and toes to aid blood circulation while at the same time allow the mind to travel to the happier days of the past and to better wishes of tomorrow. Gradually and patiently I was able to have full body movement and after about the longest four hours of my life I was on my knees praying my thanks to God and to whoever was with me. I had no worries about losing money over not being at the stall as I had a friend to help on Sundays. Part of those four hours were spent with gentle massage of my heart and I continued the treatment right up to the minute I arrived at the market. It was nearing lunchtime when eventually, I made it to the stall having travelled by taxi to arrive.

As well as being in her glory Jeannie was concerned about my ill health, she being informed of what happened the night before. The mornings takings exceeded all before it, and wasn't Jeannie delighted.

"Well doesn't it take the magical or should I say Spiritual gifts of a woman to sell such items as jewellery, cosmetics and perfumes?" Having paid my deposit to secure the horse-shoe shaped stall for the following year, I thanked Jeannie for her gratefully accepted help and advice, with a guarantee agreed for next year we parted, I to say my farewells and thanks to my neighbouring stall holders and their families and friends, Jeannie to her husband waiting in their car.

Well, I didn't return to the stall the following holiday season, I couldn't, I was and still do receive government handouts. Of course my ill health doesn't prevent me getting excited about my findings about the Spiritual Church and neither does it prevent me from my voluntary work.

164

THE ETHERIC CONNECTION

During that Spring of 1985 and on a rare Sunday away from my voluntary work and only days before my search for an indoor market stall I, for the very first time visited a Spiritualist Church. That Spiritualist Church is situated in Albert Road, Blackpool, in the hub of the resorts holiday industry.

It was a spur of the moment decision having me excited a little as I prepared myself for the fifteen minutes walk to the church. I calmed by the time I reached the steps leading up to the opened inviting double narrow doors of which led me to the hall of the church where my choice was a seat at the rear in the near empty room, only a handful of people occupying seats close to the Speakers platform. Although alone it wasn't with isolation that I sat flicking through the pages of the Spiritualist Hymn Book which was gracefully handed me on entering the church hall, the shuffling of feet and the movement of chairs interrupted by deepening interest of one of the delightful hymns I at the time was reading. As I looked up and around I took note of the almost capacity filled church and that the fingers of the small round facial clock on the wall above and to the right of me were at two minutes before the commencement of the two thirty service. Also as I was using my eyes they noticed people were on the platform, two to the left and two to the right seated themselves onto plastic bucket seats, while another approached the book-stand in the middle and to the front of the platform where immediately and out of my sight for a while sat another person.

After a most cordial and sincere welcome we were then asked if we would sing Hymn Number 113 from our hymn Book.

> We are sailing o'er life's ocean
> to a far and brighter shore;
> And the waves are dashing around us,
> and we hear the breakers roar;
> But we look above the billows
> in the darkness of the night,
> And we see the steady gleaming
> of our changeless beacon light.
>
> Though the skies are dark above us,
> and the waves are dashing high,
> Let us look, towards the beacon
> we shall reach it by and by.
> 'Tis the light of God's great wisdom,
> and he holds it up in view,
> as a guide-star to His children,
> and a help to YOU and ME.

He will keep it ever burning
from the lighthouse of his love;
And it always shines the brightest
when the skies are dark above.
If we keep our eyes upon it,
and we steer our course alright,
we shall reach the harbour safely,
by the blessed beacon light.

I, never in my wildest dreams could have expected a more welcoming hymn. I think I sang it quietly to myself and time and time again as, as at the beginning of the service it was the shuffling of feet and the movement of chairs that brought me back to the awareness as to where I was.

Because of prearranged commitments it was to be three Sundays later before revisiting the Spiritualist Church. During that three week period I had within and around me a warming and calming atmosphere inherited from my time in the church. How different a feeling it was from my everyday connections with Catholicism.

In a strange and wonderful way I was drawn towards the Spiritualist Church and, on the four Sundays that followed my absent three weeks, my internal involvement grew stronger, the Spiritualist Church just seemed to be a natural place to be, in community prayer and service. I had the feeling I was free from the ideology, the falseness of that religious statues represent, free from the college trained voice of theological false priests, bishops, cardinals and their colleagues and their teachings and preachings of their fairy tale past. I was also believing I had reached a point in life when sorrows, errors and misjudgements of the past were being put to one side. Something 'Out of this World' happened during the singing of a hymn after the Medium part of the service, on my fourth visit to the Spiritualist Church in Albert Road.

Standing next and to the left of me was the most beautiful Woman I have ever seen. It was a Woman of immense beauty, surrounding the warm gleaming smile on her beautiful serene face, tender with love and the heavenly sparkle in her eyes were glowing, shining, beaming, warming and calming rays of light. The Woman was a little smaller than I, so I had to look downwards at her face and in doing so I could hardly believe whose face was looking up at mine. At that point in time easily I could have said the apparition was that of the Virgin Mary, my common sense telling me otherwise. It was to be five years to the month before I returned to the Albert Road or any other Spiritualist Church, but in mind and soul I was a

166

Spiritualist.

Amid all the ill-health and 'business misfortunes was a great growing new inner self and the growing feeling of greater warmth, 'happiness, comfort and a greater generosity of feeling towards others, especially of those who are in need of spiritual help. Although giving more of my free time caring for others with my Samaritan work I was still without whatever it was I was without. As with Spiritualist Church the Samaritans embrace all races and all creeds and it isn't linked to any religious organisations as we understand them to be today. So I am thinking, "If having affinity with my Samaritan friends and with my friends in the Spiritualist Church what on earth is it that is missing in life? After all I have the love of my son and his family." I just had to try harder to find the missing answer.

One dark and cold winters night in late November 1988 I selected a few of my tapes and comfortably sitting in my fireside chair I shut my eyes and allowed my mind to relax and then to run free. At a time I was bringing together the scene during my taxi visit in the town of Darwin, the crying of a baby when I was in Ward 10 and the appearance of the Victorian dressed, brown plaited haired girl in Ward 11 during my stays in Victoria Hospital, Blackpool; then there was that beautiful lady who appeared at the side of me in the Spiritualist Church. It was leaving 1 a.m. and after about three relaxing and comforting hours I was still without the answer but I was confident the link was with the experiences I have just mentioned, that was frustrating as I knew I had the answer in 'the palm of my hand', yet could not see it. On Sunday 20th that week I made a phone call to a well known and trusted local clairvoyant. An arrangement was agreed for a meeting at 2 p.m. in my home on the Tuesday of that week. Nothing other than my name, address, telephone number and the time of the meeting was known to the clairvoyant during that telephone call.

On the arranged afternoon and in my lounge the clairvoyant inquired as to what he could do for me. I explained about the vision in the Spiritualist Church and that from time to time what I had seen seeped through from my subconscious to my conscious mind and I just had to find answers as to why that lady appeared next to me. The medium went into a trance. Although I have not mentioned who I did see next to me in the Spiritualist Church I can assure you I do know. Was this going to be a turning point in my life? I wondered. Having come out of his trance the medium, with an air of disbelief written all over his face came out with something like, "I have never seen anything so beautiful in my entire life. What you saw in the Spiritualist Church that Sunday was a ROMAN CATHOLIC NUN, and the brilliance was out of this world." Then the medium went on to describe in detail the description of the Nun and what was in her hands.

Everything mentioned by the medium was correct including the bunch of herbal flowers the Nun was holding in her hand. Yes; it was a Roman Catholic Nun from Nazareth House in Aberdeen that was with me in spirit that Sunday, but it wasn't one of the Nuns who inflicted cruelty upon myself and brothers and sisters, it was, I am in no doubt, the lovely Nun in charge of the hens. "Why would a Roman Catholic Nun visit ME in a Spiritualist Church," I asked. After all I still had with me that burning hatred for the Nuns who ill treated myself and my brothers and sisters whilst in the 'House of God'. "You have seen a commitment," was the mediums answer to that burning question. "A commitment," I puzzled. "You have to keep a low profile and give yourself to others." And of the other experiences I had then mentioned to the clairvoyant he said that I was obviously receptive to being psychic and that I would benefit by attending development classes and that the visions were what is termed in his field as 'Watchers'. "By the way, if you are thinking about putting your house up for sale, don't. You won't sell it!" The week before I had the Sale Sign removed from the front of the house. "Anything else?" I inquired. "Yes; you won t get married again. "That is because you don't want to get married again." "Great! I thought. "That is because you don't want to get married again." "Correct!" I thought. The last piece of information was in itself worth the small fee requested by the clairvoyant, I thought. Although the visit was worthwhile the mirror on the wall was still not clear, nevertheless I now have the compatibility of reason and desire for writing this book.

The following day and with the 'Watcher' label attached to myself and the Roman Catholic Nun I strolled along to the Sacred Heart Church in Talbot Road, Blackpool. On entering the church I felt as if I had entered a Cold Storage. Bewildered I returned home to do some deep spiritual thinking. As the days went by, more and more shops and stores were reminding us of the nearness of Christmas and it was a nice feeling knowing soon families from all over the world will be together for a few short hours of high spirits and goodwill and that the churches will again be full, as usual for about an hour.

It was with a faint aroma of incense belonging to Catholicism that had me returning to the church in Talbot Road that Christmas Eve. Midnight Mass, and the crowded church would be a deciding factor between my returning to the Catholic religion or continuing with Spiritualism. At the end of my journey on foot and on arrival at the wrought iron gates of the church my legs weighted, my stomach knotted. "Well, I tried!" Turning away from that Church I turned my back on Catholicism and, I shuddered my last cold shudder.

TRUTH

Truth is rising! See it beaming,
lighting up the darkened mind;
over flasehood's mountains streaming,
giving eyes to the blind.

Truth is rising! hear it knocking,
breaking rusty bolts of years;
tombs of ignorance unlocking,
to the deaf ones giving ears.

Truth is rising! 'Tis prevailing!
Conquering banners sweep the skies;
all old dogmas 'tis assailing,
winning brilliant victories.

Truth is rising! Stand from under!
Floods are bursting, lightings play;
all around the sky ther's thunder;
bligatory must pass away.

Truth is rising! Earth's awakening!
Spirit-voices speaking plain;
all the old dry creeds are shaking
saying man shall live again.

Truth is risen! Oh what glory!
Blessed truth dispels the gloom;
Angels haste to tell their story
of our pathway to the tomb.

    The words you have just read are the words of one of many from the Spiritualist Hymn Book and convey what I now believe to be THE TRUTH!

    With Christmas out of the way I had time to try and get a grip on my inner feelings and what I really believed about in orthodox religions. For years I have wanted to know what one can gain by the adoration and worship of imaginary Gods and Idols. Why are the churches afraid of transferring their peoples so called priceless relics into educating the minds of their people so they can become more intelligent, giving them a better standard of life. And why do those churches not transfer their peoples so called precious relics and their hidden wealth into food, clothing and bricks and mortar to help the poor and starving millions throughout the world instead of hiding behind the claim that they are in their Gods hands. The more knowledge you gain the more confident one becomes so that has me now believing Jesus was simply a Prophet, a healer and a teacher but with supernormal powers over gatherings of uneducated people and that he was put to the cross by the military, they fearing their people were paying more attention to the man they called Jesus than they were to them. That now brings me to saying that I admire Jesus, I do not adore Him. I also say to myself, "Didn't Doctor Livingstone go to the black man in Africa they not understanding a word spoken by the Dr. but they understood the love from his heart." And what about the life long devotion to the sick and injured by Florence Nightingale and what about the humanity of the founder of the District Nursing Association, William Rathbone. Surely they and others alike have done as much for the people as Jesus. Will we or our grand children be reading the names of those I have mentioned in the next altered Bible. I feel that in todays turbulent world there are signs of the mind of man seeking the truth about religion and politics and the truth will be sought where ever it can be found.

Fed up at having been misled and still without the answers sought I, on Sunday 27th May 1990 returned to the Spiritualist Church in Albert Road where in the past I enjoyed inner comfort and happiness. Before the end of the month of June I had snuggled in nicely with the Spiritualist Church. The heavenly hymns, the philosophy of the spiritually guided mediums and their messages to the people from all walks of life attending the services giving me more confidence, happiness and inspiration to face the future knowing there is life after death and that one day I will have found that of which I am seeking and that I also will have the answer or answers to that which is within and around me. I can understand why people who scoff at the Spiritualist Church because they are ignorant as to what takes place inside the churches of Spiritualism, and that the preachers and teachers are afraid their flocks will learn the truth about the Bible. It was the search for the truth that led me to being a Spiritualist. It is my belief, the reason why so many people are deserting their churches is because the theological mind can only think and preach of the past where as mankind has advanced dramatically in science, medicine and navigation etc. It is also my belief, orthodox churches should now change as the past should be treated as history and should be of interest as a story of our ancestors alongside the greats of our time.

It was with Development Classes in my mind that I set off to the

170

basement of the Albert Road Spiritualist Church, only to be told by the attendant Development Classes are not held but I was welcome to seat myself in readiness for the 'Open Circle'. "I'm here, so I may as well stay," I murmured to myself, then going towards an empty seat against the wall at the rear of the 'Open Circle', or so I thought at that time. The large finger of the rounded facial clock moved to 7.30 p.m. Then a voice from the front of the gathering wished all of us a good evening then asked us to stand in silent prayer for all our loved ones and for all in the world who are ill and in pain.

"We will start the evening by singing hymn no." whatever it was. That was followed by an interesting talk on the principles of Spiritualism. Following her talk the medium then went on to give messages to people she had received from friends and relations in the Spirit World, all of which I listened to with great interest. Then, from out of the blue; the finger of another lady pointed in my direction, immediately the other medium sat down. Modest and unassuming was I until the voice of the woman said, "The gentleman with the throat condition." Automatically my index finger of my right hand was raised, pointing towards my chest, I in staggering disbelief on hearing what was said to me. "Yes, you," was the mediums direct reply to my betoken reply. "You have a throat condition, don't you! With unbelievable surprise and with a negative voice I had to answer, "Yes!" "Then you are the gentleman I want," said the medium. Then the medium went on to describe in detail a lady who was living in the house next door to where I am still living. "The lady I have with me is saying she is concerned about your throat and she is saying you should get it seen to otherwise it might be too late." To this day I have that throat condition and my G.P. has referred me to the hospital for a check. The medium was also correct in saying Mrs Black my ex next door neighbour and friend passed into Spirit only a short while ago. The medium did get one thing wrong, it wasn't a Yorkshire Terrier that Mrs Black sat stroking in her lap ... it was a Tortoise. Happy and excited as I was on receiving my first message via a medium I sat there like a weathered Spiritualist but not knowing what was in store for me. I had obviously gone into deep thinking at what I had heard for it took a nudge from the person sitting next to me to bring me to the voice of another medium. On raising my head I could see a woman who was obviously speaking to me, and she was saying something like, "You know a small heavy built lady in the Spirit World who enjoyed taking her dogs on to the stage in the entertainments business." Puzzled and frowning and not recovered from my first message I couldn't answer. "Yes you do! She is here with me showing me her dogs walking in a circle around her." Mrs Mac. the mother of a past girlfriend whom I mentioned earlier in the book fitted the

171

description given by the medium and the dogs on 'show' were her Poodles which she bred at the bungalow in Preston New Road, Blackpool. When the Poodles were at the acceptable age and ready for 'Showing' they were taken to Dog Shows throughout the country.

Forenames of three male friends of mine who passed into Spirit were also given to me by that medium. That's handed out every time you might be thinking and I can understand why you would have such thoughts but by giving me two of the same surnames, they were not picked out of a hat. My first 'Open Circle' experience had me thinking on my way home, I could 'be getting closer to the answers I was seeking and so desperately needed to conclude. Six weeks later and on the Sunday 22nd July the visiting medium to the Albert Road Spiritualist Church surprised me when saying I was going to receive Spiritual healing for my painful leg. That problem has been with me for about 30 years and has required a regular supply of strong painkillers prescribed by my G.P. There was no way possible for that medium to know about my painful leg. The second pleasing message given to me by that medium was I would be Spiritually rewarded for all the happiness I have brought to people.

The medium doesn't know me, my name or whether I am a local resident or a visitor to the town. Several times the medium strolled from one end of the platform to the other and with clenched fists close to her chest she was saying to me in a wishing, determined voice, "You have some unfinished business that needs attending. You are holding back on something." By the look of frustration and by the frustrating movements of her walk and body signals I could clearly see the medium was desperately keen for herself to get a clearer message to me from the spirit who was with her at that time. "I have been given a 'Bowler Hat'," said the medium. "What on earth am I doing with a 'Bowler Hat'? There must be a link with whatever it is you are holding back and the 'Bowler Hat'." Neither could I link the two at that time as I have been holding back on several parts of my life. "Anyway take it with you, will you?" Then just as the medium and I thought that was the end of the message she returned to me saying, "Whatever it is you are holding back, you have been given three months in which to try and get it sorted out otherwise everything will be in vain." Immediately after the service I joined in with others for a cup of tea and a biscuit, while we mingled talking with one another mainly on how good was the service and other matters concerning day to day life. To try and find the answer to the message given to me during the service I flitted from one medium to another each in turn being recommended by another.

I slipped the last of my freshly brewed tea then walked the few yards from the centre of the room to return my cup and saucer to the Tea

172

Bar then, returning to where I was standing I continued in conversation with whoever it was I was talking with. Just as we were about to complete our farewells I was approached by a medium with whom I had conversed earlier. "Have you some unfinished writing?" As I was about to say No, I replied with, "Yes, yes I have. I had been writing a book and shelved it because I don't have an ending." Instantaneously the medium said, and I thought, "There is the answer." It surely was crass stupidity on my behalf not linking the 'Bowler Hat' with my writing. I certainly owe a lot for being a Spiritualist for without me really understanding that of which I was seeking and that of which was in and around me my friends in the Spirit world certainly did.

Rereading the earlier pages of this book for the first time in about five years, I found I no longer had with me the burning hatred for those that inflicted the cruel physical and mental torture and the vicious unkindness upon myself and my brothers and sisters.

Decades of spun intricate webs are now brushed aside and the engraved tombstone memories removed. Now the past memories are written in dust in 'THE ATTIC OF MY MIND'.

The 14th January 1991 "Ride a cock horse to Banbury Cross," reiterated a practising medium at the home of the local weathered medium Mavis Watson who holds regular Monday evening 'circles' I didn't respond to the words spoken. Several minutes later that same practising medium was saying, "It's Andrew! It's Andrew!" Then, I just had to accept the message was for me. The words 'Ride a cock horse to Banbury Cross' were the last spoken to me by my mother before we parted company on that first day in the orphanage.

Einstein's theory has established that if we were to space travel for a decade we would return to earth younger, how younger depends on how fast the spacecraft had been travelling. If that be proven, with the brain developing long before the body the more that can be discovered about the workings of the mind and brain the closer man will be to realising what a great future awaits our children of the future.

At this present time we only receive messages from the Spirit but some time in the future we will be able to communicate with them, not from this earth plane but from another planet where the vibrations are more akin to that of the Spirit.

The End.

Front row left to right,
Andrew, Yvonne, Anne and Bill Gorman.
Back, Mother Lucy holding Betsy (right) and Anthony (left).